THE BOTH OF US

A Psychological Thriller

Dan Lawton

Black Rose Writing | Texas

This is a work of fiction. Names, characters, businesses, places, events, and incidents are either the products of the author's imagination or used in a fictitious manner. Any resemblance to actual persons, living or dead, or actual events is purely coincidental.

ISBN: 978-1-68513-594-2
LIBRARY OF CONGRESS CONTROL NUMBER: 2024949364
PUBLISHED BY BLACK ROSE WRITING
www.blackrosewriting.com

Printed in the United States of America
Suggested Retail Price (SRP) $22.95

The Both of Us is printed in Book Antiqua

*As a planet-friendly publisher, Black Rose Writing does its best to eliminate unnecessary waste to reduce paper usage and energy costs, while never compromising the reading experience. As a result, the final word count vs. page count may not meet common expectations.

For KB

The Both of Us

CHAPTER 1

It was the voice. It was always the voice. The voice that first turned his head when he crashed into her at the library fifteen years ago. The same voice that agreed to let him buy her a coffee afterward, as an apology for not paying attention to where he was walking. The same voice that said she'd take him forever and always, through sickness and health, three years after that.

It was her voice. Rachel's voice. His wife's voice.

Mark leaned forward against the tug of the nylon belt across his chest and turned up the radio's volume. He was listening to a doctor hotline he didn't know the name of. Just something he landed on instead of channel surfing while stopping and going during his commute home. He'd never listened to the show before but something about it hooked him on this day. People would call in and tell the doctor their stories—though not a medical doctor, rather a therapist. Free advice from a certified shrink. Not even a copay for an office visit. Mark saw how the show could appeal if someone wanted to remain anonymous.

Which was why hearing Rachel's voice made little sense.

Rachel had never been to a therapist, as far as he knew. And he would have known because she would have told him. They told each other everything. They were close. Happy. Still very much in love. Maybe most importantly, they were still fond of one another too.

He turned up the volume even louder, to drown out the bustle of the traffic surrounding him.

"Hi, Mindy from Indy, how can I help?" the therapist said, her voice sullen and lacking tolerance.

"I … I'm a little nervous, sorry," Mindy from Indy stammered.

Or, Mark knew, Rachel. He'd know his wife's voice anywhere.

"It's my first time calling. I've been listening for a while. Years, off and on. I'm a big fan."

"Thank you," the therapist and radio host coldly said, as someone who probably heard that all the time might. "How can I help?"

"The thing is, I've been wanting to call for such a long time, but I'm nervous. I've never told anyone this before. I don't even think I've ever even said it out loud. But—"

"Listen, I don't have time for this," the therapist said with frustration. "Either get on with it or I'm going to have to move on. I've got other callers lined up and ready to go."

"You're right, of course. I'm sorry." Mindy from Indy took a deep breath and let out an even bigger sigh. "I have a secret. A big one. It'll change my life if it comes out. Which is why I don't know if I can do this."

The therapist said nothing.

Mark's breath caught.

"I've been holding on to this for so long, Doctor Lisa," Mindy from Indy said through sniffles. "But … I'm sorry, I don't think I can do this."

"Sure, you can," Doctor Lisa said, more tenderly now. "Go on."

"No, no, I can't. I'm sorry."

The line went dead.

"Hello?" Doctor Lisa said. "Are you still there? I think we lost her." She sighed. "You've got to be ready to go out there. When you're up, I need you to get to the point. Let's bring in our next caller. Looks like we have Barry from Fort Wayne. Hi, Barry, how can I help?"

Mark turned off the radio before hearing Barry's problems. His chest pounded. He pressed the phone icon on his phone and dialed the first saved number. Home. Yes, they still had a landline. Reception was sometimes spotty inside the house. The landline rang and rang, until it didn't. Mark hung up and dialed the second saved number. Rachel's mobile. The phone rang a few times then bounced to Rachel's voicemail, where Mindy from Indy told him to leave a message so she could call him back when she was able.

He hung up before the beep.

His head spun.

Around him, the traffic on State Road 67 was thinning. The city lights shone in the rearview, gray clouds hovering overhead. Mark looked over his left shoulder and gunned it, abruptly switching lanes and ignoring the blaring horn that followed. The engine rumbled through his feet as he let off the gas and thrust the clutch to the floor, then switched gears and pressed down as hard as he could. He sped through traffic, weaving in and out of lanes, his eyes darting between mirrors.

Once the city was fully behind him and he was cruising in the fast lane, humming along between eighty and ninety, he tried Rachel again. Both numbers. Same results as before.

Something was wrong. Rachel never ignored his calls.

Mark geared up and picked up speed.

Twenty-five minutes later, he peeled into his driveway and slammed the car in park, not bothering to wait for the garage door to fully open.

"Rachel?" he said as he whipped open the front door and ran into the house. The tie around his neck might as well have been a noose. "Rachel? Abagail? Maureen?"

Toys and dolls were strewn across the carpet in the playroom on the left, the TV on, but no girls.

"Rach? Girls?"

Downstairs bathroom, empty. Guest bedroom, nothing. Mark stopped at the bottom of the stairs and listened, heard nothing upstairs. Instead, he walked toward the light creeping out from underneath the saloon doors at the end of the hallway, toward the kitchen in the house's rear.

"Rachel?" he said as he pushed through, the saloon doors squeaking. "Girls?"

"Daddy!"

"Dad!"

His girls, his life, leaped off their chairs and ran toward him with their arms spread out wide. He melted as he dropped to his knees and scooped them up, exhaling a heavy sigh of relief. If anything had happened to his girls …

He squeezed them as hard as he could, desperate to fight off the tears forming in his eyes.

"Dad, I can't breathe," Abagail wheezed.

Mark pulled himself together and let go. The girls laughed.

"You squeezed too hard," Abagail said. She was eight and their firstborn. Bossy sometimes, but the sweetest, happiest girl he'd ever been around. Mark often thought she was too intelligent, too curious, for someone her age. He couldn't say where that trait came from. He didn't recall being that way as a child. Neither had Rachel.

"Yeah, Daddy," Maureen said the way a feisty five-year-old would, "too hard."

"Where's Mommy?" Mark asked them.

"I'm right here," Rachel said from somewhere behind him.

He shot up and spun toward the voice—the same voice he just heard on the radio, desperate but unable or unwilling to reveal her lifelong secret.

"You made good time tonight," Rachel said. An apron covered her front. She wiped her hands on it.

Her voice was exactly as he remembered it.

"What's the matter, honey?" she asked, stepping toward him and dropping a now clean hand on his shoulder. "Are you all right?"

Mark looked at his wife. Studied her. The apron was stained with cooking oil and buttery streaks—the same one she always wore when she cooked. She smelled like herself, looked normal. No signs of recent tears. The liner around her eyes was subtle but pulled out the blue in her irises in a way that mesmerized him so much, he temporarily lost his train of thought. It happened more than she'd ever know.

"You're sweating," she said to him.

Mark exhaled the tension away. "You're okay?"

"Of course, I'm okay." She snickered. "We're fine. Why wouldn't we be okay?"

He didn't know how to answer that. Not here, not now. Not with their impressionable girls within earshot. Instead, he pulled Rachel into an embrace and said nothing.

"Are you sure you're okay?" she whispered into his ear.

They separated and he said, "I'm okay. I promise. Let me go change out of these clothes and I'll be back."

Later, after the girls were in bed and a bedtime story had been read, their nightlights left on to keep the bad dreams away, Mark joined Rachel for a glass of wine by the fireplace. A nightly ritual. They'd spend a half-hour discussing their days—just them, no distractions, phones in a different room—and connecting before cleaning up the kitchen and preparing for the next day. If they were lucky, they'd have an hour or two afterward to watch something on the DVR before falling asleep and zombie-walking up the stairs to go to bed. Wash, rise, repeat. It was a simple life, but it was the life they both wanted. And they couldn't have been happier.

"What's on your mind?" Rachel asked him. "You seemed a little frazzled when you came home tonight."

Mark put the glass up to his lips and breathed in the aromas of the red liquid. Chocolate and cherry, a hint of apricot. He took a sip and let it sit on his tongue before swallowing, to give him more time to figure out how he was going to address the situation.

Their chairs were so close, he could have reached out and touched Rachel. When her fingers caressed his forearm, the hairs stood up straight and he flinched. He hoped she didn't notice.

"Hey," Rachel said with tenderness. "What is it? Did something happen at the office today?"

"No, no, nothing like that. It's just …"

Rachel put her glass on the end table, leaned forward, and faced him fully. "You're scaring me, Mark."

"Do you ever listen to the Doctor Lisa Show?"

"Whose show?"

"Come on, Rach. Don't play."

"I'm not playing. I've never heard of it."

"Doctor Lisa. You know, the therapist hotline. People call in with their problems and the therapist, Doctor Lisa, she—"

"Yeah, I get it. I understand the concept. My answer's the same. Never heard of it."

Mark went for another sip, if for nothing else than to buy himself a few seconds to process. Rachel's reaction threw him. She seemed defensive. Why?

"Sorry," Rachel said. "I didn't mean to snap at you."

Mark swallowed, felt nothing.

"What about it?" she asked.

"Have you ever called in to the show?"

"I just told you I've never even heard of it."

"Will you just answer the question, please?"

"No, Mark, I've never heard of or called into the Doctor Liz Show."

"Lisa."

"What?"

"Lisa. Doctor Lisa, not Liz."

She sighed. "Lisa, fine. Same answer."

Mark took another sip. The evening wasn't unraveling quite the way he expected. He hadn't planned on starting an argument tonight.

"Why are you asking me about a radio show?" she asked.

"I was listening to it earlier tonight, on the way home, and—"

"Hold on, pause. You were listening to a therapist hotline? Why? Since when? If there's something bothering you, you can talk to me. You know that, right?"

"No, it wasn't like that. I was flipping through channels and landed on it. Today was the first time I've ever listened."

"Okay. And?"

"And is there something you need to tell me? Something you've been holding onto for a while, maybe?"

"What are you talking about?"

"Mindy from Indy."

"Who the hell is Mindy from Indy?"

"You tell me."

Rachel shook her head and looked away. Avoidance.

"I heard your voice, Rachel. I know it was you."

She turned back and their eyes locked.

"I heard your voice," he repeated. "You're my wife. I know your voice."

She looked hurt. Or caught. "I … I don't know what to say."

"Do you have something you want to tell me now?"

Rachel didn't respond right away. Her gaze fell toward the fireplace, which crackled and snapped next to them. It threw a little heat but not much; mostly it was for ambiance. Rachel's shoulders drooped and she slouched deeper into the chair, as if it were swallowing her up like quicksand.

"It wasn't me, Mark." She twisted her torso and faced him. "I'm telling you, it wasn't me. It must have been someone who sounded like me." Rachel paused. Quickly and subtly, her eyes widened before returning to normal, as if they hadn't changed at all.

But Mark saw it, whatever it was.

"What?" he asked.

"Nothing. I just thought about something I forgot to do today."

"Are you sure? Your eyes just now, they—"

"No, it's fine. I was supposed to send in a permission slip for Abagail's field trip next week, but I don't think I did. I'll have to send her teacher an email."

Mark nodded. Was she even paying attention?

"You believe me, don't you?" she asked.

"Huh?"

"About the radio caller. It wasn't me."

Did he believe her? He wanted to, but he heard what he heard. Certain things were hard to ignore. Especially when they were as obvious as this.

"But it was your voice," he said.

As if shot out of a pistol, Rachel leaped out of her chair and fell to her knees in front of him. Below him. She took the wine glass out of his hand and placed it on the table next to him, next to hers. After, she grabbed his hands and held them, pulled them close to her lips.

"Honey, look at me," she said.

He did, even though he didn't want to.

"I have never heard of that radio show. I have never called that radio show. And I certainly haven't heard of Mindy from Indy. I'm Rachel Starr from Brooklyn—not that Brooklyn, the other Brooklyn, the one nobody outside of Indiana has ever heard of. I'm married to the most handsome, most loving, best husband and daddy on the planet in Mark Starr. We have a beautiful family and an amazing life. The perfect life. And I love my husband very much."

Mark felt himself softening and the tension fading. Looking down into his wife's eyes—at the passion and intensity burning behind them, and with the words she spoke—he couldn't help but believe her.

"Do you understand?" she asked, their hands still intertwined. "I love you, Mark Starr. I have since the moment we first met. I don't know who you thought you heard on the radio today, but it wasn't me. I can promise you with everything I have that it wasn't me."

He looked deep into her eyes. Into her soul. There wasn't a single word that could summarize well enough how he felt about this woman.

"Let's go to bed," she said. "It's been a long day. You're clearly stressed. Let me rub your shoulders and help you relax. Okay?"

She had him. Hooked him. It wasn't the first time. There was something about her—there always had been—that pulled him in. A magnetism that shattered his walls and crumbled him to pieces.

"Come on," she said, standing up and pulling on his hands until he was too. "If you play your cards right, your shoulders won't be the only thing I'll be rubbing tonight."

·   ·   ·   ·   ·

Mark lay awake, listening to the sound of Rachel's breath. A tree threw a shadow on the ceiling that looked like a monster, with its claws swaying and its arms broad enough to squeeze the life out of a person. Midnight was approaching and the temperature was falling. The bitterness of fall in Indiana reared its head when everyone was supposed to be asleep. And unfortunately for Mark, it didn't wait around for those who weren't.

After a dozen years married, he was amazed at how often Rachel still surprised him. She had tricks up her sleeve he neither asked nor wanted to know where she learned them, and there was a tinge of mystery that shrouded her—nothing short of intoxicating. He'd do just about anything for her and their girls, for their family.

But he didn't like, or understand why, she was lying to him.

CHAPTER 3

I have a secret. If I tell you what it is, can you handle it? Can I trust you with it? Don't let me down. Ready? Here it is. I'm just going to come right out and say it.

I had an affair.

I know—trust me, I know. But it's not just that. The guilt has eaten me up since the day it happened. If I could take it back, I would in a second. No questions asked. Give me a mulligan on my life choices. I'm not perfect. And before you criticize me, neither are you, so you can slow your roll.

Sorry about that. I'm defensive, I guess.

Unfortunately, I know that's not how these things work. There are no second chances when it comes to the choices I've made. So I need to deal with it. Up until now, I really haven't. It's been my little secret, but the burden of holding a secret for so long can suffocate you. That's what happened to me. I'd wake up in the night sometimes, drenched in sweat and short of breath, with the weight of it sitting square on my chest as my unknowing husband lay beside me.

Feeling guilty about it doesn't make it justifiable, I know that. I also know that the classification of what happened doesn't either. I consider it more of a fling than an affair, a onetime moment of weakness. But that's neither here nor there. It happened, and I was a part of it. A willing, eager, consenting adult. The only person to blame is me. I own that truth.

I'm sure you must think I'm the worst kind of wife. On one hand, it's easy to understand why you feel that way. On the other, put yourself in my shoes for a minute. Should one moment of weakness ruin everything you've worked so hard for over years? Everything you thought you've ever wanted. If it were you and you knew your spouse wouldn't ever find out, would you admit to it knowing it would likely end your relationship and the life you've built? Be honest. If you think you'd admit to it, kudos to you. I don't believe you, but who am I to judge you? Maybe you're a better person than I am. Certainly possible.

But look, this isn't about you. It's about me and my mistakes. Yes, plural mistakes. One mistake that turned into multiple. Honestly, it's pretty bad. If you thought badly of me before, it's about to get a lot worse for you.

My name isn't actually Mindy from Indy, though I guess by now you already know that. I'd have to be a fool to use my real name. I hope nobody does. I get it—privacy rights, yada yada—but visiting a therapist's office isn't truly anonymous. Think about all the people who see you walk into the office, aside from the therapist—the receptionist, other patients in the waiting room, those on the street who might watch you park and walk in. You never know who could see you, and make assumptions about you. What if you ran into someone you knew? How cringe would that be?

Which is why I called the hotline. To avoid all that. Isn't the whole point of calling a therapist hotline rather than visiting one in an office to remain anonymous? No intake paperwork, no credit card receipts. No paper trail at all. I'm so broken, I couldn't even tell the therapist my secret behind the protection of a fake name over the phone. How pathetic is that? Maybe if I'd been able to, none of this would have ever happened. Maybe if I had gotten it off my chest and learned how to cope with it, learned how to manage my feelings better …

But it's too late for that now, isn't it?

So, here we are.

Yes, I was unfaithful to my husband. One time. And no, my real name isn't Mindy from Indy. Think of me what you want. Now that everything's out in the open, I might as well spill it all. The truth is, the fling I had happened around the same time my husband and I were trying to conceive for the first time. Which means—and I know, it's bad—there's a chance our firstborn child might not be his.

There, I said it. That's my real secret. Now do you see why I kept it to myself for so long?

Do you hate me yet? I wouldn't blame you if you did.

I've been reminded of my mistake every single day. The kids adore their dad. It's easy to see why. He's an amazing father to them. The mistakes I've made don't change the way I feel about any of that. If anything, I've grown to appreciate what having a family is like and what it does to a person. It's easy to take something like that for granted. I've been guilty of that. Maybe for good reason.

Yet, the truth has been burning inside of me like an inferno, desperate to escape. As much as I try to extinguish the flame, it burns even hotter.

Which is why I'm telling you my side of the story, the whole truth. You, and only you. It's for selfish reasons, I admit, but what choice do I have? Seriously. By telling you, I get it off my chest by finally telling someone everything from start to finish, which will help me move on and forget about what I did. Or at least try to. That is what this is all about anyhow, isn't it? Not only that, maybe it'll help you understand me and what I've been dealing with all this time too. All I ask is that you reserve judgement about me until you know the whole story. Can you do that?

For full disclosure, I'll tell you now that it's going to get worse before it gets better. But stick with me and it will get better. I promise it will. At least, I hope it gets better. I think it will. Time will tell, right? You can decide for yourself. Ultimately, your opinion is the only one that matters at this point, isn't it?

CHAPTER 4

The longest night of Mark's life finally ended even before the sun rose. He lay awake, staring at nothing in the darkness, freezing his balls off until the programmed thermostat kicked the baseboard heater on. His internal clock told him his alarm would go off in fifteen minutes. At least the first one. The second one five minutes after that. He waited ten before leaning over and grabbing his phone to dismiss what would be the most obnoxious sound on the planet.

Even with an area rug covering the wood, the floor still felt cold on his naked feet. But at least the hard part was over. Now that he was up, he could slip into the bathroom and crank the shower faucet to near-scalding. The next ten to twelve minutes were the most important minutes of his day to rejuvenate his system. The house was asleep, the neighborhood dark. The world felt like his and his alone, and he used the time to straighten out his head for the day to come.

Mark was in finance. A financial advisor—but not one of those scumbag ones. He took great pride in his honesty in his professional dealings. He worked for a large firm in the city, which was why they lived on the outskirts. He wouldn't raise his girls in any major city, no matter the size, no matter how highly the state rated the schools. That, for him, was always a nonnegotiable. Cities stripped children of their innocence. And while he wasn't naïve enough to think Abagail and Maureen would remain innocent forever, he also thought it was his duty as their father to preserve their bliss for as long as he could. The time would come when the girls could independently decide to move to a city if they chose to, but that time wasn't now. Until then, it was green grass and shrubbery and white picket fences—though not really, only metaphorically; they didn't have a fenced-in yard. Rachel didn't fight him on it. She was agreeable most of the time, while not submissive. Her opinion held weight, and that was the way he liked it. A true partnership.

Which was why her lying to him about the radio show baffled him.

He thought about it all night. Couldn't sleep because of it, unable to shut off his brain. Could he have been wrong about what he heard? In theory, certainly plausible. But the way his body reacted to hearing her voice—the perked ears, the intense focus on what Mindy from Indy teased but didn't say—made him think otherwise. If it wasn't Rachel, everything about his being was fooled.

Mark cut the water and dried off in the shower. The hot steam cleared his sinuses the way a sauna might. He wiped off the mirror just enough so he could see to trim his beard. After, he went to wake Rachel. He rested his still damp hand on her shoulder and caressed her silky skin with his thumb, the way he did every morning. She woke before long and breathed in the morning through her nose, then rolled over and slipped her fingers into Mark's.

Usually, he reacted to her touch in a way that relaxed him and gave him a semblance of peace. But today was different. His first reaction was to pull away, and he used all he had to fight against that urge. He was still upset, that was all; that explained the reaction.

"Can you get the girls up?" Rachel groggily asked. "I'll meet you downstairs in five."

A welcome distraction from the woman he used to know, Mark pulled his hand away and got dressed before waking the girls. Downstairs, the girls snuggled on the couch with their favorite stuffed animals and blankets. Maureen's blanket had a hole in it the size of a basketball. No matter how many times Rachel sewed it up, the hole returned, usually bigger than before. He dreaded the day the blanket tore completely and had to be discarded. Maureen would be devastated.

Coffee was a must. Breakfast optional. Today, it wouldn't happen. He could always grab a bagel from the basket at the office if his appetite returned, but that was the least of his worries.

He heard Rachel before he saw her. Her voice was too chipper for first thing in the morning as she greeted the girls. They responded just as they usually did—enthusiastically, loudly. Mark had a headache.

"Morning," Rachel said as she shuffled into the kitchen, her slippers dragging.

She grabbed a mug from the cabinet and he filled it with the black gold from the pot for her. They each added a little something to their mugs and stirred. He felt the jolt as soon as the liquid touched his tongue.

"What's on the agenda today?" he asked, although he knew. Abagail had dance at four o'clock after school, and Maureen had a playdate with one of the girls her age in the neighborhood.

She told him everything he already knew. Then: "What about you?"

"Nothing unusual. Will be home for dinner."

She smiled and nodded, took another sip. He did the same. Except he watched her as she held the mug with both hands, a faint billow of steam floating above it. She hadn't looked at him straight-on yet. But to be fair, neither had he. Not unless she was looking in another direction.

How had they become strangers so quickly?

Rachel's eyes shifted and looked at him. He tried to avert his, but he knew it was too late; she caught him staring.

"Hey," she said. She waited until he looked at her. "Everything okay?"

He nodded.

"Is it about last night? The radio show."

He took another sip.

"You believe me, right? I was cooking dinner while Maureen colored at the table. Abagail wouldn't stop talking, so there was no way I could have called that show."

The point was hard to argue. Logistically, it made little sense. There was silence in the background of Mindy from Indy's call. There was never silence in this house when the girls were awake. It didn't make sense.

Maybe he was wrong.

"You're right," he said. He smiled at his wife, and he felt a little better. What she said made perfect sense.

"I love you, Mr. Starr," Rachel said.

"And I love you, Mrs. Starr."

Rachel stepped toward him and rested her head on his shoulder. He draped his arm around her and pulled her close. They held their positions for a few seconds. On the clock on the stove, a new hour flipped. Right on time.

"Well," he said as he pulled away.

"Yep." She faced him and gave him a weak smile. "Have a great day. See you tonight."

CHAPTER 5

The best part about being a financial advisor was that Mark got to make his own schedule, within reason. He had a core set of clients who maintained regular appointments he could work around, but he had to be in the office during pockets of normal business hours for drop-ins and occasional staff meetings. All that to say, sometimes he went into the office early so he could slip out early. Other times, he'd run an errand in the city—pick up or drop off dry-cleaning or a prescription, run to the bank, get the oil changed in his car—before heading in, depending on his meeting schedule for that day.

Today, he had a meeting first thing with the Wildes. Tom was a soon-to-be retired police chief and Helen was an already retired school teacher of forty years. Between both of their pensions and the shrewd money-growing investments Mark had set them up with years ago, they weren't what some might consider filthy rich—but they would retire in style, just about wherever they wanted.

The most infuriating part about growing wealth over time was that it was so simple and yet, so few people did it. Routinely small investments with moderate risk over a long time would grow into an amount large enough to sustain a reasonable lifestyle upon retirement, thanks to the power of compound interest. It didn't take a genius. Mark was evidence of that. So many people didn't understand the concept, for whatever reason. Good for him; kept him in business. He did his part in spreading the word the best way he could, one client at a time.

Tom Wilde greeted him with a big smile and a firm handshake, like he always did. Mark never paid much attention to Tom's police uniform before, but that was different today; it was the first thing he noticed. Even with Rachel's reassurance, Mark still couldn't stop thinking about Mindy from Indy.

After they went through the Wildes portfolio and Mark showed them the status of the detailed retirement plan he'd outlined for them—as he did for all his longstanding clients—they wrapped up their meeting. Helen dismissed herself to find a restroom and Tom shook Mark's hand again.

"Thank you for everything you've done on this," Tom said. "You're a real professional."

"Thank you, Tom. I appreciate it."

"How are the girls?"

"They're so good, thanks for asking. Abagail is in dance now and loving it, and Maureen might be the cutest kid on the block."

They both laughed.

"But I might be biased on that one," Mark added.

"Not from my perspective. Hard to argue with you on that one. And Rachel?"

How was Rachel? According to her, everything was perfectly normal.

"Everything all right?" Tom asked.

"Everything's fine. Why?"

"Your face. You cringed when I said her name. You two having problems?"

Damn police officers. They could read people like a book.

Mark thought about his options. Tom had opened the door and invited him in. He could take the opportunity and walk through it. Or he could keep the details of his marriage private and pound his head against the wall trying to find the truth. Tom, ultimately, was just a client. Although Mark had been to Tom and Helen's son's high school graduation, and to his wedding—so maybe they were more than that. Maybe that made it okay.

"Actually," Mark said. "Can I ask you something?"

Tom stepped closer and leaned in.

"What would you do if you thought Helen was lying to you?"

"Easy. I'd bring her downtown and put her in one of our interrogation rooms. No windows, no distractions. I'd sit there until she told me the truth."

Mark didn't know what to say. He offered a weak smile but quickly took it back. He couldn't read Tom's expression.

Tom burst out laughing. "I'm just busting your balls."

Relief flooded through Mark's veins. He forced out a laugh.

"In all honesty," Tom said, "I'd just ask her about it. Be straight with her. More often than we might think, people want to be honest. Give her the chance to do that."

Before Mark could ask a follow-up, Helen returned.

"Ready?" she asked Tom.

"Only if you are."

Helen faced Mark and said, "Thank you, Mark."

"My pleasure," Mark said.

"We're going to be there when Abagail has a dance recital," Tom said. "You tell us where and when."

Mark smiled at that. "I'm going to hold you to that."

The men smiled at each other, shook hands again, then Tom and Helen left.

Mark walked behind his desk and threw himself into his chair. He sighed. He couldn't get Rachel out of his mind. A dull ache lingered in his skull.

Across the room, knuckles rapped on the door. Mark looked up and saw the person he knew it would be, who was also the person he didn't want to see right now.

Todd.

"Markster. What's up, my man?"

"Hi, Todd."

Todd was a good ten years younger than Mark, but it felt like a hundred. They lived on different planets. Todd was in his late-twenties, a bachelor, and with no responsibilities. He wasted his money at nightclubs and on a collection of trucker hats with state names on them that held zero monetary value. Mark found it a bizarre investment of money and time for someone in their field. Todd only had eight hats remaining before he had all fifty states, which apparently would be an accomplishment worth celebrating once achieved. Mark didn't understand it. He found Todd exhausting.

"You want to sneak out for an early lunch?" Todd asked.

Mark glanced at the clock. "It's not even eleven."

"And? I didn't sleep at all last night, man. I'm surviving on Red Bulls and Spearmint." He blew a tiny green bubble, as if to prove it. "I'm starving as shit."

At the mention of food, Mark remembered he hadn't eaten all morning. His stomach growled at the thought. "I have to be back for a meeting with a client at noon."

Todd clapped once. "Tony's?"

Tony's was a Mexican restaurant near the office. Was Mark in the mood for Mexican? No, not really. But was he ever? At least it would be quick.

"Fine."

Todd enthusiastically pointed at Mark, his face lit up with excitement. "You're my boy, Blue."

Mark put his computer to sleep and reluctantly followed Todd to the elevator.

• • • • •

Todd talked like a teenager, acted like a teenager, and ate like a teenager. Mark felt nauseous looking at the heaping pile of food on Todd's plate. Refried beans on top of refried beans on top of cheese on top of every kind of stuffed tortilla ever made. To Mark, they were all the same. How Todd would ever go back to work and be productive was beyond him. But it also wasn't his problem, so he let it go.

"Not eating, bro?" Todd asked.

"Not that hungry, I guess."

Todd nodded and took a huge, mouth-wide-open-sized bite of whatever was in his hands. Black beans exploded out the back of the tortilla.

"How was your night last night?" Todd asked while chewing.

Mark was repulsed.

"Get any ass?"

Well, actually …

"What my wife and I do really isn't any of your business."

Todd laughed. "Okay, Gandhi. I forgot you were such a prude."

"There's a difference between being a prude and not sharing intimate details of my marriage."

"If you say so." Todd took another disgusting bite.

Mark had to look away.

"You know what I did last night?" Todd said. "I dropped a grand at The Pony." He laughed again. "Best grand I ever spent."

The Pony was a gentleman's club in Indianapolis. Mark had never been and didn't get the sense he was missing out.

"This one chick, Charity, she said for five hundred bucks she'd—"

"I really don't want to know."

Another bite. "But I made the smart decision and didn't. I went home and wanked it instead."

"That's great, Todd."

"You should be proud of me. Fiscally responsible." Todd laughed again and took one more bite, devouring what was left in his hands. "So, what's up with you, dude?"

"What do you mean?"

"You're being kind of a dick."

Was he?

"No offense."

Mark sighed. "I'm sorry, Todd. I just had a long night. Hardly slept."

"Too much fucking?"

Mark glared at him.

"Sorry."

"It's just ..." Did he want to discuss this, especially with Todd of all people? "I think Rachel's lying to me about something."

"Why do you think that?"

Mark told him about the radio show and Mindy from Indy, and about how he confronted Rachel and her defensive reaction.

"And you're sure it was her?" Todd asked.

If Mark didn't know any better, he might have thought Todd was being sincere—like an actual friend. "She's my wife. I'm positive."

Todd looked away, as if pondering. "That sucks, dude."

Leave it to Todd to come up with the big ingenuities.

"It could be anything, though," Todd added.

"You're right."

"I think I have an idea."

"Let's hear it."

"It's simple. Call the radio station."

"And ask them what?"

"Make up some story. See if they can trace the call. They can tell you where the call came from, at least. Maybe not exactly, but a rough idea. An area code or something."

That was a decent idea. Except one thing. "You might be on to something."

Todd spread out his arms and wiggled his fingers, as if expecting praise.

"Except, they'll never give me that information. But I know someone who might be able to help."

CHAPTER 6

Before we can get to the end, we must start at the beginning. My story really begins ten years ago. Back then, my husband and I were happily married and enjoying one another's company. We'd spend weeknights on the town, enjoying a bistro or searching for the speakeasy we'd heard about but never met anyone who'd been. We'd hold hands as we strolled under the streetlights and watch the stars together. He'd point out constellations like the lovable nerd he was, and I'd nod my head and make sounds like "ooh" and "ahh" to show him I was listening and was as fully invested in it all as he was. I wasn't. The truth is, it all went in one ear and out the other. I didn't care about the stars or the constellations, especially not when it was so cold that my nipples were about to fall off. But I said nothing. I just smiled and let him talk about it, let him finish. That's a bit of a metaphor for our marriage, I'd say.

Back then, my husband and I both went into the city to work. We'd always lived on the outskirts—close enough to enjoy the nightlife, but far enough away where we could take a break from the never-ending bustle of it all. I enjoyed the lifestyle—slipping into heels and too short and too tight dresses during the day, then stripping down and removing my makeup and changing into yoga pants and running errands around town over the weekend. I miss that life. I'm not sure I was cut out for shuttling the kids back and forth to extracurriculars, to and from school, meal prepping, and pretending to be a happy housewife. Yet, that was the life I lived. My husband had a thing about his wife staying home and raising the kids in the country, so I went with it. Maybe I shouldn't have. Maybe if I would have held my ground and told him what I wanted, none of this would have ever happened. Never know, I guess.

During the day, when it was just me, I'd gone into my closet more than once to try on every one of those dresses that still hung there collecting dust. There aren't many things more depressing than struggling to slide an old dress over your hips, or failing to zip it all the way up, even after skipping breakfast and lunch for three straight days. I could suck in as much as I was able, but I'm not the woman I used to be—in more ways than one. It sucked, but it was my life. Sometimes, I just wanted more. Can you blame me?

Anyway, back when I was going into the city to work, I had a satiating social life. By social life, I don't mean mom groups or PTA meetings. An actual social life. Tequila shots and onion rings after work at the bar a couple of blocks away from the office. The occasional bachelorette party or girls' weekend. Or, my favorite, the company holiday parties where everyone let loose and put their disagreements and prejudices aside, if only for a few hours.

His name was Jimmy. He was introduced to me as James during his onboarding at the office, but his friends called him Jimmy. He and I became fast friends. It wasn't an attraction that connected us—although, admittedly, he was attractive. But I think many people are attractive. Everyone does. We're all human, no big deal. It wasn't like that; we worked in the same department. Our desks were close. I considered myself his office mentor. I showed him around, pointed out the bathrooms and the snack drawers and let him know which bottle filler had the coldest, freshest water. I told him to let me know if he had any questions about anything—anything at all. I was an open book.

Our friendship started over instant messenger. At first it was funny memes about office life—a hump day camel or red stapler reference. Then it was teasing about the junior employees getting chewed out by their manager in front of everyone. Then inside jokes, invitations for a coffee break downstairs, lunch meetings. Nothing unlike any other office since the beginning of time. Naturally, the conversations intensified as time went on. First, office gossip and professional paths. Next, hobbies and life journeys. Then, personal tragedies and hardships. Hopes and dreams, certainly.

One afternoon while we pretended to enjoy the house salads on our plates, it was Jimmy who finally asked the question.

"So, you're married?" he asked.

The ring felt like a tourniquet around my finger then, cutting off all circulation to my brain. Instinctively, I tucked my left hand under my right and fidgeted with the stone. I always thought it was too small; this was the first time it felt too big. I thought I was worth more than that to my husband. Maybe I was delusional.

"It's just, you've never mentioned anyone," Jimmy added.

"Never came up, I guess."

"What's his name?"

"I don't want to talk about him."

"Why not?"

"Just feels icky."

"Icky?"

"Well, yeah. Here we are, eating lunch together. How's your salad, by the way? There's so much dressing on mine, it's like the lettuce is revolting."

"Horrible. I think they used an entire bottle of Ranch between the two of us."

We laughed.

I sucked on the straw.

"You were saying?" Jimmy said.

"Anyway, right," I said. "It just feels wrong to talk about him when I'm having lunch with another man. That's all."

"Just colleagues, right? I'm sure your husband has female colleagues he spends time with."

"I know. You're right."

"But?"

"What do you mean, 'but'?" It wasn't meant to be flirtatious, but as soon as the words left my lips, I recognized it sounded that way.

Jimmy smirked and said, "We are just colleagues, aren't we?"

"Of course."

He smirked again. "Then what's the big deal?"

Looking into his eyes made my universe spin. I had to look away to avoid being absorbed into the vortex. We were just colleagues. Nothing had happened between us. Just friendly, harmless conversation.

"Are you happy?" Jimmy asked.

"What?"

"With him, I mean. With your husband who doesn't have a name."

"He has a name."

"Then what is it?"

"Why do you want to know?"

Jimmy folded his hands and gazed into my eyes. I tried not to look at his bulging biceps, but I couldn't help myself. I was certain he noticed.

"Yes, I'm happy," I said.

"That's good. I'm glad."

Was I happy, though? Of course, I was. At least I thought I was.

"What about you?" I asked. "Married?"

He lifted his left hand. No ring. "Not married."

"Seeing anyone?"

"Nothing serious."

I didn't know what to say. It was the first time with Jimmy that I felt flustered, lost for words. Something was definitely brewing between us. I had the sense he felt it too. How could he not? The heat between us was practically fire.

"So," he said.

I pulled out my phone and glanced at the screen. It was approaching one o'clock. "Probably should head back now. Before Beavis throws a fit."

The boss's name was Evan Beamis, but we called him Beavis—like the character from the cartoon we watched as kids. They both shared the same elongated face with huge nostrils, so the nickname was all too perfect. Evan's overeager shadow was named June, but we called her Butt-Head, for obvious reasons.

"Don't want to piss off B and B," he said.

B and B. Beavis and Butt-Head.

Jimmy grabbed my plate and tossed it, along with his, into the nearby trash can.

"Remind me to never get the salad from here again," I said as we walked back to the office.

"Seriously. I'm going to have to grab some crackers on my way back to my desk. I'm starving."

We laughed.

Our shoulders brushed as we walked and I had to resist the urge to touch his fingers with mine. My skirt vibrated.

"All right, I'll see you over there," Jimmy said when we got back into the office. "First, I need to pee. Then, I really do need some crackers. I wasn't kidding."

I laughed some more. I laughed a lot when I was with Jimmy. I didn't laugh like that at home anymore.

"See you around, *colleague*," he said before disappearing into the men's room.

Part of me wanted to follow him and do him right there, right then, in a stall in the men's room. The danger of it was intoxicatingly tempting. But another more logical part of me wasn't willing to risk it all to satisfy a lustful desire that surely wouldn't last. Giving in to Jimmy's temptation didn't happen until many months later. And it was both the best and the worst thing I ever did.

CHAPTER 7

Mark met with his twelve o'clock appointment, did what he had to do, then asked his assistant to clear his schedule for the rest of the afternoon.

"Everything okay?" she asked.

"Yes, Carly, thank you," he said. "There's just something I need to take care of today."

Carly smiled and nodded without prying further. That was one of the many things Mark liked about her. His last assistant asked too many questions and needed too much hand-holding for his liking. He had two children at home; he didn't need another at the office. Just like that, the rest of his day was free. Another advantage of making his own schedule. He packed up and left.

What he planned to do next seemed obvious, if not too easy. He wondered where the line was—how far could he push or how much should he share?—and if he was crossing it. Matters of business and personal affairs should be separate—and usually they were. But Tom was more than a client; hadn't he just proven that? Mark really needed a friend's advice right now, and there was nobody better than Tom to talk to this about. For more than one reason.

He pulled up to the Indianapolis Metropolitan Police Department headquarters and found an open spot on the street. He lined up the side-view mirrors and cut the wheel, then straightened it out as he glided into place three solid inches from the curb. No matter how many times he did it, he still proudly admired his work from the street before heading inside.

Officers dressed in military-like black uniforms paid him no mind as he adjusted the tuck in his shirt while he walked. Unexpectedly anxiously, he stood in line, a cool breeze blowing on him from the overhead vent, and waited his turn. A hush fell over the vestibule.

When his turn came, he walked up to the counter and spoke to the woman behind the glass. He gave her his name and asked to speak with Tom Wilde.

"Have a seat," the uniformed woman said, motioning to the row of chairs against the wall. "I'll ring him."

Mark thanked her and sat, and he waited.

Minutes passed. Then more minutes. Fifteen became twenty, twenty became twenty-five. Mark glanced at the woman behind the glass, hoping to nab her attention, but she was preoccupied with other visitors and a phone that refused to stop ringing. He wondered if Tom wouldn't come.

Then he saw him. At the end of the corridor, Tom strode toward him, his peaked cap profound on the top of his head. Mark had seen Tom in full uniform many times, but never in the hat. Something about the formality of it made his stomach roll. For a few seconds, he considered forgetting this altogether and sneaking out before Tom saw him, but then he thought about how ridiculous that sounded. He was simply a friend visiting a friend, to ask for some friendly advice. It just so happened that his friend was the metropolitan department's deputy chief of police.

Tom greeted him the way he always did — with a smile and firm handshake. His hand felt especially meaty, his long fingers swallowing Mark's thinner ones.

"I've got to say," Tom said, "when Lawanda called and said Mark Starr was here to see me, my heart skipped a beat. You're not the person I was expecting today."

"Is that so?"

"Afraid not. You're not one to make a house call, if you will. Is there something I should have signed when I was in your office earlier? Or something you forgot to tell me about our portfolio?"

"No, nothing like that."

Tom visibly exhaled, his shoulders shrinking. "That's a relief. You had me nervous. One year out from retirement, your financial advisor unexpectedly showing up at your office isn't something you want to have happen." He forced out a laugh. "Trust me."

"Sorry to make you nervous, Tom."

"Water under the bridge, my friend."

Friend.

"What can I do for you?" Tom asked.

"Is there somewhere we can go to chat? Somewhere private. It's personal."

The smile faded from Tom's face. A stoic, detective-like expression replaced it. "Of course. We can talk in my office. Follow me."

●   ●   ●   ●   ●

Tom's office was predictably intimidating. One glass wall, multiple framed degree certificates hanging on another, a dark mahogany desk with bright lighting and dual monitors. A photo of Helen on the desk provided the reality check Mark needed. Tom was just a person, a man, like Mark — and a friend.

"So," Tom said. "What's going on?"

Mark felt more at ease now, but he considered his words carefully. He didn't know what kind of situation Rachel had gotten herself into—trouble, even—and he had to tread cautiously. Friend or not, Tom had a duty to uphold the law, and Mark knew he'd do just that if faced with the scenario.

"About that conversation we had earlier at my office," Mark said. "That question I asked you."

What would you do if you thought Helen was lying to you?

"Yes, I remember. What about it?"

"What would you say if I told you it wasn't really a hypothetical about Helen?"

"I'd say that I already knew that."

"You do?"

Tom scrunched his face and leaned back as if to give Mark space to take in the surrounding room.

"Right," Mark said.

"Is it Rachel?"

"It is."

"Want to tell me what's going on?"

Did he? It was ultimately why he was there.

"As a friend, of course," Tom added, as if sensing Mark's hesitation.

Friend.

"You ever heard of the Doctor Lisa Show?"

"The radio show? Sure."

Mark sprang up. "Do you listen to it?"

"Me? No. I mean, there have been times over the years, once in a while, but not recently. That Doctor Lisa is quite the firecracker, isn't she? She's always putting the callers in their place. I've found it mostly entertaining every time I've listened. Why, what about it?"

"I stumbled on it yesterday while in the car, and there was this caller, Mindy from Indy. She said she had a life-changing secret that no one else knew, but she hung up before saying what it was. The problem is, the caller wasn't Mindy from Indy. It was Rachel."

Now Tom was the one who sprang up. "Your Rachel?"

Mark nodded.

"Are you sure?"

"It was the same voice. I know my wife's voice. Would you recognize Helen's?"

"No question. We've been married for forty-five years. I'd know her voice anywhere."

"Exactly."

Silence hung between them. Processing time.

"Okay, I'm sure there's an explanation," Tom said. "Did you ask Rachel about it?"

"Of course. And she denied it."

"Figures. These things are never that easy. How did she react to it? Did her expression change? Did you look into her eyes? Did she look away or avoid eye contact? Get fidgety? Anything like that?"

"I don't know, Tom. She seemed fine. Normal. Maybe even offended that I asked. Was barely listening, to be honest."

"Is it possible you're wrong?"

"I've wondered that too. I've replayed it over in my mind a thousand times, and I keep going back to the voice. It was hers. I get chills thinking about it. So no, I don't think it's possible that I'm wrong." Mark took a breath. He watched Tom, waited for his reaction. Tom gave him nothing. "I'd like to find out for sure, though. And I was hoping you could help."

"What did you have in mind?"

"I was thinking if the radio station could give me its call log, I could see if Rachel's number is on it. That way, I can get a definitive answer and figure out what's going on."

"They'll never give it to you."

"You're right. Which is why I'm here."

"You think I can get it?"

"I thought if you showed up in your uniform, maybe they'd be more open to it."

Tom considered it silently before saying, "I can't do that."

Mark sunk. "Please, Tom. I'm not asking you to lie to anybody or do anything illegal. I'm simply asking you to take a ride with me, maybe stand next to me. I'd do all the talking. I just thought if they saw a man in uniform, it'd help bring some credibility to the situation and show that I'm not some lunatic trying to creep on their callers."

Tom spun his wedding band, listening, considering, but said nothing.

"I promise you, if they refuse or ask us to leave, that'll be it. I'll accept their answer and forget about it. I'll figure out another way. Please. I'm asking for your help on this, as a friend."

Friend.

Mark waited.

"As your friend," Tom started, "I find myself curious about this situation. As the deputy chief, there's nothing here. I can't do anything that even remotely resembles police work. I'm talking tracing numbers or license plates, anything like that."

"I wouldn't ask you to."

"I'm too close to retirement to take any risks. I won't jeopardize everything I've worked for."

"If anyone knows that, it's me."

Tom thought some more. "But because you're my friend, and because I like Rachel, I don't see why anything you're asking is crossing any lines."

Relief flooded through Mark. "Tom, thank you. Truly. This means more to me than you know."

"I've been around the block a few times, kid. I've seen a thing or two. If this were Helen instead of Rachel, I'd want to know what's going on too."

Mark nodded because he didn't know what else to say.

"All right, head back and wait outside," Tom said. "I'm going to drain my snake and grab a muffin for the road, then I'll meet you out there. I'm driving."

CHAPTER 8

Finding the radio station's address was as easy as Googling it. Mark knew the station broadcasted out of the city, so combining a few keywords gave him more results than he could ever use. Luckily, he found what he needed right at the top.

It was nothing like when he was younger, when he had to log on to MapQuest and download directions ahead of time — all while crossing his fingers that there was enough ink in the cartridge to print the sheet without lines covering up the steps. Printing was the first of many challenges, he remembered. Another, which he knew from firsthand experience, was accounting for potential detours due to roadwork or auto accidents. One time before he and Rachel were married, they drove to Chicago, Illinois, to attend a Foo Fighters concert at the arena downtown. They arrived on time, drank some beers, and rocked their faces off during the show. It was amazing. Tremendous entertainment. The show ran late, though, and they got stuck in a night roadwork detour that brought them deeper into the city, through a homeless village, right into the nucleus of a litter-stricken slum. Turned out, he took a wrong turn somewhere along the way that added two full hours to the drive home. They made it back unscathed, but Rachel made him promise to never drive her into Chicago again. To date, he'd kept that promise. Although he was fairly certain the statute of limitations no longer applied to that promise now that he had a map on his phone at all times.

The main door to the radio station was locked. Unsurprising. Mark took his shot with the intercom system next to the door. He pressed the call button.

"Yes?" a man's voice said through the speaker.

"Hi, yes," Mark said. "I'm here to see Doctor Lisa Schneider."

"Do you have an appointment?"

"No."

No response.

"Hello?" Mark tried.

"If you don't have an appointment, you can't see her."

"It's important. It's about one of yesterday's callers. I think someone might be in danger."

Tom shot him a glare and whacked him with an elbow.

"Hold on," the voice said.

"Not asking me to lie, huh?" Tom said.

"It's not a lie, per se. Just a minor exaggeration. It could be true. Never know."

Tom grunted in response but stayed where he was, his shoulder touching Mark's.

The intercom cracked. "Is that a cop with you?" the same man's voice said.

"How'd you know that?" Mark asked.

Tom nudged him again and pointed above their heads. A security camera angled directly at them. Mark nodded.

"Yes, I'm a police officer," Tom said into the intercom.

A few seconds later, the door buzzed and unlocked. Mark grabbed the handle and pulled it before the intercom guy changed his mind. They were in.

A man with a scraggly beard appeared in the corridor and walked toward them, one hand hiking up his oversized jeans. Mark would have been surprised if the man was a day over twenty-five. The scraggly man stopped in front of them and said nothing, fidgeting with his waistline.

"Hi," Mark said. "I'm Mark, this is Tom."

"Hi," the man said.

"You are?"

"Tom."

"Two Toms," Mark said. "That's funny."

"Not really. Thomas is routinely in the top fifty for boys' names every year. It's quite popular, actually. The probability of two Toms being in the same space together is higher than you think." This time, the bearded Tom used two hands to hike up his pants.

Apparently, he'd never heard of a belt.

"I'm going to call you Tom Two then," Mark said with a smile. "To avoid confusion."

"Why?" Tom Two asked.

Mark was at a loss for words.

Behind Tom Two, clanking heels echoed as they rounded the corner. A thin but healthy-looking gray-haired woman approached. Her face was friendly but she walked with a bravado that matched the woman he heard on the radio the day before. She, he presumed, was the famous Doctor Lisa Schneider from the Doctor Lisa Show.

"Hello, gentleman," she said upon approach. She held her hand out first to Mark, then to Tom, and they took turns shaking it. "I'm Doctor Lisa Schneider."

"Mark Starr."

"Tom Wilde. Deputy chief of police for Indy Metro."

"Impressive," she said, eyeing him, possibly undressing him in her mind. "What can I do for you?"

"I wanted to ask you about a caller from your show yesterday," Mark said. "I think there's something strange going on."

"Strange?" she said. "I was led to believe someone was in danger."

"Well, that's the thing," Mark said, suddenly feeling unsure of himself. "That's what I wanted to talk to you about."

Doctor Lisa looked at her wristwatch, then back up. "I'm in the middle of show prep right now, but if it's important, I can spare you ten minutes. No more."

"It is," Mark said.

Doctor Lisa looked at Tom Two. "Tommy, you can go back to your station now. Thank you."

Tom Two didn't move. Instead, he creepily stared at Mark, blinking occasionally but not often enough.

"Thomas, go," Doctor Lisa said, more firmly.

Tom Two broke eye contact and huffed. "Fine, Mom!" he said, then stormed off and rounded the corner.

"Sorry about him," Doctor Lisa said to Mark and Tom. "He tries, but he struggles to stay in his lane sometimes, if you know what I mean."

Neither Mark nor Tom responded. It was safer that way.

"Come along," Doctor Lisa said. "You're down to nine minutes and the meter's still running."

•　　•　　•　　•　　•

The first thing Mark noticed about Doctor Lisa's office was the smell of a litter box — definitely urine. A peach cobbler-scented candle on Doctor Lisa's desk attempted to mask it, but failed. Clumps of hardened litter made a path on the carpet from the box to the desk, but the cat that made the mess was nowhere to be found.

"Seven minutes," Doctor Lisa said. "Talk."

"First of all, thank you for seeing us," Mark said. "I appreciate you taking time out of what I'm sure is a packed schedule to give me a few minutes."

"Uh-huh. Six minutes."

"Right. So, I was listening to your show yesterday, and I heard this caller who said something rather jarring."

"The more you do this, the less the calls seem to bother you," Doctor Lisa said. "At least that's been my experience. I've heard just about everything, I think."

"Yes, well, I'm not a regular listener, so …"

"I'm sorry to hear that."

"Nothing against you, certainly. Until yesterday, I'd never even heard of you." Mark forced out a laugh. Even to him, it came out harsh.

Doctor Lisa offered a weak smile.

"This caller," Mark continued, "they said they had a secret that they hadn't told anyone before."

"You're going to have to be more specific. I couldn't tell you how many secrets I hear on a daily basis. Five minutes."

Something pressed against Mark's leg, and he swatted at it. "Mindy from Indy. That was her name."

"Ah, yes. I remember that one. Unusual caller. Sounded a bit distressed, if I recall. She hung up before she spilled her secret, though. Happens all the time. Before you ask, no, she hasn't called before."

"I'm fairly certain she's my wife."

That hung between them.

Doctor Lisa shifted in her seat. "Okay. And?"

"But her name's not Mindy. And she's not from Indy." Mark flung his knee forward, trying to move whatever continued pressing against him.

"I don't think I can help you. I suspect most callers don't use their real names, but I have no way of knowing that. Did you ask your wife about it?"

"Yes, of course. She denied it."

Doctor Lisa shrugged. "Well, I'm not sure what else to tell you. People call in to remain anonymous for a reason."

"Yes, but" — Mark looked down as something sharp pinched his shin—"What the?" He kicked out of reflex and a cat went flying. It angrily meowed when it landed near Doctor Lisa's foot.

"Mr. Murphy!" Doctor Lisa said. "Come to Mama."

The cat leaped up and landed on Doctor Lisa's lap. The two snuggled their faces together. Mark looked away when Doctor Lisa pursed her lips.

"Anyway—"

"Tell him you're sorry," Doctor Lisa said.

"Who? The cat?"

She waited, kept her eyes on him.

"I'm sorry, cat."

"Mr. Murphy is his name."

Mark sighed. "I'm sorry, Mr. Murphy."

Doctor Lisa put her face against the cat's again. "I'm sorry about the mean man, sweetie-pie." Doctor Lisa then looked up at Mark. "Four minutes."

"Doctor Lisa," Tom interjected, to Mark's surprise, "I'm led to believe the caller, Mindy from Indy, might be in trouble. For her own safety, I'd appreciate it if you could share your call log from yesterday so I can look into it. Just a printout of the phone numbers will do, then we'll be out of your hair."

Mark was stunned.

"Well, officer—" Doctor Lisa began.

"Deputy chief," Tom interjected.

"Yes, of course, excuse me. Deputy chief, if it's a matter of law enforcement, I don't see why that would be a problem." She eyed Tom again. Mark wasn't sure if it was the cat or Doctor Lisa who meowed next.

"It is."

Doctor Lisa broke her gaze, then picked up her desk phone and pressed a number. "In that case." She waited. "Hello? Tommy, can you please print yesterday's call log? … Yes, I'm serious. … Thomas, please just do it." She hung up.

"Thank you for your help," Tom said. "I really appreciate it." He stood up and motioned for Mark to follow.

They took turns shaking hands with Doctor Lisa. She held on to Tom's hand noticeably longer than she did Mark's.

"Sorry again for Mr. Maxy," Mark said to Doctor Lisa.

"Murphy! Mr. Murphy!"

Mark cringed. "Right. Apologies."

Outside the door, Mark couldn't hide his embarrassment. Without seeing it, he knew his face was red; he felt the warmth.

Tom chuckled.

"Thank you for doing that," Mark said. "But you didn't have to."

"I did. I really did. That conversation was painful and going nowhere."

Mark didn't argue.

Downstairs, Tom Two waited for them with a stack of stapled papers. He glared at Mark as he handed them to Tom.

"Did you see the look he gave me?" Mark asked Tom once they were in the car. "What was that about?"

Tom smiled and shook his head. "You have so much to learn, my friend. So much."

Mark didn't understand what he was missing, but he let it go. He had other things to worry about. Tom handed him the stack of papers. Mark started scanning the numbers from the top, looking for Rachel's.

Many months later. Company Halloween costume party, to be exact. Which was really just an excuse for all the twentysomething women to hike their skirts up, pull their blouses down, wear those push-up bras that were saved for special occasions, and show more skin than was allowed by the office dress code. I was no different. My husband told me he thought my outfit was too revealing, but he didn't press the issue. Dressing like a whore was accepted one day a year. He had his own party to attend, for which I was certain there would be plenty of eye candy for him to ogle over, so what could he say? He thought it was sexy, just like every other heterosexual man did. And hell, I felt sexy. With it, my confidence was sky-high that night—and it wasn't always; quite the opposite most of the time. There was so much truth to looking good, feeling good.

I was dressed like a vampire—a revealing vampire with a sheer halter top that was held up by threads—complete with blood-red lipstick and enough black eye shadow to beautify the neighborhood. I walked in and nobody looked twice, which said more about the other women than it did about me. One woman in business development, Mariah was her name, wore a leather miniskirt that was so mini, I swore I saw her twat. Which explained why she had a group of ten or so men huddled around her like shadowing dogs, all the testosterone sickening.

B and B wore matching oversized peanut butter and jelly costumes, which wasn't surprising but was just as cringeworthy as it sounds. June's laugh was so high-pitched and obnoxious, I could tell she was already two or three drinks deep, at least. I would have taken the under one hour for how long it would have been before June and Evan were in his office with the door shut, their PB&Js strewn across the carpet.

I found Jimmy drinking alone on the sofa near the punch bowl. A giant panda head sat on the floor next to him.

"Hey, stu-pand-ous costume," I said as I approached.

Jimmy looked up and feebly smiled. "Weak."

"What can I say? Some of my puns are un-bear-able."

He looked away. He seemed troubled.

"Hey, what's wrong?" I asked. Then I remembered. "Your doctor's appointment! How'd it go?"

Jimmy had been struggling with massive, debilitating headaches for weeks. Some days he'd be fine, others he'd have to leave the office early or go sit in a vacant room in the dark. He'd popped so much pain medication, one might have thought they were breath mints.

"Not good," Jimmy said, looking back at me with dejected eyes. "It's bad."

The look on his face was emptiness. Hopelessness. There was nothing behind those gorgeous eyes of his. It gave me a pit in my stomach.

"Last week, I forgot where I put my keys," he said. "I spent forty-five minutes one morning looking for them. Where do you think they were?"

"I don't know, Jimmy."

"Just guess. I want you to guess."

I'd only just arrived, but I already wasn't having fun anymore. I felt self-conscious. "I don't want to play this game. Just tell me."

"They were in my pants pocket. The pants I had on." He took a sip from his red Solo. "Forty-five minutes. On Sunday, I shit you not, I slept for twenty straight hours. I woke up and took a piss, then went back to sleep for six more hours. That's not normal."

"You didn't tell me that."

"It was probably because I forgot. I don't have the slightest clue where I parked my car tonight, either. Not even sure how I got here, to be honest."

The party was loud. Techno music blasted my ears. Piercing laughter. Off-tune singing. I was in hell and much too sober.

"What did the doctor say?"

"It's a brain tumor."

I gasped.

"They're not sure just how bad until they cut me open, but I didn't leave there encouraged."

I was breathless. I sat next to him and leaned back, trying to absorb what he'd just said. I couldn't seem to process what it all meant.

"I'm moving to Florida," Jimmy said. "I'm handing over my resignation letter tomorrow."

I looked at him. The pain in my chest was so strong, I half-wondered if I'd been stabbed. "Why Florida?"

"The Mayo Clinic in Jacksonville has one of the best neurosurgery hospitals in the world. The outlook is grim, but they give me the best chance. They've agreed to admit me on Monday."

"Monday? As in three days from now?"

Jimmy nodded. Sadly.

"But that's too soon. I'm not ready for that. I need more time. Jimmy, give me more time!"

"There isn't any more time to give. It might already be too late."

As if a flood of tears had been dammed and were just waiting for it to burst, I wept. Snotty and slobbery and pitifully.

"Don't cry," Jimmy said as he rested a hand on my wrist. "Please."

His touch sent a jolt of electricity through me. It shot from my toes to my scalp and back again, stopping at every extremity on the way through, all in the blink of an eye. Aside from shaking hands on the first day we met, this was the first time we'd ever touched outside of accidentally.

What happened after that was only predictable in that it was a long time coming. The worst-kept secret I'd ever had. I was happy in my marriage, I was, but I was also so infatuated with Jimmy that the intensity was beyond my control.

I threw myself at him with an unexpected ferociousness. Right there on the sofa in front of everybody. I didn't care who saw. There was nothing I could do to stop it, even if I wanted to. Which I didn't. Jimmy didn't hesitate in reciprocating, his hand on the back of my head pulling us closer. Our bodies had been deprived of each other's intimacy for grueling months, only made worse by seeing each other almost every single day. I saw Jimmy more than I saw my husband, and when I wasn't with him, I was thinking about him. I needed to see this through. I needed to be with him, at least once. Before it was too late.

I took his hand and pulled him to his feet. There was a coat closet maybe twenty feet from where we were, and I made a beeline for it. Risky or not, I didn't care. Jimmy would be gone in three days, and I might not ever see him again. It was the definition of now or never.

"Are you sure?" he whispered into my ear as we pushed inside.

I answered him with my lips. And I didn't even bother covering my mouth as he lifted my skirt and penetrated me in the tiny closet not meant for people.

Three months later, Jimmy was dead. An unabashed email from human resources came through on a Friday of all days—I'm convinced they get off on ruining weekends with bad news on Fridays—with the news. Jimmy, our former colleague, had succumbed to brain cancer after a long (not long enough) and courageous battle. They provided an address where sympathy flowers could be sent, if interested.

Of course, they used the word colleague. I broke down at my desk.

So, yeah.

I loved my husband. I also loved Jimmy, just differently. Both things can be true. That was what made it so difficult. After spending all day gushing over Jimmy at the office, I'd go home and eat dinner with my boring, pathetic husband, pretending everything was normal. We'd cuddle on the couch and fall asleep while trying to watch a movie, and I'd dream about Jimmy. I also woke up happy every morning that it was my husband by my side and my kids down the hall. I was struggling.

There are days when I still miss Jimmy—I'm not going to lie, I do. But those days are far and few in between now. When I think about him, I wish he were still alive and could send me a GIF that would make me smile. I wish I could hold his hand, just to see how it felt. Life was sad in that way. One day you were given a gift, and the next it was gone. Sometimes in the cruelest way possible, like in Jimmy's case. Even so, I consider myself one of the lucky ones. I got to say goodbye, at least, unlike many who don't.

That says a lot about me, doesn't it?

What makes it better—or worse; some days it's hard to tell where that line is—is that I'm reminded of Jimmy a little every day, every time I look at my firstborn. There are parts of Jimmy in there — it's as clear as day to me — but there are also parts of my husband too. Absorbed quirks, learned behaviors. While I don't know for certain who the biological father is, I know. Just like how mothers know when their kids are struggling or hurting. Deep down in my core, in my soul, I know. And I carry that guilt with me every day. I keep thinking it'll get easier, but as time goes on, I think it's doing the opposite.

What's up with that? You must have some insight into that, don't you?

The first gut punch was that Rachel's number was missing from the call log. The landline too. Mark checked several times. Then when he came up empty, he checked several more times for good measure. Wasn't there. Neither were.

What did that mean?

It meant he had more work to do.

He couldn't pinpoint the exact time he'd tuned in to the radio show, but he gave himself a window. If he left work shortly after 5 p.m., which he did, and was home by 5:45 on a normal day, that gave him less than an hour to sift through. The rest could be disregarded. What he couldn't quite remember in the flurry of it all was by what time he'd made it home. He'd sped, he remembered, and made good time, but he hadn't bothered to look at the clock. It didn't matter much; there were only five calls logged within that forty-five-minute window anyhow. He could handle making five calls.

Tom had to get back to work, he said, so he drove them downtown so he could do that and Mark could grab his car. Mark fidgeted with the stack of papers on the way. The anticipation gnawed at him.

"Are you going to be okay?" Tom asked once he parked.

"Yes, fine. Thank you for all your help. Seriously."

Tom nodded. "Off the record, I hope you'll keep me updated."

"Of course."

"And if you need anything … Let me know and I'll see what I can do."

"I appreciate it."

They each stepped out of the car, shook hands, and went their separate ways. Mark hurried to his car where it was flawlessly aligned parallelly in the spot, repeatedly pressing the unlock button as he approached. Part of him wondered if he should move his car so he didn't make calls in front of the police station, but there was no time for that. There was nothing illegal going on anyway, as far as he knew, so no trouble. He was just a guy making some phone calls in his car. Nothing to see here.

He went in chronological order. To avoid making a fool of himself if he knew someone on the other line, he typed each of the five numbers into his contact list in his phone and searched. No matches. Which left him with two options. Either Rachel had a second phone, a burner, which seemed unlikely; Mark would have known. Or something else was going on. Maybe he was wrong about all this. Maybe what Rachel had said was right—maybe what he heard was someone who sounded like Rachel rather than Rachel herself. Could that be possible?

Only one way to find out.

He pressed the phone icon, typed in the numbers from the 5:01 p.m. call on the call log, and … waited. His thumb hovered over the call button. What was his plan? If somebody answered, what was he going to say? He paused and thought about it.

He peeked in the rearview. Staring back at him was a face he hardly recognized. Dark bags hung like anchors beneath his eyes, showing the world the exhaustion he didn't realize he carried. Using his wrist, he wiped the beads of sweat from his brow and looked back at his phone, determined to find out what was going on.

His thumb pressed the green button until it vibrated, then he put the phone to his ear. It rang until it didn't. The call connected.

"Hello?" The woman's voice was cheery. She sang the word more than spoke it.

Mark knew it wasn't who he was looking for. "Hi. I'm sorry to bother you, but is your name Mindy, by any chance?"

"I'm sorry?"

"I know it sounds strange. Sorry."

"Who is this?"

"My name's Mark. I'm looking for my wife."

"Well, it's not me."

"I gathered that. I must have the wrong number. I'm sorry. Thanks for your time." He hung up.

That wasn't bad, he thought. Expectedly awkward, but not as painful as it could have been. He dialed the second number from the log. This one was from 5:14 p.m.

The phone rang twice, then went straight to voicemail. Call declined. A nasally woman identified herself as Sandy. Before she had the chance to finish her recorded spiel about leaving a name and number—if people even did that anymore; with caller ID, why bother?—Mark hung up. He moved right on to the next one.

The third number was logged at 5:22 p.m. The one after that was 5:36, which Mark thought was too late. He would have been close to home by then. With that realization, he leaned back and took a breath. A lot was riding on this next phone call. He was jittery and anxious. If it wasn't Rachel, or the eerily similar voice of Mindy from Indy, he'd be stuck with an unknown next step. He wouldn't know where to go from here.

He typed in the number and initiated the call.

"Yes?"

Mark's breath caught. He felt it in his chest—the sudden furious pumping under his skin, the pressure against his rib cage. His world spun and he thought he might pass out.

There wasn't even a sliver of doubt in his mind about who was on the other end. It was her. It was Mindy from Indy. Rachel.

His wife.

Mark tried to respond, to say something, but he choked on his words.

"What did you say?" she said.

He tried again but failed, his tongue like adhesive in his mouth.

"Okay, I'm hanging up now."

"No, wait!" Mark managed. "Just wait."

Silence.

"Who is this?" she asked, her voice low, her tone questioning.

Mark didn't know how far to push it. Should he confront Rachel right now or wait until he got home? Whose phone was she using? Where was she? Where were the girls? There were so many questions he needed answers to and so little time to process it all.

"What do you want?" she asked.

"Rachel?"

Mark's chest thumped. He quivered with anticipation at what her response might be. What happened next told him everything he needed to know.

The woman on the other end of the line—his wife Rachel, the woman he committed his life to and entrusted with raising his girls, the voice he heard every single day—hung up and the phone went dead.

CHAPTER 11

Mark headed home. He kept the radio turned off so he could focus on his thoughts. The vibration of the rubber against the pavement numbed him. Nothingness filled his mind, despite the quiet allowing for his thoughts to run rampant.

He didn't know what to think. Rachel all but confirmed it was her on the phone by the way she reacted. It didn't make sense. Did she think he wouldn't say anything to her about it? They lived in the same house! The whole situation was baffling. And of course, this now meant that Rachel had a secret that had been eating her up for years. What was it?

A text message arrived. Keeping one hand on the wheel, he grabbed the phone and scanned the message. It was from Tom, asking how he made out. He'd wait to respond until he had more, or any, information. He tossed the phone back in the cup holder and kept driving.

Home was supposed to be a man's sanctuary. A place where he could go after a long day's work to kick his feet up and unwind. Somewhere to blow off steam, where he could put his guard down and be his genuine self, not the façade of a man he showed to the outside world. Usually, that was how Mark felt about being home.

Today was different.

Today, he sat in his car in his driveway, just waiting, before going inside. A pit formed in his stomach. He didn't even want to open the garage door. Not yet. Doing that would put him one step closer to doing what he dreaded—walking through the door and seeing Rachel, and having to confront her. They wouldn't have time to talk for hours, until after the girls were in bed. Before then would be filled with so much unspoken tension, he was already exhausted thinking about it. Hopefully, the girls wouldn't notice anything was wrong, with their youthful naivety Mark envied in a situation like this. He needed a few more minutes to compose himself, before he could handle what was to come.

A door opening slipped into his periphery. To his left, he heard Maureen's laughter before he saw her. Cackles rang out, followed by playful screams. She ran through the doorway and into the yard, her mouth wide with bliss. Pigtails with pink bows swung like pendulums as her head moved front and back, checking to see how close Abagail was behind her.

Abagail crossed the threshold next. She held her hands in front of her, scrunched like claws, as she slow chased her younger sister, who continued screaming. Even through the closed window, Mark heard Abagail roar like a tiger or a friendly monster—something spooky but not terrifying for the younger Maureen. Abagail was good about that, about shielding her little sister from the big bad world like she wasn't afraid of it herself. Maureen looked behind her and tripped over her feet, tumbling to the ground.

"Uh-oh!" Abagail said. "Looks like Mina's going to get you now! Roar!"

Maureen screamed another playful scream. Abagail fell on top of her and pretended to eat her with her hands and her mouth. They both giggled.

Maureen looked toward the driveway and her eyes lit up. "Daddy!" She sprung up from the grass and wobbled toward the car as fast as she could.

In an instant, Mark's tension faded. At least temporarily. A smile overtook his face and he sensed his sour mood floating away. He reached for the seat belt and released it, setting himself free. His feet hit the driveway just in time to catch Maureen as she launched herself at him.

"Daddy, you're home!" she yelled out.

He closed his eyes and squeezed her. They were a touch moist.

Abagail was next. Being three years older than Maureen, she wasn't as enthusiastic to see her dad, but that meant her excitement had more meaning to it. At eight years old, Abagail could be moody and irrationally emotional sometimes. Her expression usually told Mark what kind of mood she was in when he got home at night. He took great pride in turning her frown upside down, so to speak, as he often did.

"Hi, Dad," Abagail said. She smiled and hugged him.

His girls. There was nothing on the planet that was better than this. Their presence couldn't have been a more welcome distraction from the evening's inevitability.

"I'm going to go tell Mommy you're home!" Maureen shouted. She hurried back toward the house, disappearing inside before Mark had time to stall her.

"Oh, great," Mark mumbled under his breath. The smile faded away just as quickly as it came.

"So, Dad, how was your day?" Abagail said, bringing him back.

He almost laughed. Abagail spoke like a miniature adult sometimes. They had real conversations when they were alone, about life and feelings and the world. He felt like he could tell her almost anything. Under no circumstances could he or would he choose his favorite child—not ever. There was no comparison and his relationships with his girls were unique to just them. With that, he could acknowledge the special bond he and his firstborn shared. Whether it was as simple as they had more time together since she was older, or if there was something deeper, something embedded in their DNA, there was no denying their connection was extraordinary.

"My day was fine," Mark said. "Better now."

Abagail smiled at that. He smiled back.

"Daddy!" It was Maureen, back outside.

With her, to Mark's dismay, was Rachel. He tried avoiding making eye contact with her, but it wasn't as easy as it seemed; his face was pointed at her.

"You all right?" Rachel asked as she approached. She always knew when something was bothering him. Usually, he adored that about her. It was an amazing trait. Today, it irritated him beyond comprehension because she already knew the answer to that question. She reached out and tenderly touched his shoulder.

He winced and immediately regretted it. The jolt was subtle, unintentional, but there was no taking it back. He looked at Rachel, who took a step back as if he'd offended her. Which he had. He felt like an ass.

"Daddy, will you play monsters with us?" Maureen asked. "Abby is Mina the monster, I'm Princess Patty Cakes. Who do you want to be?"

Mark kept his gaze on his wife, who now dejectedly crossed her arms and looked away. She wasn't angry with him; she was devastated.

"Do you want to be Prince Peter Pan?" Maureen asked. "You can help save the princess from the monster."

"I don't know, sweetheart."

"Come on," she said, grabbing his hand.

As Maureen pulled him away, Mark kept watching Rachel. The hurt weighed heavily on her face, drooping her lips. Her fingers caressed her opposite arms to comfort herself, something her husband should have been doing. All Mark could think as Maureen pulled him farther and farther away was, what had he done?

·　　·　　·　　·　　·

The girls were in bed. Mark was so exhausted from playing with them while trying his best to refrain from showing any of the tension he carried, that he wanted to be in his too, but that wasn't possible. He and Rachel had hardly looked at one another all afternoon, never mind spoke. They needed to discuss what was going on, regardless if either of them liked it. They took their usual chairs in front of the fireplace, which smelled ashy but wasn't lit. No wine was on the docket tonight, for either of them. Clear heads were needed.

"Rachel, I—"

"—I don't. Oh, sorry. Go ahead."

"No, you go."

Rachel nodded but it took her a few seconds to speak. "What happened outside earlier?"

"I'm sorry. I don't know what that was. I had a long day. I guess I'm on edge a bit."

"Why were you home so early?"

"Was I?"

She stared at him, blinking.

"Rachel … I just don't know what to say."

"About?"

"Did you think I wouldn't know it was you?"

Rachel scrunched her eyebrows and pursed her lips. "What do you mean?"

"Earlier. When I called."

"We didn't talk on the phone today."

Mark sighed. "This is exactly what I'm talking about."

Rachel folded her arms. "Excuse me?"

"Mindy from Indy. The call today. Whose phone were you using, by the way? Or do you have a second one?"

"What? Mark, what are you talking about? Who is Mindy from Indy? … Wait, from the radio show? You're still on that? I thought we talked about that."

"I got the call log from yesterday's show, Rachel. I called the numbers on it. I called and spoke to you earlier, remember?"

Rachel shot up out of the chair. "Mark! What the hell are you talking about?"

He sighed again. "You're making this way more difficult than it has to be. Why won't you just admit it?"

"I honestly don't know what to say to you right now." Rachel paced, her arms still folded.

Silence fell.

"Why do you have two phones?" Mark gently asked. They were both getting heated, and he knew that wasn't productive. He was calmer than he thought he was going to be. "It's not a big deal, I just want to know what's going on. I'm sure you have a good reason."

"I don't have two phones."

"Then whose phone were you using earlier?"

Rachel smiled and laughed, but not happily. "I can't believe this. You're not listening to me."

"I hear the words that are coming out of your mouth, but I don't believe them."

Rachel stopped moving.

"Sorry, but I don't."

She looked at him and wiped her cheeks, then she sat.

"I called the number from the call log and I spoke to you. You hung up on me."

"Is that what you were doing today instead of working? How'd you even do that? There must be privacy laws against that."

"That's what you've gotten out of this conversation? Really?"

"What am I supposed to say, Mark? I don't know who you think you spoke to on the phone, but it wasn't me!"

"Keep your voice down. You'll wake up the girls."

Tensions were rising.

"Why are you doing this to me?" Rachel said through tears. "Why are you accusing me of something I didn't do?"

"I want to believe you, I do. But how do you explain your voice? I heard your voice."

"You must have misheard."

"You're my wife! I know what your voice sounds like!"

Tears streamed down Rachel's cheeks now. "Don't yell at me, Mark. Don't you dare yell at me."

Mark stood up, clenched his fingers, and made a loop around the room. The sense of calm he had before had vanished. He took a few seconds to take deep breaths and center himself. His skin was getting hot and he needed to cool down.

"Okay, listen, I don't want to fight," he said.

Rachel sniffled, wiped her cheeks, then recrossed her arms.

"So, if you'll just admit—"

"No, Mark! No! I won't admit it, because it wasn't me."

"The call—"

"There was no damn call!"

"Mommy?" Maureen's voice startled them both.

"Why are you up?" Rachel asked her, miraculously switching her tone into mommy mode without skipping a beat.

Maureen just stood there with her rag of a blanket hanging from one hand. She looked half-asleep. Mark feared knowing how much of their conversation she heard.

Rachel wiped her face once more and stood up. "Come on," she said to Maureen. "Let me put you back to bed."

"Goodnight, sweetheart," Mark called out, but it came without a response.

Rachel put her hand on their daughter's shoulder and led her from the room, leaving Mark alone with his thoughts and his doubts. He was no closer to the truth. If anything, he couldn't have been any further from it. And perhaps worse, now there was some serious friction in his marriage.

CHAPTER 12

I love my husband, but I don't always like him. There's a difference, and it's significant. That's what I told myself for far too long. People look at him and see perfection. Calm demeanor, fantastic jawline, bright smile, a package almost as thick as his wallet—though they wouldn't know that from the outside, I suppose, but it's true. His kids adore him. A beautiful, I hope, wife.

What they don't see is what happened when it got dark outside and the doors were locked.

I'm not going to exaggerate and say it was all the time, because it wasn't. Most of the time, he was charming and kind enough. He wasn't one to shower me with extravagant gifts or bring home flowers just because, but that's okay. I didn't need those things from him. I don't even like flowers. They remind me of funerals and make me sneeze. He'd offer to do the dishes most nights, and he'd even give the kids a bath without me asking. Rarely did he forget to put the trash out at the end of the driveway on Thursday mornings. If a pipe leaked, he'd tighten it. If the screen door stuck, he'd lubricate it until it opened and closed freely. He reliably cut the grass. He's an admirable father.

Our problems were nothing mundane like that. My husband was mostly a good man. Except for when he wasn't. The man who came out when he got angry was one I wish I never knew. While I was more vocally emotional—abrasive, even—he was the opposite. His anger manifested itself in a slow simmer and put a scowl on his face that I'm convinced he didn't know was there. It made him so unapproachable. It's not necessarily what he'd say that was the problem, it was in the delivery of how he'd say it.

To put it frankly, he was a bully. He'd talk at or down to me with a smugness a fool could mistake as confidence. Not by me. Like the way he'd tell me to "think" or to "listen to the words that are coming out of your mouth right now," as if I didn't choose them intentionally. He thought he was above me, that I didn't have the intelligence or intuition to make it in this world. He's verbalized none of those things to me, but that's what makes it worse. A subtle eye roll here, an exasperated pinching of the tension spots in his neck there. It was his body's way of showing me what he truthfully thought about me.

Those were the things outsiders didn't see.

A person can only take so much. I've lost count how many nights I lay awake next to him while he slept without a care in the world. He doesn't have any clue how many tears I've shed about the way he's treated me or the nasty ways he's spoken to me.

The worst part is, he'd wake up the morning after a fight and look at me with the charm I used to be defenseless against, and I couldn't be mad at him. He wouldn't even apologize for hurting me, but I'd forgive him in my heart and mind. It's pathetic, I admit, but it's the truth. Maybe I'm weak.

Even so, I acknowledge what happened with Jimmy isn't fair to anyone, so the guilt still gnaws at me. Maybe that's why I've changed so much. I used to be fun to be around. Lively, energetic. I'd laugh a lot. Recite silly puns. Belt out karaoke and dance on a table if I was tipsy — or close enough to it where I could say I was. That part of me died along with Jimmy, and I've never been able to get it back. Now, I'm just existing, just there and taking up space. Gray and gloomy and unhappy. Never satisfied. Nothing, no one, has ever been good enough since Jimmy.

My relationship with my husband had no bearing on that situation anyhow. Listen, I get it, that sounds ridiculous. How does a wife sleeping with another man have nothing to do with her husband? Of course, it does. That's what I'd say too. But I'm telling you, in my case, that just isn't what happened. Before kids, back when I was working, I can't recall one time where my husband said something to me that could be taken cruelly. Not one. I wouldn't have married him if he treated me like that. I'm not an idiot.

Some days when I'd feel especially blue, once everyone was out of the house, I'd pull out my laptop and pour a midday glass of wine and poke around the web. I'd read Jimmy's obituary and bawl embarrassingly often. Obviously, I had no one to talk to about it. I bookmarked the webpage as Dinner Recipes in case my husband ever went snooping. But why would he? If he ever asked me who Jimmy was, I would have told him the truth: that we were coworkers once upon a time, an old friend, and I must have mistakenly bookmarked the wrong page. I would have laughed it off and my guess is, he wouldn't have pried any further. He probably would have shaken his head as he walked away, wondering to himself how his wife could be so stupid all the time, even with the small things.

I've tried to forget about Jimmy. I have. We didn't know each other very well — not in a way that mattered, at least. It was harmless flirtation, until it wasn't. But even then, it was just one time. The only time we'd ever been physical outside of a casual handshake or incidental touch was on the sofa, then inside that coat closet during the Halloween party. It just so happened that my skirt was higher than it should have been and his pants were at his ankles at the same time.

So, like I said, I loved my husband. But I also loved Jimmy, even though that's a connection that can't ever be explored again. At some point—I can't say for certain when—I had these thoughts. Horrible thoughts. I wondered if my life would have been happier if the roles were reversed. What if it were my husband who had the brain tumor and not Jimmy? How might things have turned out differently for me?

Which, of course, led to my thoughts spiraling even further. Like, what if my husband were dead? I tried not to think like that, but I couldn't stop it. I just couldn't. I started daydreaming about it, visualizing how I might feel afterward.

At the time, I never thought I'd do it, of course. They were just thoughts. You can't get in trouble for thinking something. But then, I wondered if maybe they were more than thoughts. I loved my husband. But sometimes that isn't enough.

CHAPTER 13

Mark sat at his desk in his office, obliterated with exhaustion. Carly had already gotten him two coffees, plus he had one on the way into the office, and it wasn't even noon. His afternoon schedule was jammed, but he didn't think he was going to make it through. It may have been in everyone's best interest — his clients especially, since it was their money — for him to cancel all appointments again this afternoon, but he would have rather not. Besides it being a bad look two days in a row, he thought forcing himself to focus on something other than Rachel might do his mind some good.

So far, that theory was failing.

Last night was cold, long, and horrible. Mostly sleepless. After the spat he had with Rachel, he didn't dare go upstairs to bed. He didn't want to be near her and he knew she felt the same way. Instead, he slept on the couch in his work clothes — and by slept, it actually meant not sleep. He couldn't. His mind was in a tailspin, replaying their conversation on a continuous, infinite loop leading to nowhere.

What threw him the most was how convincing Rachel was. She was adamant she wasn't involved in whatever Mark had stumbled into. Between the tears and the passion with which she displayed, he almost believed her. He wanted nothing more than to believe her. If it were up to him, he'd forget about everything—what he heard on the radio, the voice, the phone call, the confrontations that ensued—but he just couldn't. He'd heard Rachel's voice as clear as day not once but twice, and he had to understand why. He had to know what she was hiding.

Someone knocked on Mark's door. He looked up.

"Markster, my guy," Todd said from the doorway.

"Hey, Todd."

"Whoa. You look like shit."

"Thanks." Mark grabbed for the mug on his desk but missed, tipping it over instead. Thankfully, it was empty. "Carly! More coffee, please."

Todd took a seat across from Mark. "What happened to you yesterday?" he asked.

"Yesterday?"

"Yeah. We went to Tony's for lunch, then I heard you peaced out."

"Where'd you hear that?"

"Just around. It's a small office."

That was true. It was relatively small.

"So, where'd you go?"

"Something came up."

"Might that something have anything to do with what we talked about?"

It took Mark a bit to figure out what Todd was referring to. "Oh, right. Yeah, sorry. I'm exhausted. My mind's not working right."

"How'd it go?"

"Really well, actually. I mean, I guess. I got the phone numbers."

"You did! How did you pull that off?"

"Had some help from an old friend."

"Cool, dude. Did you figure out what's going on with her then?"

"Well, not exactly. Not yet. It's kind of a long story." Mark's head pounded. "You don't have any Advil, do you?"

"No, but I can get you some Oxy if you want it."

"Seriously?"

Todd shrugged. "Not me, but I know a guy who could hook you up. Just trying to help."

Mark buried his head in his hands. This was going to be the longest afternoon of his life. "Carly! Coffee!"

"Here you go, Mark."

He looked up. Carly stood above him with a steaming mug of coffee cradled in her hands and a tight smile on her face.

"Oh, thanks."

"Are you okay?" she asked him.

He forced out a smile. "I'm fine."

"Good, because Tom Wilde is on the phone for you. He says it's urgent."

Tom?

"I'll take it," Mark said. "Patch him through."

"I'm outta here, Markster," Todd said. "If you change your mind about … you know … let me know."

"Yeah, yeah. Thanks, Todd."

Carly gave Mark a questioning look. He shook her off. She left, and thirty seconds later, his desk phone rang.

"Tom?"

"Hi, Mark. Bad time?"

"No, not at all. What's up? Oh, wait! I got your message yesterday but I totally spaced responding. It was a bit of a crazy afternoon."

"No, it's not about that. Not directly." Something was off about Tom's voice. He sounded like … a policeman. Mark didn't like it.

"What's going on, Tom? What's wrong."

"Something's come across my desk that you're going to want to see."

Mark's breath momentarily caught. "What is it?"

"I'd rather not get into it over the phone. Can you come to the station? I know it's the middle of the day, and with everything that happened yesterday—"

"No, no, don't worry about it. If it's important, I can make it happen."

"It is. Very."

Silence.

"Mark, you there?"

"Yes, I'm here. Sorry. Just processing."

"I understand. When you arrive, check in with Lawanda and she'll ping me right away. I'll let her know I'm expecting you."

"Thanks, Tom."

Tom hung up.

Mark sighed and massaged his temples. This was the last thing he needed right now. He gathered his belongings and shut off his computer.

"Hey, Carly," he said. He stood in front of her, hovering over her desk. "Sorry to do this again, but I need to take the afternoon off."

She looked at him blankly.

"I know, I'm sorry," he said. "Please tell my clients that when you call them. And you can tell them I promise to make it up to them. Can you do that for me?"

"Of course."

He thanked her and left the office.

Call it intuition or maybe it was just a pessimistic state of mind. Either way, the tone in Tom's voice told Mark what he was about to learn was going to rock his world in ways he couldn't imagine. But then he wondered, how much worse could things get?

Lawanda didn't seem to recognize him. Mark smiled and waved as he approached the counter, as if they were friends, but she didn't return either gesture. She looked him up and down, sizing him up.

"Yes?" she said.

"Hi. Remember me from yesterday?"

Lawanda stared at him.

"I guess not. My name's Mark Starr. I'm here to see Tom Wilde. He's expecting me."

"Uh-huh."

"Should I just wait here, or?"

"Have a seat." She pointed. "Over there. Like everyone else."

He sat down. His eyes were heavy. He considered closing them while he waited but thought better of it. Falling asleep in a place like this might not be the best look. Thankfully, Tom didn't keep him waiting long. Four or five minutes at most.

"Mark, thanks for coming," Tom said upon approach.

Mark stood and shook Tom's extended hand.

"Follow me."

When Lawanda was behind them and out of earshot, Mark leaned into Tom and said, "I don't think Lawanda likes me very much."

"I don't think Lawanda likes anybody very much. Which is the way it should be. This isn't a hotel."

They walked the rest of the way in silence. The point was taken. Tom pulled on his office door and held it open for Mark, ushering him inside. They took what was becoming their customary seats on opposite sides of Tom's desk. Mark waited.

"Are you familiar with Indy Guns and Ammo?" Tom asked.

"Sounds like a gun shop."

Tom just stared.

"Just a guess."

"You ever been?"

"I don't even know where it is."

"Is that a no?"

"That's right. What's going on, Tom?"

"What about Rachel?"

"What about her?"

"Is she familiar with Indy Guns and Ammo?"

"I really don't know. Why?"

Tom reached forward and grabbed the computer monitor that was closest to him. He spun it so it faced Mark. A video was cued up. "I want to show you something." Tom pressed a button and the video started.

Mark leaned in. With the dull lighting in the room, the screen was dark and the video was grainy, but he could see well enough. The video feed was from overhead, pointing down at a long glass counter. A range of guns, most with long barrels, hung on the wall behind the counter. Mark wasn't a gun guy, so they all looked the same to him. He gathered he was looking at the sales floor of a gun shop. Indy Guns and Ammo, he presumed.

A man with a big belly and a tight shirt stood behind the counter. His lips were moving, but the video didn't have any audio, so Mark couldn't make out the conversation. Facing the big-bellied man was a customer — a woman with her back to the camera. Her hair was pulled back in a loose ponytail, her waist trim. The man nodded and held up a finger as if to indicate he needed a minute, then he walked to his left and disappeared into the back, leaving the woman alone.

The man couldn't have been in the back for five seconds when the woman, without hesitation — it was as if she planned it — leaped onto and over the counter. She reached underneath the counter, grabbed something, and tossed it inside her opened handbag. Just as quickly, she leaped back over the counter and casually walked out of the shop. The big-bellied man hadn't returned from the back. The footage ended.

"Why are you showing this to me?" Mark asked.

"Did you recognize the woman?"

"Should I? I wasn't looking that close."

Tom moved the mouse and clicked to rewind the footage. "Look again. Watch closely."

A knot formed in Mark's throat. He sensed where this was going.

What about Rachel?

Is she familiar with Indy Guns and Ammo?

The video played again, just not from the beginning. Mark watched as the customer, the woman, leaped over the counter again. He leaned in closer to the screen to get a better look. It looked like the woman grabbed a small box, something that fit in her hand, but he couldn't tell what it was. He continued watching, studying, as the woman leaped back over the counter and started for the door.

The screen paused.

"There," Tom said. "Look at her face."

Mark leaned in even closer. So close, the LCD screen warmed his face. He squinted at the woman, trying to make out who he already knew it was.

Rachel.

Mark's jaw fell open. "Is that …"

"Rachel? Looks like her to me. What do you think?"

Mark wanted to say it wasn't her, but it was. It was definitely her. The same face he'd seen smile tens of thousands of times. The one person on this planet who he thought he knew inside and out, aside from himself. The woman he married, the mother of his two precious daughters.

Rachel.

"I don't understand," Mark said. "Why would Rachel be in a gun shop? We don't even own a gun."

"Are you sure about that?"

"Positive."

"Apparently your wife does."

"Excuse me?"

"I asked the owner of the gun shop to check his inventory, and he's missing a box of 9mm ammo. He stores them in the glass case right where Rachel grabbed from, or so he says."

The reality of what was happening was suffocating. Mark was short of breath.

"You okay there?" Tom said.

Mark held up a hand. "Fine. I just need a second." He took a few seconds and breathed. In and out, out then in, until he was calm.

"I'm going to need you to do something for me, Mark. Are you with me?"

Mark nodded. "I'm with you."

"I need to talk to Rachel about this. Urgently."

"Okay."

"The gun shop owner is being reasonable about this. He doesn't want to press any charges right now. He just wants his inventory back."

"That's good then. Right?"

"For now, sure. But things can change, Mark. I'm sure he's going to advise with his counsel about logical next steps. Who knows how he might feel after that."

"Got it. So, what do you need me to do?"

"I need you to convince Rachel to turn herself in."

"Turn herself in? But you just said —"

"A crime was still committed here, Mark. Just because the shop owner may not press charges doesn't mean my job stops. I have to book her and talk to her. I have a job to do. I'm sorry."

"I understand." And he did. But he didn't like it.

"I need you to talk to her and convince her to come in tomorrow, in the morning. Can you do that?"

Could he? They weren't on good terms right now. They hadn't even spoken today. At all. "I'll see what I can do."

Tom leaned forward over the desk and lowered his voice. "I'm going to be straight with you, Mark. As a friend."

Friend.

"I can keep this to myself for twenty-four hours at most. After that, I'm bound to take the next step. Do you understand what I'm saying to you?"

"I … I'm not sure."

"If Rachel doesn't come here tomorrow before the clock turns noon, I'll need to send out a crew to your house. I don't want to see her taken out of your home in handcuffs, Mark. I don't think you want that either."

He didn't. Of course not. Not for her and not for him. What would the neighbors think? The girls would be at school, but they had friends in the neighborhood. What if they overheard their parents talking about it, or what if they were banned from playing with them going forward? The girls would be devastated. For Mark, what if the firm got word, or his clients? A scandal like this could end his career.

"Bring her in, Mark. These things go a lot smoother in the courts when the accused is cooperative rather than combative."

Mark nodded. He understood. "I get it. I appreciate the heads-up about all this. I'll talk to her. I'll make sure she stops by."

"This is important."

"I know. I'll get her here. Whatever it takes."

CHAPTER 15

Mark couldn't go home early again. Not today. Not after the bomb Tom just dropped on his life. He could have gone back to the office and made some apologetic phone calls to the clients he'd blown off, but he wasn't in the right headspace for that. He could have asked Todd to join him for a late lunch. But he didn't want to talk about what was going on, and he knew Todd would ask. What he wanted was to be alone, to think.

Johnny's.

He wasn't a frequent bargoer, but everyone knew about Johnny's. It was the spot to go to burn off steam after a long week or a difficult day at the office. Todd had bullied him into going once or twice. Mark remembered enjoying the vibe enough. A bar was a bar.

Nobody turned and looked at him when he walked in. The lights were so dim, it could have been the middle of the night. Three billiards tables went unused. A jukebox with splintered glass played a glam metal track from the eighties Mark recognized but couldn't remember the name of. Two men threw darts, their backs to him. Mark sat at the bar, leaving two stools between him and the next patron. He eyed the tray of nuts but thought better of it.

"What can I get you, darling?" the bartender asked.

Mark looked up at her. A neck tattoo was the first thing he noticed. A cat. Flesh tunnels left ginormous holes in both of her ears. One eyebrow, one nostril, and her bottom lip were pierced.

"Well?"

"Oh, sorry," he said. "What was the question?"

The bartender rolled her eyes. "What do you want?"

"Just get me a beer."

She stared at him.

"Please."

She continued to stare.

"What?"

"I have ten beers on tap and twenty more cold. I'm going to need more information than that."

He felt like an idiot. He panicked and said the first beer that came to mind. "Right. Um, I'll take a Budweiser." He hated Budweiser but changing his mind now would have made him look like even more of a moron than he already did.

The bartender left to retrieve his order. A much older man two stools down chuckled at something — at Mark? — and sipped from his glass.

Mark considered leaving. He was clearly out of his element here, an amateur. His mind was elsewhere, but that wasn't an excuse. Where was Todd when he needed him? This was Todd's scene.

The bartender returned with a glass filled to the brim, a smooth layer of foam on the top. Somehow, it didn't spill over. Not even a single drop.

"How much?" Mark asked.

"Four bucks. Do you want to start a tab?"

He shook his head and reached for his wallet. He pulled out a twenty-dollar bill and slid it across the counter. A corner of the bill grabbed on to something sticky on the surface, tearing slightly.

The bartender grabbed it. "I'll be back with your change."

"No, keep it."

She raised her eyebrows and a smile briefly formed.

Mark rubbed his finger along the top of the glass. Foam latched onto his finger and stayed there, fizzing. More of it slid down the side of the glass. Slowly, steadily, a journey to nowhere.

"You good?" the bartender asked him. She lifted his glass and slipped a napkin underneath.

"Thank you," he said, not answering her question.

"You don't come in here much, do you?" she asked.

He snickered. "Is it that obvious?"

"It's not that. It's just that I would have remembered you."

He looked at her, questioning.

"You're not like my usual clientele."

He shifted his eyes left, to the older man on the stool, then to the others throwing darts. He hadn't noticed before, but they were all bikers. Or they were at one time. Or they were wannabees and dressed like they were. Each sported a Harley-Davidson logo somewhere on their person—a bicep tattoo, a sleeveless shirt, and a bandanna. Mark bit back a laugh.

"See?" the bartender said. She smiled. Fully this time. Her teeth were straight and, he imagined, white.

"What's your name?" he asked.

"Sarah."

"Sarah?"

She scrunched her eyebrows now, cocking her head; she was quite expressive.

"You don't look like a Sarah, is all."

"Why not?"

"It's just the … and your … nothing. Forget I said anything." He took a sip of the Budweiser. Foam tickled his nose. The beer was cold, but it tasted horrible.

She laughed. "I'm just busting your balls. It's because of my pussy, isn't it?"

The biker two stools down howled with laughter. Mark tried to swallow but coughed instead. The beer burned his throat and the back of his nose. "Excuse me?"

Sarah craned her neck to the side and pointed to her tattoo. "My ink. Mr. Pussycat. I know, it gives off a certain vibe. I was drunk one night in New Orleans. It seemed like a good idea at the time. Live and you learn, right?"

Mark's nose and throat still burned but he pushed through it. "I think it's nice." He coughed again.

"Hold on." Sarah stepped away, filled up a glass with water, and handed it to him.

He nodded his thanks and took it. He sipped until the burn faded and the urge to cough stopped.

"So, Mr. …" Sarah said.

"Mark."

"Mark, what brings you into Johnny's at one o'clock in the afternoon in the middle of the week?"

He sighed. "I think I'd rather not talk about."

Sarah looked surprised, or hurt. Or both. Mark had a feeling she didn't get told no very often. Her bubbly personality certainly made her easy to talk to, so it was easy to imagine why most patrons probably did. Sarah nodded and grabbed a damp rag. She did a number on the sticky spot from earlier.

"Can I ask you something?" Mark asked a minute later.

Sarah kept wiping the counter. "Sure."

"Do you ever get lied to?"

The rag stopped moving and Sarah looked up. "With the guys who come into this bar? Every day."

"How do you deal with it?"

Sarah moved closer to Mark and leaned over the counter. He tried his hardest to keep his eyes focused on anything and everything above the neckline.

"The key, for me, is to read between the lines. Most of what people say has some truth in it. It's about finding out what that truth is, then ignoring the bullshit surrounding it."

"But how do you know what the truth is?"

"It's all in the eyes."

"How do you mean?"

"When someone's telling the truth and wants you to believe it, they look at you right in the face without blinking. It's like they think you can see it in their eyes." She laughed. "Stupid. It shows their hand. Because then when they're not telling the truth, you can tell by looking at their eyes. If they're not locked in to you, either blinking too much or too little, chances are, they're either lying or at least embellishing."

"So, you're saying it's like that thing where you can tell when someone's lying if they look up and to the left, right? Or is it to the right?"

"That doesn't work. Everyone's heard of that, so liars are consciously aware of it and won't do it. Blinking, or not blinking, is subconscious. People don't think about it; it just happens."

"Is there any science behind this?"

"All I know about science is what happens in the real-world. And this bar is as real as it gets."

"And it works? The blinking thing."

"Every single time." She stood up straight and smiled. "Why do you ask?"

Mark took another sip of the water. After swallowing, his throat felt much better. "No reason."

CHAPTER 16

Mark left Johnny's and headed straight home. If he made good time, he would have twenty-five or thirty minutes to talk to Rachel before she had to leave to pick up the girls. The timing was perfect. First, he could talk to Rachel; then, he'd have ample time to look for the gun while he was alone. He wasn't at home alone very often. Typically, he didn't mind.

This situation was anything but typical.

He pulled into the garage and slid the car into park. He closed the door behind him and walked into the house. "Rach?" he called out. "Where are you?"

Rachel didn't respond, but he heard something. A voice. It sounded like it came from the kitchen. He went toward it.

"Rach?"

Rachel gasped. Something slipped from her grasp and crashed onto the floor. "Geez, Mark!"

"Sorry. I called for you."

"Didn't hear it."

"I opened and closed the garage."

"I guess I didn't hear that, either."

He nodded. It didn't matter. Music played from her phone. She'd probably been singing, wrapped up in the four-minute heartbreak story marketed as romance. Rachel bent down and came back up with a small knife in her hand. Mark noticed the fruit containers on the counter, saw the edge of the strainer in the sink.

He put his things down. Rachel ignored him, keeping her head down and singing softly to herself. He couldn't blame her; the last two days had been tense.

Mark walked over to his wife and stood beside her. "Hey," he said.

"Hey," she said back without stopping what she was doing. Colorful sliced berries filled the strainer.

"Will you put the knife down and look at me, please?"

She did, but with a heavy sigh. "What, Mark? I'm in the middle of something. What time is it? Why are you even home right now?"

"That's what I wanted to talk to you about."

A paleness overtook her face.

"Can we go sit for a few minutes? Please."

She let him take her hand and lead her to the table, where they sat. A slight tremor transferred from her hand to his as he held onto it.

"What happened?" she asked.

"Tom asked me to go visit him at the police station this morning."

"Tom Wilde?"

"Yes."

"What did he want?"

Mark studied her face. He paid close attention so he wouldn't miss anything. "He showed me a video. From inside Indy Guns and Ammo."

"The gun shop?"

A lump formed in his throat.

She knows.

"You know it?" he asked.

"I've heard of it. Why was Tom Wilde showing you a video from a gun shop?"

"There was a robbery." He watched Rachel carefully.

Nothing.

"Again, why did Tom show you this? Isn't something like that ... confidential?"

"Have you ever been to the shop?"

"The gun shop? No. Why would I go to a gun shop? I'm a democrat."

He almost laughed. But he didn't. "So that's a no?"

Rachel's jaw flexed. "Yes, Mark, that's a no. What's up with this new thing where you don't believe a word that comes out of —"

"I saw you."

Rachel said nothing. The silence was so heavy, the pressure of it pinched his chest.

It's all in the eyes.

"What did you say?" Rachel finally said.

"I saw you in the video, Rach."

The breath fell out of Rachel; she deflated like a balloon. "I've never been inside any gun shop ever, Mark. I hate guns. You know that about me."

"You're right. I know that. Which is why seeing you in that video —"

"It wasn't me."

"Rachel, it wasn't just me who saw you. Tom recognized you first. That's why he called me, to show me. To see if it was you. And it was."

Rachel wouldn't make eye contact. She looked down, then away, then anywhere but at Mark. "I ... I —"

"Do you own a 9mm handgun?"

"What? Of course not! Why would you ask that?"

"Because a box a 9mm ammunition was stolen from the gun shop. And there's video of you taking it."

Rachel cried.

It's all in the eyes.

"Tom needs to talk to you about what happened."

"Nothing happened. It wasn't me."

Mark's frustration was boiling over, but he knew that if he was going to convince Rachel to turn herself in, he needed to stay calm. It was a must. "Maybe there's another explanation. That's why we need to talk to Tom. Together. You can see the video for yourself."

Rachel wiped her tears away then looked at the side of her finger for evidence of a makeup smudge. "It wasn't me."

"Fine. But we still need to talk to Tom about it."

She shook her head. "I need to think about it."

Mark leaned forward and took his wife's hands. She trembled.

"Look at me," he said.

She did.

It's all in the eyes.

Tears pooled in her eyes and streamed down her cheeks. Blinking made the tears worse, but she had to. She looked right at him but Mark couldn't get a read on her.

"Rach, Tom is doing you, us, a courtesy by telling us. If you don't turn yourself in by noon tomorrow, he's going to send someone to the house to arrest you."

Her hands shot up to her mouth and covered it. A tiny gasp escaped.

"He's giving you the chance to do this on your own, in private. Away from anyone who might see. Do you understand what I'm saying?"

She nodded.

Relief washed over him. At least when it came to this, Rachel had come to her senses.

Rachel looked behind her, at something in the kitchen. "Shoot," she said. "I need to go pick up the girls."

Mark nodded. She stood up and went into the bathroom, assumingly to clean up her face. The toilet flushed. A few seconds later, the garage door opened then closed. Rachel was gone, without saying goodbye.

Mark wasted no time. He leaped up from the chair and frantically searched for somewhere Rachel may have hidden a gun. He didn't have long before Rachel would be back with the girls, and his opportunities to do this were limited.

He went room by room. In the kitchen, he opened all the cabinets, looked behind and around everything. Inside the oven, refrigerator and freezer, microwave. On top of the cabinets. Behind all the food. Underneath the table. Nothing.

He checked the hallway closet, every crevice of the bathroom. Inside, behind, and underneath the washing machine and the dryer. Nothing. In the living room, the end tables contained the usual—remotes, phone charger, four hundred lip balms. No gun. Nothing in between or underneath the sofa cushions aside from some crumbs from late-night snacking.

"Damn it!" he yelled. He was getting frustrated.

The girls' playroom was a disaster. As a parent, he couldn't fathom the idea of Rachel hiding a gun in their playroom. Rachel was a phenomenal mother. Caring, loving, attentive. Smart. The best. No way. He swept the room and found nothing even remotely resembling a gun. Thankfully. He moved on. A quick search of the guest bedroom resulted in nothing either.

Upstairs, he flipped over every hand towel and bath towel and face cloth in the closet, moved every box of bandages and bottle of every type of medicine the family could ever need, with a backup bottle of each for good measure. You never know when you'll need it, Rachel often said. No gun. Rachel kept their house meticulously clean—one of the things Mark appreciated most about her; there was nothing like coming home to a freshly cooked meal and a clean house, the girls' playroom and bedrooms aside—which made Mark's search so much easier because there weren't messes to sift through or piles of nonsense to look under.

The upstairs bathroom was clear. He scanned both girls' bedrooms for the same reason as the playroom. No surprise, he found nothing. Just toys they didn't play with anymore and too many stuffed animals to count. He spent the most time in he and Rachel's bedroom, for what seemed like obvious reasons. Her walk-in closet had bins filled with old purses, and there were stacks of shoeboxes that touched the ceiling in spots. It was overwhelming. He'd never have time to look through them all.

What he did instead was try to think logically about where someone might hide a gun. Somewhere that would be easy to access, but not too easy. Somewhere hidden out of plain sight if someone wasn't looking for it, but obvious if they were. He checked both nightstands and bureaus, under the mattress and the bed frame. He even checked under Rachel's pillows, and his own, just in case. Found nothing unusual. He checked the time. He had no more than ten minutes before Rachel would be back with the girls.

He went back downstairs and into the garage. Rachel avoided the garage at all costs; that was his baby. The only time she spent in it was getting to and from her car. Which could make it the perfect hiding place for a gun; somewhere no one would expect.

For as organized as Rachel was, Mark couldn't have been further from it. Shelves containing one of just about everything—and two of the important things, because he never knew when he might need it—lined the garage's walls. Tools and spare parts to who knew what were strewn all over. Frankly, he didn't know where to start. Before he could decide, the garage door squeaked and started pulling upward.

Rachel was home.

Quick to find an excuse, Mark turned his back to the door and toyed with tools on the workbench. He stayed that way, moving his arms to look busy, until he heard a voice.

"Daddy!" Maureen called out with her usual giddiness.

Mark put a smile on his face and turned toward them. Maureen ran up to him and wrapped her little arms around his waist. Abagail soon joined them.

"What are you doing, Dad?" Abagail asked.

"Just looking for a screwdriver to fix that loose door finally," he said. He turned toward the pile of tools, found one on the top, and picked it up. "Here we go."

Abagail smiled at him.

"Can we help, Daddy?"

"Of course, you can!"

"Yay! I'll meet you in the bathroom. I'll get the paper towels!"

"We don't need—"

Maureen was already gone, shot like a cannon into the house.

"Never mind," Mark said. He looked down at Abagail. "You helping too?"

"Sure," she said, then she grabbed his hand and pulled him toward the door.

Mark snuck a glance at Rachel as he walked past. Her head was buried inside the driver's side door, her backside out of the car. She came out with her purse in one hand, her phone in the other. She turned and their eyes briefly met, but there was nothing there. No smile, no acknowledgment, no anything. Mark lost her as he ascended the stairs, Abagail leading the way.

Whatever was going on in that head of Rachel's, he couldn't imagine. None of it made any sense. Despite all the evidence presented to her, Rachel was still in denial. Understanding how that was possible was beyond his competence. He still had some work to do to convince her to turn herself in, he realized, and that was a major hurdle they needed to get over. Mark had so many questions.

What was she doing with a box of 9mm ammo?

Where was the gun the ammo loaded into?

Where did she get the gun from?

How long had she had it?

Most importantly, what was she planning on using it for? Or whom?

He couldn't see Rachel's face, but he felt her energy at his back, undoubtedly from her piercing eyes. The force of her presence was strong, intense. Not good. He knew he had a battle on his hands.

It's all in the eyes.

CHAPTER 17

Mark woke in a panic. It was one of those moments where he knew in his gut that he slept through his alarm. That feeling of dread knowing the day couldn't get off to a worse start. There was a commotion downstairs — the girls getting ready for school, Rachel clanging around in the kitchen. He was irked that Rachel didn't bother waking him, but it wasn't her responsibility; she wasn't his secretary. Usually, he appreciated that about her. Today, it felt like a slight.

He slipped out of bed and checked his phone. He was behind, but not by much. There was still time to make it out the door on time, if he hurried. So, that was what he did. With everything. A quick shower, spent less time than normal on the toilet, a quick but good enough shave. He could skip the coffee with Rachel, if needed, and get his fix at the office, even if it tasted subpar.

Downstairs, the girls' breakfast plates were on the counter and the TV was off. They were getting their shoes on in the hall leading to the garage. Backpacks were zipped and ready to go.

"Bye, girls," he called out to them. "Have a beautiful day."

"Bye, Daddy!" Maureen said.

Abagail smiled and waved.

It was then that Mark noticed someone was missing. Rachel. "Where's Mommy?"

"Right behind you," she said, startling him.

Mark turned around and faced her.

"About what we talked about yesterday," she said. "I'll do it."

Mark was so surprised that he didn't have any words. The girls were too busy to notice the conversation.

"You'll be here when I get back, right?" Rachel asked.

"Oh. Well, I …"

"Please. Will you go with me?" She looked at him with pleading eyes. Or fearful.

There were a select few moments in a husband's life where there was a correct answer and an incorrect answer. Regardless of how much tension lingered between them, Rachel was still Mark's wife. Whether he believed or understood her didn't matter in this situation. It was his duty to be there for her in a time of need, and he would be. He'd make it work.

"Yes, of course," he said. "I'll be here. We can go together."

"Where are you going?" Abagail asked, always the curious one.

"Just an errand," Rachel answered. "You girls ready?"

"Yep!" Maureen said. "Bye, Daddy!"

Then they were gone.

Rachel being willing to turn herself in without an argument was good. Very good. A relief, really. Mark wasn't prepared to deal with the aftermath of a police ambush if Rachel didn't go willingly. Tom wasn't bluffing, either. Like he'd said, he had a job to do, and he'd do it, friends or not. This part was good. What wasn't good was the next phone call Mark had to make. After what happened each of the last two days, not being around again today was a horrible look. But he had no choice. He pulled out his phone and dialed Carly.

"Mark?" Carly said upon answering.

"I'm sorry to call so early."

"Is everything okay?"

"Yes, of course. Actually, no, not really. I'm in the middle of a bit of a personal crisis."

"Oh no! Is there anything I can do?"

"That's why I'm calling. I hate to do this, but I'm going to need you to clear my schedule again today. I'm really sorry."

"Oh. Uh. Okay."

Something was off about her tone. "What is it, Carly?"

"I was going to tell you today. At the office. You've seemed off the last couple of days, so I didn't want to add more stress."

"What's going on?"

"It's just … earlier this week, the first time you had me clear your schedule, Mr. Lyons was on the calendar."

"Okay, and?"

"And there's something urgent he needs to talk to you about, he said, so I booked him for yesterday afternoon instead."

Uh-oh. He had a feeling he knew where this was going.

"He told me he won't be treated this way. With all the capital he brings into the firm, he was adamant that his business should be prioritized."

"And it is."

"Right. That's what I told him."

Stanley Lyons. A local business mogul. He owned three apartment complexes in the city, a restaurant, plus a handful of commercial properties and other non-real estate investments. He grew up with a trust fund but was far from a trust fund baby. All of his investments made fists of money year-over-year, at least since Mark had him as a client. What Carly said was right; Stanley Lyons's portfolio was at least ten times larger than anyone else's on his roster. The reality was, the commission earned off Stanley's portfolio alone kept the lights on. He was the big fish in a sea of small ones who Mark somehow reeled in all those years ago. He still wasn't sure how he did it, but he had. Possibly his greatest professional success. Letting him get away would be devastating.

"He was pissed to be rescheduled twice in the same week," Carly said.

"Let me guess, he's on the schedule for today too?"

"He was."

Mark rubbed his eyes. He'd been awake for thirty minutes, and he already felt a migraine forming. "Okay. Thanks, Carly. I'll call him personally. I'll handle it."

"Are you sure there isn't anything else I can do?"

He thought about it. He liked Carly. She was good at what she did, and she kept him in line the best she could without overstepping. He wasn't sure he deserved her. "I don't think so. But I appreciate the offer. If you can call everyone and let them know, you can take the day. I'll cover it."

"Thank you, Mark. And I'm sorry I didn't tell you about Mr. Lyons earlier. I didn't think—"

"No, not at all. You did the right thing."

She exhaled. "Thank you."

"Take care, Carly."

"Yeah, you too."

They disconnected.

Things had gone from bad to worse in a hurry. Rachel was one thing; that situation spoke for itself. But now, work was piling on. His professional identity. Their sole source of income. Their lifeline, in many ways. If Stanley Lyons pulled his money out of frustration, it might bury Mark. Not might, would. It would bury him. Then he'd have to explain to Marty Joyce— Marty was the firm's president—how he let one of the firm's biggest clients walk out the door. Marty was detached from the day-to-day, but there were a dozen or so clients he met with quarterly to ensure their happiness. Stanley was one of them. If Stanley walked, Marty would fire Mark on the spot with no opportunity to explain himself. Not that Mark had a reason Marty would ever deem acceptable. Marty was cold like that. That could have been why he was so successful.

Add that to the pressure Mark already faced with Rachel's mess, and it was enough to suffocate him. Desperate for air, he yanked on his suddenly tight collar.

Rachel would be home soon. Or not. He didn't know. He was usually gone by now, on his way to the office. When he thought about it, he realized he knew very little about Rachel's routine. He made a mental note to ask her about it sometime, after this all blew over.

It was strange. They knew each other so well, yet, he knew so little about her daily life as a mother. How had he let that happen? Before kids, they'd take daily walks around the city, where they both worked, or around their condo complex. They used to exercise together. Run 5Ks. They even once drove up north and participated in a Tough Mudder. They didn't place particularly well, the strength event doing them in, but they had a blast. They drank beers with the new friends they made, shared a shower in the hotel, made love in the jacuzzi. Laughed over breakfast the next day about how poor their combined upper body strength was.

Now, they spent a half-hour talking over a glass of wine at night, but were both often too tired to do anything together much beyond that. They were intimate occasionally. He sometimes wondered if he was in the minority, but he found occasionally to be good enough these days. It was all part of the marriage cycle, he supposed, especially with young kids. But that wasn't an excuse. For as strong as he thought their marriage was, maybe there were some chinks in the armor he'd been overlooking. Was there a chance Rachel wasn't as happy with their lives as he always assumed? Could this have something do with her recent out of character behavior?

When this was all over, he'd attempt to ensure they spent more time together. Just the two of them. They could find a babysitter for the girls or they could go to Rachel's parents' house more often. His family was the most important part of his life; he needed to get back to treating them that way.

Mark retreated upstairs and changed into something more comfortable with less strangulation involved. He chose something casual but not too casual; professional but not stuffy. He wasn't sure how he should look to accompany his surrendering wife to the police station. Would there be cameras? Did anyone else know what was about to happen? What would happen next?

And then it hit him.

Rachel didn't have a lawyer. In books and movies, the accused seemingly always wanted to call their lawyer. He and Rachel didn't have one. They never needed one. Why would they? They lived a normal, law-abiding life. They filed taxes in March every year. Neither of them had ever been convicted of a crime, never mind been arrested. Mark had one speeding ticket from seven years ago, but otherwise had a clean record. Rachel didn't have any, as far as he knew. Their lives were, in the eyes of the law, boring.

Which was another reason Mark simply couldn't believe this was happening to them of all people.

There was no time to find an attorney. Rachel should have been home any minute, and they'd head into the city. It wasn't possible for him to find an attorney that quickly. None of their offices were even open at this hour. But he knew many people, working in finance. He could get a recommendation to—

Too late.

Beneath his feet, the garage door opening rumbled.

Rachel.

He headed downstairs. "Hey," he said when he saw her.

"Hey."

"All good at school?"

"Yup." She didn't look at him.

"So—"

Now she looked at him. "Let's make one thing clear. I've agreed to do this because I have to see that footage for myself. I'm not admitting any guilt because I did nothing wrong. I didn't steal anything from a gun shop. I've never even been to a gun shop! If you're going to try to gaslight me again, I don't want to hear it."

Mark was too far taken aback to respond. He hadn't expected her to attack him like that. Rachel was laser-focused on him, her eye contact intimidating.

It's all in the eyes.

"I'm not in the mood, Mark. Unless the next words out of your mouth are an apology, I don't want to hear it. I'll be waiting in the car."

Mark stayed back for a beat to gather himself. Rachel hadn't ever spoken that way to him, or anyone. She wasn't a pushover, but certainly not confrontational. Typically, she avoided it at all costs—even eating a meal at a restaurant that wasn't made as she ordered it, just to avoid having to send it back. He lost count how many times they'd been through that throughout the years. Had he really driven her to the dark place she was in now? That he was witnessing such a stark change in her character—which could be credited to the way he's treated her, she said in her own way—was unfathomable. Had he really been tearing her down like that? That burden felt horrible. Where had he gone wrong as her husband and life partner? He owed it to her to do better.

But still, he saw what he saw. The footage didn't lie. Neither did the voices he heard, one he even spoke to directly. He was just trying to find the truth. She was the one gaslighting him, trying to cover her tracks. Putting it all on him must have been part of her tactic here, though the end goal was about as clear as mud. Besides, he wasn't the only one to see what he did on film. Tom did too, before Mark even. That had to mean something.

Everything would be cleared up today, once Rachel saw the video. Then, she'd have no choice but to admit it. How could she deny what would be thrown in her face so bluntly? The biggest question was: Why did she continue lying about it?

The answer would come soon enough. Mark grabbed his wallet and his keys and joined her in the car, determined to find out the answer to that lingering question.

CHAPTER 18

Rachel said nothing to him on the way, and he didn't dare press his luck. He drove in silence, strumming his anxious fingers on the steering wheel. He switched on the radio and, like fate, the Foo Fighters were on. All the memories came flooding back in an instant. The Fighters were their band. Aside from their one hellish trip into Chicago armed with the MapQuest directions, they'd seen them three other times. Dave Grohl's rasp was something that always connected them, for whatever reason. Concertgoing was another one of those things he and Rachel did together before the girls were born, back when she used to be down for anything—and he was too.

The memories choked him up. He glanced at Rachel to gauge her reaction, but all he saw was the side of her face as she looked out the window, trapped in her own world. He considered turning the radio up so she might react to the song the way he did, but he didn't want to force it. He could only imagine what she was going through, what she must have been thinking. How abandoned she felt. He wanted nothing more than to reach over and grab her hand as a show of unity, to remind her he was still there for her through the best and worst of times, regardless of how she felt about him right now. But he didn't. Maybe he should have. Whether he believed in her innocence—and the truth was, he didn't; with all the evidence he'd been presented with, how could he?—he could still be there for her and support her.

But the moment passed and he missed his opportunity. Dave Grohl lectured about watching his hero walk out of his life. He could have been talking directly to Mark.

There goes my hero.

Watch him as he goes.

There goes my hero.

He's ordinary.

Dave Grohl was right; Mark was being an ordinary husband. He should have been better than ordinary for her. She deserved more than that. Rachel was his wife, the mother of his two beautiful daughters, and he was letting her down.

They arrived. Mark parked as close as he could, a block away. Inside, Mark led the way. He walked up to the counter, Rachel at his heels, where his old friend Lawanda sat in her usual spot. She eyed him as he approached, as if she might recognize him this time.

"You're here again?" she asked.

"Afraid so," he said.

"Tom Wilde again?"

He nodded.

Lawanda made the call and Mark showed Rachel to the waiting area without needed prompting. He sat and sighed. He wasn't looking forward to this.

"How many times have you been here?" Rachel asked.

"Enough."

She scoffed.

Mark picked at his fingers. He usually didn't, but he needed something to do with his hands—an outlet for his negative energy. Where was Tom? The waiting was killing him.

Tom finally showed up and Mark just about leaped out of his seat. While he wasn't happy to see him—he really wasn't; nothing personal—he couldn't stand the waiting anymore.

Mark first knew something was wrong when Tom didn't greet him with his customary handshake. Tom's face showed nothing. Not hurt or disappointment or anger. Certainly not sympathy. Mark shielded Rachel. He stood slightly in front of her, if only a little. Hardly noticeable, but he felt the instinct kick in; the need to protect her.

"Thank you for coming in," Tom said.

Mark nodded. Rachel dug her hands into her pockets.

"Come on up," Tom said. "Let's talk."

They followed. Mark had gotten so familiar with the walk that he could have done it with his eyes closed. That didn't seem like a good thing.

He wished he could have closed his eyes to what was about to happen, too.

Just like he had the day before, in Tom's office, he cued up a video on his computer and spun one of the monitors toward them. He didn't say anything because he didn't have to; he simply hit play and let the video do all the talking.

Mark couldn't watch. He'd seen it twice already, and that was two times too many. And that didn't count the four thousand times it replayed in his head, over and over again, while he tried to fall asleep last night. Instead, he watched Rachel to see her reaction.

It's all in the eyes.

Rachel leaned forward and squinted as if trying to get a better look. Mark remembered the footage; just wait. Rachel watched the monitor while Mark watched her. He felt Tom watching them both.

The gasp—though Mark thought it sounded forced, or maybe he was imagining it—came before her mouth fell agape.

"Play it again," she said.

Tom did.

"One more time."

He did.

Tears pooled in Rachel's eyes, eventually dancing down her cheeks.

"When was this?" Rachel asked.

"Two days ago," Tom replied.

Mark knew her wheels were spinning.

"I ..." she stammered. "That's not possible."

Tom leaned in. "Rachel, what were you doing at Indy Guns and Ammo?"

"I ... I ..."

"More importantly, why did you steal a box of 9mm ammunition? What are you planning on doing with it?"

Mark's chest pounded so hard that his bones hurt.

Tears poured out of Rachel's eyes now.

"Why did you do it?" Tom pressed her. "I need to know why."

"I ..." she tried. "I know what it looks like. That woman, she—"

"It's you, Rachel," Tom said. "I know it's you."

She shook her head. "It's not me. It wasn't me."

Mark couldn't believe his ears. She just saw it, saw herself, and yet ... she continued denying it.

"I gave the footage to my video department," Tom said, "and I gave them your photo. They used artificial intelligence software to compare the two."

Rachel frantically shook her head. She knew where this was headed. They all did.

"And Rachel," Tom said. "The faces are a perfect match. The same shape, identical symmetry. Everything. We ran it through the software a dozen times to make sure. I hate to say this, but I know it was you. There's no doubt."

Rachel sobbed. "No! No, no, no! You have it wrong. You don't have any idea how wrong—"

"The footage, Rachel," Tom said. "We all saw it."

Mark felt helpless watching her react like this. He reached over and attempted to grab her hand, but she violently yanked it away.

"Stop," she said with vile. She quickly stood up, nearly knocking her chair on its back. "Don't follow me." She stormed out.

Mark stood up to go after her, but Tom stopped him.

"Let her go," Tom said. "There are a couple officers outside my office. They'll wrangle her."

"Wrangle her? I don't want to do that," Mark said. He started for the door to stop Rachel, but she was already gone.

"Stop!" Tom snapped.

Mark did, but not because of Tom. He stopped because of the sound on the other side of the door.

Rachel was screaming.

"It's okay, Mark," Tom said. "Sit down."

Mark didn't. His head spun.

"You did the right thing, bringing her here."

"I don't know if I did. She's my wife."

Tom nodded and motioned for Mark to sit. "I understand. Trust me, I understand. There was no other choice."

Mark shook his head. He wasn't so sure. He wasn't sure about anything anymore.

"You saw the tape. You saw her reaction. AI says it's a one hundred percent match. So, if you had any doubt before, you shouldn't. It's been all but proven now. It's her, Mark. It's her."

The facts were hard to argue with. Especially the latest one. Impossible, really. But Rachel ... she was distraught. Her reaction was puzzling. And now, she was being wrangled—whatever that even meant—and there was nothing he could do about it. The sound of her wails was gut-wrenching.

"Sit."

Mark finally obliged. He practically collapsed into the chair.

"Good, good," Tom said. He handed Mark a paper towel. Mark took it and dabbed his forehead. "Are you all right?"

Mark nodded.

"Rachel's fine. I promise."

Mark nodded again. He took a minute to breathe. He could no longer hear Rachel; he trusted Tom knew what he was doing. "So, what happens now?"

"They're bringing her down the hall. One of our investigators will talk to her and try to convince her to confess. He'll find out what's really going on here. He's phenomenal at what he does."

"What do I do?"

"As a police officer? I say get out of here. Go home. As a friend? If it were me and this were Helen, I'd get a large coffee and park my ass in the waiting room for as long as it took."

Friend.

This didn't seem like a friendly encounter today, though. But as Mark looked at Tom, he saw it. Beneath the walls, he saw the man he knew, the trusted confidant. He saw the man he had turned to for help when Rachel was first in trouble.

He saw a man he could trust.

A friend.

"Thank you, Tom."

"Don't worry. We'll get to the bottom of this. I promise you, Mark."

The funny thing was, for as horrible as he felt in the moment, Mark believed him. He believed Tom would do the right thing.

CHAPTER 19

Mark didn't know what to do with himself. Not in the sense that he was bored and had time to kill, but in an agonizingly painful way. He couldn't go home and try to keep busy while waiting for a phone call from Tom or someone from the police department. That simply wouldn't happen. But he couldn't sit in the hallway outside Tom's office all day, either, or in the waiting area next to Lawanda, where she could judge him.

Something he considered was heading a block or two over and finding a newspaper or magazine he could sink himself into for a while, but he didn't think he'd have the focus to even bother trying to read, so that was out. Maybe he could find something to eat. The problem was, he wasn't hungry. He was too worked up to have an appetite.

Waiting for news about how things were going with Rachel, and that she was okay, was the most anxious he'd ever felt to where he was almost nauseous. The waiting was excruciating. And that included when he was kicked out of the delivery room during Maureen's birth due to stress on the baby the doctor wouldn't elaborate on. At least back then, Mark felt confident that both Maureen and Rachel were in good hands under the doctor's watchful attention—whose name he forgot a long time ago. One of the nurses assured him everything was going to be all right, and ultimately she was correct. Having gone through the experience once before when Abagail was born helped to ease his mind. He couldn't say the same thing now; he had nothing to compare it to.

Maureen had an elevated heart rate, he later learned, and the doctor wanted to clear the room to eliminate some of the stress. Mark waited just outside the door and heard everything—Rachel's screaming as she pushed out Maureen's shoulders, the doctor sternly but encouragingly telling her to give it one more good push, followed by Maureen's first cry. As soon as Maureen was out, a nurse ushered Mark into the room so he could snip the umbilical cord and celebrate with his wife and new daughter. At least then, he was close enough to hear everything. Unlike now, where all he knew was that Rachel was somewhere in the building, talking to an investigator. All alone. Probably afraid.

Not good enough.

He should have been there for his wife, wanted to be, but he wasn't even given that option. That infuriated him. Mark trusted Tom and his method, but he couldn't help but wonder if Tom was pushing hard enough for answers. Tom should have been in the room with Rachel.

An hour passed as Mark mindlessly scrolled on his phone outside Tom's office. The numbness of the activity may have worsened the boredom. Even with the distraction, he couldn't get Rachel off his mind. In particular, her reaction especially bothered him. How, after seeing herself on the video and being presented with the evidence about it perfectly matching her photo, was she still in denial? And not just argumentative about it or making up an excuse; she was adamant about it. What was he, and Tom and everyone else, missing?

The photo aspect of all this didn't bother Mark. He and Rachel had spent time with Tom and Helen in social settings, so

Tom could have pulled one from anywhere. He could have logged into Facebook/Meta and gone to Rachel's profile—Mark assumed they were friends, which made this even more difficult—or clipped one from her Instagram. Social media was an open forum, so if you didn't want your picture out there, don't post one. Rachel posted frequently. More than Mark would have liked, maybe, but who was he to say? Tom didn't need Mark's permission to grab one. If Mark was honest with himself, he would have admitted he was glad Tom did it. The more evidence the better, he thought. That way, he wouldn't be forced to choose a side. Everyone thought Rachel was guilty. Except for Rachel. Now it was Mark's job to support her through it the best he could.

Tom's door creaked open and Mark shot to his feet. "How are you doing out here?" Tom asked as he walked through the threshold. He held a coffee mug in his hand that said he was the best dad ever. Mark wondered how many years ago Tom was given that as a classic, rite-of-passage Father's Day gift.

"Not great," Mark said. "Any news?"

"Nothing yet. Just came to check on you."

Mark nodded, disappointed.

Tom lifted the mug. "I'm going to get a refill. You want anything?"

"No, thanks."

"You sure? Coffee? Might still be some muffins left."

"No, thanks. Not hungry."

Tom accepted the answer and walked off.

Mark was making himself crazy. He looked at the time. It was approaching 10 a.m. Not too early to make a phone call. He searched through his contact list and found the number he was after.

Stanley Lyons answered on the second ring.

"Stanley, it's Mark Starr."

"Hello, Mark. I've spoken with your assistant too many times this week, and I've got to say, I'm disappointed."

"I understand, Stanley. I'm very sorry for the reschedulings. I've had a family emergency this week."

"I'm sorry to hear that. I hope everything will be all right."

"Still working through it, but thank you. Carly tells me there's something you wanted to discuss with me."

"There is, but now I feel terrible. I didn't realize there was a personal matter at stake. I just assumed … well, I apologize for that."

Mark felt a wave of relief. This was one problem that wouldn't extend beyond this conversation. "No need. You're one of the firm's highest priorities, Stanley, and that hasn't changed. I apologize for not calling you myself earlier this week."

"Well, thank you. I'm happy to hear my status hasn't changed."

"Absolutely not. Like I said, you're critical to the firm." *And to me.* "So, what is it you wanted to discuss?"

Stanley explained about a new opportunity he'd come across. An acquaintance of an old colleague stumbled upon an upstart tech company, and the opportunity arose to get in early as an angel investor. A bit of out his usual wheelhouse, Stanley acknowledged, but he thought it was the perfect opportunity to expand his portfolio. He wasn't calling to ask Mark's advice or permission — that wasn't how their relationship worked; he told Mark what he was going to do, and Mark executed it or adjusted the previously made plans accordingly.

"I'm going to take 1.5 million out of my 401k," Stanley explained. "I have no problem paying the penalty on the early withdrawal because in two to three years max, I'm going to double my initial investment."

Mark didn't remind Stanley that close to ninety percent of startups failed, many of them within the first year. That wasn't

Mark's job. Besides, Stanley was an intelligent man and a wise investor, so he understood risk versus reward.

"I wanted to keep you informed about this so you can adjust the numbers accordingly when running the next report," Stanley said.

"I appreciate the heads up."

"I didn't want you to be concerned when you saw the reduction in capital."

"The foresight is much appreciated. Was there anything else?"

"No, that's all. I'm sorry for being upset. Please tell your assistant that, will you?"

"Of course."

"And my regards to your family. I hope everything turns up well."

"Thank you, Stanley."

Stanley hung up.

Mark exhaled and pocketed his phone. That was one problem resolved for today. If nothing else, it would keep Marty Joyce off his ass, which was all any one of them at the firm ever wanted. If Marty pretended like you didn't exist, you were in good standing. If he kept hearing your name—unless it was for all the new clients you were bringing in—you might want to start looking for a new place of employment. It wasn't a bad thing; it was just the way things were. Take it or leave it.

Mark looked up and saw Tom rounding the corner with his dad mug in one hand and a Styrofoam cup in the other.

Tom approached and handed Mark the Styrofoam. "Here. I know you said you didn't want anything, but you should drink this. I'm not sure how you take it, so it's black. I have some sugar in my office if you want some. All the muffins are gone—sorry about that—but this will at least give you a little sustenance. Better than nothing."

Mark took the cup. The warmth of the coffee inside tingled his fingers. "Thanks, Tom. This is fine. Great, actually."

Tom offered a weak smile and retreated into his office and closed the door. Mark held the cup in both hands and blew on the liquid until it was cool enough not to burn his tongue.

•   •   •   •   •

After what would have usually been lunch time, Tom's door swung open. Mark looked up through tired eyes.

"Follow me," Tom said. "The investigator wants to talk."

Suddenly Mark wasn't as tired anymore. He stood up and crushed the empty Styrofoam cup with his hands. Tom started walking and Mark followed him. He discarded the cup in the nearest waste bin as he passed.

Tom opened an office door and let Mark inside. Waiting at the table was a clean-shaven man with a tight crew cut and wearing a dark suit. He stood up and firmly shook Mark's hand, then offered him a seat across the table. Noticeably missing from the room was Rachel.

"Mark, this is Investigator Burroughs," Tom said as he joined them at the table. "Like I was saying earlier, he's one of the very best we have."

"Where's Rachel?" Mark asked the investigator.

"I spoke with Rachel this morning," Investigator Burroughs said. "We met for quite a while."

"And?"

"And I'm afraid to report there's no progress."

Mark didn't understand what that meant.

"Which means," Investigator Burroughs went on, as if recognizing Mark's uncertainty, "she's still in denial about everything. She insists it wasn't her on the tape, that she's never even been to that particular gun shop. She won't budge on that."

With that, Mark struggled to retain his grasp on what little hope he had left. "How is that even possible?"

"My thoughts exactly. Has she ever done something like this before?"

"Like what?"

"Refusing to acknowledge the truth."

Mark thought about it. As unusual as it may have seemed, he couldn't recall even one time she'd lied to him before this week. Of course, he supposed he wouldn't have known if she had; that's what lying was. Putting it into those terms made him question everything she ever said or did, as unfair as that may have been. He knew he'd be up all night replaying everything even remotely questionable now. Could there have been something else Rachel had been lying about too? Something major?

I have a secret.

He might not ever know.

"Nothing that comes to mind," he said.

"Is she taking anything?"

"What, like drugs? She's not like that."

"What about prescriptions? Antidepressants or antianxiety medication? Anything like that?"

His first reaction was absolutely not. But then he started wondering. How much did he really know about Rachel and what she did during the day when the girls were at school? Until today, he didn't even know the school drop-off time. He realized he didn't know what Rachel did, because he never asked. He'd ask about the girls and how the morning went, but he didn't ask too many details about his wife's life. Maybe she was Mindy from Indy. Maybe she saw a therapist on a regular basis, despite what she told him. Maybe she had lots of secrets he knew nothing about.

Maybe she was unhappy in their marriage.

"No," Mark said. "At least, not that I know of." He would have known, right? He would have seen a prescription bottle in the bathroom or in one of the cabinets in the kitchen. He would have seen a change in her behavior. He knew his wife.

Didn't he?

Investigator Burroughs leaned back in his chair and spun a pen between his fingers. "In my area of expertise, after what I've witnessed—"

"What is your area of expertise?"

"Psychology. I'm a psychological investigator."

Mark glanced at Tom, who was avoiding Mark's gaze. "I don't understand," he said, turning his attention back to Investigator Burroughs.

"After analyzing your wife, I'm concerned."

"Concerned?"

"What we're dealing with is plausible deniability. Even with all the evidence supporting the accusation, Rachel refuses to acknowledge any involvement. In these cases, there's often an underlying cause for the deniability, and that's something I think we need to explore."

Mark's head spun. This wasn't where he thought this was going. "What are you saying?"

"Based on my initial assessment, I believe your wife may be a danger to herself or others."

"What? How is that possible?"

"Rachel showed signs of deceitful tendencies. Considering what we've all seen, what she's being accused of, I'm concerned for your safety. Many times, it's the people closest to the patient who struggle to see the signs. Living with her every day, it's easy to overlook the minute details sometimes, so don't blame yourself."

Blame himself? For what?

Mark took a second to let that all sink in. Had he really missed something so obvious that it took a psychological investigator sitting with her for just a few hours to see?

Mindy from Indy.

Plausible deniability.

Stolen ammunition.

A suffocating secret.

Reality hit Mark square in the face; he even felt the sting of it. What was Rachel planning on doing with the gun the ammunition went in to?

The gun Mark hadn't found.

"I can see you're surprised," Investigator Burroughs said. "And I can understand that. For your safety, and the safety of your girls, my professional opinion is to admit Rachel to Evansville for further psychiatric evaluation."

"The mental hospital?"

Investigator Burroughs nodded. "Yes, sir. I'd like to hold her there until an extensive evaluation can be performed."

To say Mark was shocked would have been an understatement; he was flabbergasted.

"I've confirmed with the hospital, and there's a bed available for her," Investigator Burroughs said.

"I don't know what to say," Mark said. And he didn't. Of all the possibilities he'd considered, this wasn't one of them. Not in a million years had he fathomed this would be the outcome. He found Tom's eyes. "Do you think this is a good idea?"

"I do. For everyone's safety."

"Is Rachel under arrest?"

"No, not at this time," Tom said.

Mark felt dizzy with confusion. He turned back to the investigator. "For how long?"

"For emergency detention, the state can legally hold Rachel for up to seventy-two hours. Beyond that depends on your cooperation, and how the evaluation goes."

Mark's world spun so fast, he thought he might throw up. He desperately needed some air. "Can I at least see her first? If I talk to her one more time, explain to her what she's looking at, maybe she'll—"

"I'm sorry, but that's not possible," Investigator Burroughs said. "She's already on her way to Evansville."

"That's two hours away! What about the girls? What about my job? You can't just upheave our lives like this without consulting me first."

"I'm sorry, Mr. Starr, but we can. Like I said, the state has a right to—"

"Seventy-two hours, right. Got it."

"That's right."

Mark's skin was on fire. He was so angry he could have screamed. Could they do this? Could they take her away against her will? Apparently, they could.

"I'm sorry, Mark," Tom said. "I know nobody wants this."

"What am I supposed to do now?"

"Go home and be with your girls," Tom said. "Squeeze them tight. Tell them you love them. Tell them their mother loves them too, because we know she does. And regardless of what happens, she'll always love them. No matter what."

"We'll be in touch, Mr. Starr," Investigator Burroughs said. "The hospital will take excellent care of your wife."

CHAPTER 20

I'm not crazy. I successfully convinced my child psychologist of that when I was younger. Even now, I don't think I was being manipulative. Did I tell him what I thought he wanted to hear? Sure, I did. Was it the truth? Depends. Sometimes it was embellished, other times it may or may not have been. You call it deceptive; I call it being resourceful.

Whatever craziness I had — though, again, not a word I'd choose — started when I was in sixth grade, right around the time I had my first period. The doctors figured it was hormonally driven. Personally, I think it was because my parents were dicks and I'd finally grown up enough to start verbally defending myself. It wasn't a coincidence that two weeks after the first time I told my dad to fuck off, I was sitting in the office of a child psychologist to figure out what my issues were.

I can tell you what they were. I hated my life and my parents were to blame. Wasn't that hard to figure it out.

I grew up in a toxic environment. To my dad's credit, he never put his hands on me. Not once. Which meant there were never any marks; it was his word versus mine. A respected man against a moody almost-teenager. My mom, naturally, believed him. I was exaggerating at best, lying at worst. She saw nothing of concern, she said. That was because he was on his best behavior when she was around. Hence why I was sent to counseling while she continued to get on her knees for him—in more ways than one. I never understood her infatuation with and loyalty to the man. He wasn't even handsome, with his crooked teeth and balding head and gross man boobs.

The first time I brought home a school report card with what he considered a poor grade—I considered it average—he beleaguered me about it. Day after day, for weeks on end.

"What are you doing to bring the grade up?" he asked. Or, "Can you ask for extra credit?" Or my favorite, simply, "Be better."

It was insufferable. It was just a C in a class I had no interest in. Math. Who cares about math? I knew the basics, so I thought that was enough. That's why this amazing, futuristic gadget called a calculator was invented. Dad disagreed.

When I told the psychologist this, he nodded and chewed on the pencil's eraser, but he wrote nothing down. He wrote when I told him I hated my parents and how I'd rather read than do math, and how I'd once asked a friend if I could copy her math homework so I didn't have to do it myself. At the time, I didn't know any better. Now, I realize my parents paid the psychologist to say what they wanted to hear. I was the problem, not them, his analysis said.

Whatever.

As the weeks went on, I grew tired of seeing him. I didn't feel any better about my parents or some of the trouble I was having with certain classmates, and I was sick of him taking my words and spinning them to be used against me. So, I started faking it.

The first conversation about antidepressants came up, and I read the entire list of side effects—I was, after all, a reader. I saw weight gain as one of them, and I knew right then that I wouldn't take them. I'd already felt chubby as it was, my tummy never flat enough and my thigh gap too narrow, so gaining even more weight to take a stupid pill that wouldn't do anything because there wasn't anything wrong in the first place wasn't going to happen.

I walked into the next appointment with a forced smile on my face. I told the psychologist how I'd been thinking about things differently, and how I thought maybe I was triggering my dad's anger toward me. If I did what he asked without arguing and studied hard to bring my grade up, he'd get off my back about it. He was being a good dad by pushing me; he was doing it because he wanted the best for me, just like any dad wanted for their child. Predictably, the sham of a psychologist wrote that down.

Two weeks later, I was deemed cured and no longer had to visit the pencil-chewing psychologist. In some ways, what the psychologist advised actually worked. Once I got my grade up and obeyed my dad, he stopped being so mean. But I could tell by the way he looked sideways at me that he didn't love me, at least not in the way a dad should. Parents are supposed to love their children unconditionally, so I never understood how he couldn't.

That was until years later, when I did.

Life went on. I bit my tongue despite my best instincts and did what I was told. I earned adequate grades. I still hated my dad and only disliked my mom. She wasn't mean to me like he was; she just did nothing about it, regardless if she witnessed anything. How could she not know what was going on? I didn't believe that for a second, and still don't. As a mother myself, that's just bullshit. After I graduated from high school, I went off to college and never went back home. I rented an off-campus apartment with friends, worked part-time at the college bookstore, and started my life.

I haven't spoken to either of them in over fifteen years.

My mom will text me every so often, always about the kids, never about me. I text her photos of their school photos, never the photos themselves. She'll send birthday cards and holiday gifts, always slapping his name on them too, but she doesn't call. Dad probably won't let her. I'm not sure I'd pick up anyway. My kids don't know her, so they don't care.

One of the reasons I married my husband was because he was nothing like my dad. He was sweet, affectionate, kind. At first. But then life's dust settled and the daily routines set in, and I learned he's so much like my dad that it makes me sick. It's often said that daughters will inevitably wind up with someone like their dad. As hard as I tried to avoid that, I was clearly so wrong about him. Might have been the biggest mistake of my life.

That's why I despise him. Despite the love I had for him — which, we've established, was there at one time — I've seen the worst parts about my dad in him. Luckily for our children, he doesn't treat them the way my dad treated me; instead, I was the outlet for all his anger and passive-aggressiveness. For that, I'm thankful. The kids don't deserve that.

The big problem I'd realized was that I couldn't make it on my own financially. To my name, I have very little. All our joint money — which, let's be real, it's his money — is stored in accounts with his name on it. He's one of those people who checks his bank accounts as part of his morning routine, so he'd have known within twenty-four hours if I ever tried something.

Which is why I started considering something far more drastic. A more … permanent solution.

I liked my life's arrangement, mostly. I enjoyed where we lived, where the kids attended school, our home, some of our neighbors. In my mind, I could only come up with one scenario where I could keep all that and have my husband out of the picture. Divorce wasn't it. I've never been good at sharing.

So, I bought a gun. I acquired it through the proper channels with cash. I told my husband I needed a hundred dollars for a fundraiser at the kids' school one week, two hundred for new shoes for the kids the next, one-fifty for an oil change and new air filters in my SUV the week after that. Before I knew it, I'd saved enough money to buy it in cash, and my husband was too oblivious to take notice of the other things, like how the kids didn't have new shoes. I was banking on it.

This was the way I lived my life. Now do you see the type of shit he put me through?

Like I said, I'm not crazy; I'm resourceful. A woman has to do what a woman has to do when her husband is overbearing and controlling, like mine was. I wonder if he realizes he is the way he is.

I lied to him to get some money, then I saved that money to buy a gun. Legally. I want to stress that point. I'm not a monster. I've never owned one, but I've seen enough stories on the news about unregistered guns killing innocent kids to know how important safety is. I hid it where the kids couldn't reach, and where my husband wouldn't have ever thought to look.

I can't pinpoint when the realization hit me, but at some point, it clicked and I decided I wanted my husband dead. I saw it as the only way out of an undesirable situation.

Maybe that does make me a little crazy, but you shouldn't judge someone if you don't know their situation. You know a little, but I can't possibly tell you everything. I admit, this all could go back to my dad. If he wasn't the way he was, it's possible my tolerance for my husband's treatment would have been greater. Likely, even. But that's not what happened. I refused to live my entire life that way. It wasn't fair. And it was only a matter of time before he started turning on our kids the way my dad had turned on me.

Especially once he learned our oldest isn't even his.

I'm kind of a mess, huh?

But everything started changing. In a good way. It wasn't ever part of the original plan, but when something — someone — unexpectedly enters your life, you'd have to be a fool not to listen. I was listening, all right.

From what I saw from afar, he seemed like the perfect man. The perfect father. Take it from someone who's seen what a bad father looks like, and a bad husband. He was nothing like the men I know. I thought he deserved someone who knew his worth. Someone who'd treat him like the king he is. Someone who'd be there for him unconditionally, no matter what, the way he does his wife. It irks me that she has no idea how lucky she is — and how could she? Her life's been handed to her on a silver platter. If one tiny thing happened differently, she'd see how the other side lives. That husband of hers deserves so much more than she can ever give. He deserves someone who's seen it all and can appreciate it when someone as amazing as he is walks into her life.

He deserves someone like me.

It was remarkable how fast life could change. In the blink of an eye, Mark's life had just taken a one-eighty. Not only was Rachel all but gone, at least in the short term, but now he had to step into her role in the home too. He wasn't sure he was ready for all this. Except he didn't have a choice but to figure it all out. And fast.

For today at least, the timing worked out. As soon as he left the police department, he headed for the girls' school. He was unaware at precisely what time the girls were released from school—something strange, he knew, either 2:17 or 2:22 p.m.—so he called. He could have, and maybe should have, felt embarrassed about not knowing—what kind of dad didn't know what time his kids got out of school?—but he wasn't. He didn't have time to worry about embarrassment or feel shame for not being involved enough; he had to step into full-blown dad mode.

The pickup line at the school wasn't something he expected. It stretched out of the parking and into the road, past some nearby houses and over a crosswalk. Cars and SUVs and a minivan or two lined the street, making way for the school buses to pass them on the left. Mark pulled up behind one of the SUV-driving moms and waited. Around him, people. In front, a mom read a mass market paperback. Behind, another scrolled through her phone with a scowl on her face. A crossing guard crouched down and scratched a jumpy puppy behind its ears while the owner wrapped the leash around her hand and tried to control it.

The line took forever. Fifteen minutes after school was dismissed — which, he learned from the office when he called, was 2:19 — he still hadn't moved. If he would have known, he would have shut the car off. It explained the paperback. Finally, twenty-two minutes after he first got in line, the line moved. When his turn came, he rolled down his window and offered his best tired smile to the woman — the principal, he remembered, though he hadn't a clue what her name was. She didn't seem to recognize him. Why would she? He went to the school twice a year usually, for parent–teacher conferences, occasionally for extracurriculars. Rachel was the one who usually handled all the girls' after-school activities.

He told the principal the girls' names and something changed in her expression. Recognition. She smiled and asked how he was, and noted she was surprised not to see Rachel today.

"She's not feeling well, I'm afraid," Mark said. Which was both true and untrue.

"Well, give her my best," she said, and she radioed the girls one at a time.

He said he would, but he wouldn't.

A few minutes later, he watched as Maureen skipped out of the building, her too large backpack practically swallowing her whole. Turned out, hundreds of tiny voices could make quite the ruckus. He rolled his window up and still felt the car vibrate with the stampede of overenthusiastic children.

"Daddy!" Maureen said when she saw him. She ran toward him, but was stopped by a teacher or staff member. The woman leaned down and said something to Maureen, who looked like she was going to cry. After, she walked the rest of the way to the car, her face pointing downward.

"Hi, sweetheart," he said when she climbed in the back. Her hands were strong enough to clip her harness in over her chest, but Mark had to lean back and snap it into the buckle for her.

"Hi," she said sadly.

"What's the matter?"

"Miss Gray yelled at me."

"Why?"

"For running."

"Well, she just wants you to be safe, right?"

Maureen nodded.

"How was school?"

"Good." Maureen looked out the window and rubbed her eyes.

"Dad?" Mark turned at the sound of Abagail's voice, who stood outside his window. "What are you doing here?"

"Surprise!"

Abagail climbed in the back next to her sister, the middle seat between them. She buckled her harness in all by herself — bottom included. It wouldn't be long before she was ready to graduate to a booster seat. Rachel would make that call when the time was right. It was hard to believe that was possible already; it felt like yesterday when she was small enough to relax on his forearms and suck on her fingers as she slept.

"What's wrong with her?" Abagail asked.

"Miss Gray yelled at her."

"Again?"

"Happen a lot?" Mark asked.

"Every day."

He really was out of touch with these small details. He hadn't heard the name Miss Gray before.

At home, he wasn't sure what to do next. He conspicuously let Abagail take the lead, hoping she wouldn't notice he had no clue what he was doing. The girls tossed their backpacks on the bench in the laundry room and kicked off their shoes. They ran into the bathroom and fought over who could wash their hands first.

"Can I have a snack now, Daddy?" Maureen asked.

"Uh …"

"Mommy always lets us have a snack after school," Maureen told him.

Mark looked at Abagail.

"She does," she reaffirmed.

"Of course, you can have a snack," he said, as if he thought of it himself.

The girls hurried into the kitchen to argue over who could eat the remaining Goldfish. They settled it by splitting what was left of the bag. Mark had no say in the matter, though he was impressed with their problem-solving skills. After, they played for a bit in their playroom while he sat in the tiny chair and watched. What else was he supposed to do? What did Rachel usually do? He snuck a glance at his phone to see if anyone had called or if he had any work emails. No, on the former. Many, the latter.

He felt ridiculous. He'd spent a lot of time with his daughters in the evenings and on weekends, yet, it felt like his first time. Usually — and by usually, that meant always — it was Rachel who would be the timekeeper and say when enough was enough or what the girls could and couldn't do. She seemed like a natural from the get-go. From the first time she held both girls, so tenderly and motherly, to the way she cradled them while they nursed. Then as they'd gotten older, how she bandaged and magically kissed boo-boos to make them go away and the way

she read bedtime stories and ensured they ate their vegetables —
even if that meant tricking them by buying the dinosaur-shaped
nuggets that were made from them instead of chicken. Without
her guidance, Mark felt like a fish out of water.

The girls started arguing again shortly after four o'clock. He
tried to determine what the problem was and offer a fair but
stern solution, but he didn't know what the right thing to do
was. He saw both sides of the disagreement and didn't know
how to decide who was right.

"I have an idea," he said, and the girls perked up. "Who
wants to help me make pancakes?"

Maureen almost jumped out of her skin. "Me!"

"For dinner?" Abagail asked.

"Why not?"

"Mom never makes pancakes for dinner. Where is Mom?"

"Yeah, Daddy," Maureen added as if just noticing for the first
time, now that her sister mentioned it. "Where is Mommy?"

"Mommy's not here," he said. How much should he tell
them? How much did they have a right to know?

"But where is she?" Abagail pressed.

"Girls, Mommy isn't feeling well, so she went to the doctor."

"Is she coming back?" Abagail, always with the questions.

"Not right now. But she'll be back in a couple days."

"Can we go see her?" Maureen asked with a pouty bottom
lip.

"Not today."

Maureen cried. Abagail wrapped her arms around her little
sister in comfort, their latest fight all but forgotten. That was
something he admired about kids; they could bounce back
remarkably quickly. They didn't hold grudges the way adults
did.

"It's okay," Mark said. He opened his arms and both girls fell
against him. By now, both of them were crying. His throat
twisted. "Mommy's going to be fine. I promise." Except he

couldn't promise that. Nobody could. But he'd do whatever it took to put his girls' minds at ease. "So, who's ready for pancakes?"

"Me," Maureen said through sniffles with less enthusiasm than before.

"How about you?" Mark said to Abagail, who shrugged. "You can put the chocolate chips in the batter."

Abagail smiled at that. Kind of. But it was good enough. The three of them made pancakes, albeit messily. As much as Mark enjoyed it, the mess overwhelmed him and there being still over three hours to fill until bedtime didn't help. It was just him and his girls, stranded on a desert island together, and their ration of water was already drying up. Home felt like a different planet without Rachel.

$$\bullet \qquad \bullet \qquad \bullet \qquad \bullet \qquad \bullet$$

The rest of the evening was familiar. After dinner, the girls took turns taking baths and putting on their pajamas. The three of them had another snack before watching some TV together, then it was time to go upstairs. The girls argued about who brushed their teeth the longest and whose turn it was to pick out the book. Mark's temples pounded. He read a story about a frog that lived in a bog that both girls seemed appeased with. He read the words but didn't process any of them. When he finished, he asked the girls to use the bathroom then tucked them into their beds, kissed their little noses, and kept their doors cracked while he went back downstairs.

By the time the mess in the kitchen was cleaned up and the girls had what he thought was an acceptable amount of food in their lunchboxes for tomorrow—and reasonably balanced with what he found in the cabinets—he was so tired he could have gone straight to bed. Even once he did, an hour later, he felt like there was still so much to do to prepare for the next day. But it was a struggle to keep his eyes open any longer, so he gave in and crawled into his empty bed and fell asleep faster than he had in months.

Morning came in a flash. He hurried to do what he needed to do for himself before waking the girls and getting them ready for the day. Everything felt rushed—his shower, the time the girls had for breakfast, the show they watched. They left the house six minutes later than he wanted to, but they both had their backpacks, jackets, and were dressed and wearing shoes. Their teeth were even brushed, at least a little. It was a start. He was stressed out and on edge, and the girls arguing in the backseat about whose turn it was to use the coloring book was enough to make him scream. But they made it to school on time and he didn't yell at them, though he couldn't promise himself that would always be the case going forward. How did Rachel do this every day?

He arrived at the office exhausted. It took all he had not to fall asleep in the elevator, with the soothing music and relaxing vibrations. Amid all the chaos, he realized he hadn't had even a few seconds to think about how Rachel was doing. In the free hour he had before he went to bed last night, he sent some emails to rearrange his work schedule so he wouldn't miss any client meetings. He was coming in a half-hour later and leaving over three hours earlier than usual. It wasn't sustainable. This wouldn't work beyond this week. He knew that. But right now, he had no choice. His girls needed him.

"Mark?" Carly said when he walked in. "I didn't know if you were coming in today."

"Sorry I'm late. Had to bring the girls to school. Did I miss anything?"

"Nothing important. Your first client is due in fifteen."

He checked the clock. That gave him just enough time to grab some coffee, maybe a bagel, and review his client's files for a refresher before they came in. He tossed his belongings on the floor in his office and collapsed into the chair.

"Knock, knock," Todd said from the doorway before Mark even had a second to catch his breath. "Did you pull an all-nighter or something?"

"No, why?"

"You look like ass."

"Thank you, Todd. I can always count on you for a boost of self-confidence first thing in the morning."

Todd laughed as if it were a joke and invited himself in. He sat across from Mark. "What's going on with you, man? I don't feel like I've seen you much this week."

"That's because you haven't."

"How are things at home?"

"Really shitty, Todd. But I'd rather not get into it right now, if you don't mind. My head's killing me. I had to pinch off my loaf earlier to get the girls to school on time so my stomach hurts, and I haven't had any coffee yet. A client named ... Carly! Who the fuck is coming in this morning?"

"Jodi Southerland," she yelled back.

"Jodi Southerland is coming in to see me in thirteen minutes and I don't even know who the fuck Jodi Southerland is!"

"She's the widow," Carly called out. "Husband fell off the roof last year."

"Right. Now I remember." Mark sighed.

"Yikes, man," Todd said.

"Yeah."

"I just came to say hey to my guy, but I can see now's not a great time, so ..." Todd slowly stood up and walked backward out of Mark's office.

"Todd, hold up."

But Todd was gone. He practically ran away.

"Sorry," Mark whispered to himself. He felt like an asshole. He hoped he could pull himself together before Jodi Southerland arrived.

•   •   •   •   •

That was how day one without Rachel went. To put the cherry on top, he forgot that Abagail had dance—class was sometimes once a week, sometimes twice, depending on several factors Mark wasn't attuned to. By the time he realized it, class was already over and Abagail was pissed. She gave him the cold shoulder the rest of the night, refusing to say a word to him.

Day two was much of the same, except it was Friday, so that helped. Abagail still wasn't speaking to him. Due to Mark's condensed schedule, he saw clients back-to-back from 9 a.m. until 1 p.m., not even having time to use the restroom or eat or clear his head. Once the last client left, he was famished and irritable and thought his bladder might explode. He'd held it in so long, a sharp pain pierced his lower back. Of course, since he had to go so badly, he sprayed all over the urinal and his pant leg when he finally let it out. Dabbing the spots with a damp paper towel only made it look worse.

He retreated to his office, passing Carly's desk on the way. Todd leaned over it, whispering something in her ear that made her laugh.

"Hey, man," Todd said. His eyes exploded when he saw Mark. "Dude, what happened?"

"Don't ask," Mark said, shaking his head. He went into his office and gathered his things, including the stack of paperwork he needed to execute for his clients. Usually, he'd do what he needed to do in between clients, when it was still fresh on his mind, but there hadn't been any time for that this week. "I'll see you later," he said when he passed by Carly's desk again.

"Have a pissing good weekend," Todd said, choking back a laugh.

Even as Mark heard Todd and Carly laugh hysterically once the elevator doors closed behind him, he wasn't mad. He flatly didn't care anymore.

On the way to school, his phone rang. The caller ID told him it was Evansville State Hospital. Rachel! His mood changed in an instant. He felt more alert, hopeful. He quickly answered.

"Is this Mark Starr?" a woman's soft, soothing voice asked him.

"Yes. How's Rachel?"

"Rachel is doing fine. Stable."

Stable? He hadn't a clue what that was supposed to mean. "When can I see her?"

"That's why I'm calling, actually. The doctor wanted me to see if you can come tomorrow. He'd like to have a sit-down with you."

"On a Saturday?"

"We have multiple doctors on a rotating schedule."

"Oh, well, of course. I'll just need to find a sitter for my girls, then I can make the drive."

"How's noon?"

"I'll be there."

They disconnected and he felt a surge of energy. If Rachel was coming home, that must mean they had a breakthrough. She could come home and he could go back to his normal schedule, and everything would be right in his world again. But then he wondered if he was getting too far ahead of himself. The woman on the phone said nothing about Rachel going home. All she said was the doctor wanted to meet with Mark. About what? Would he learn the doctor wanted to keep Rachel even longer? Was something wrong? The thought made him sick.

He picked up the girls and they started arguing almost immediately.

"It's my turn to color!" Maureen snapped.

"No, you used it this morning!"

"No, I didn't!"

"Yes, you did!

"Girls! Stop it!" Mark reached behind him and snatched the coloring book from whosever hand it was in. He threw it on the floor next to him and the car fell silent.

Both girls started crying.

Great. Just what he needed.

"Oh, no, girls, don't cry. I'm sorry."

It didn't work. Neither of them stopped.

"It's been a long week without Mommy. I'm sorry." He peeked in the rearview and saw Abagail grab onto Maureen's hand. "Good news! I talked to Mommy's doctor today, and it sounds like she's feeling better!"

Abagail perked up. "Is she coming home?"

"Yes. I mean, I hope so. I think so." The moment wasn't lost on him that Abagail acknowledged him, even if it wasn't about anything to do with him. Progress.

Abagail blankly looked at him in the mirror.

"I'm going to go see her tomorrow."

"Can we come?"

"Not tomorrow, sweetheart."

Abagail looked out the window now, unsatisfied with his answer. She kept holding Maureen's hand.

"I miss Mommy," Maureen said.

"Me too," Abagail said.

Me too.

Thankfully, the girls' usual babysitter was available to come over on short notice. She could spend Saturday with the girls while Mark made the two-hour drive to Evansville. Mark offered to pay her double.

Hannah arrived right on time—Hannah was the babysitter— and knocked on the door. Mark let her in and graciously thanked her for coming. Hannah was a junior at the STEM Academy in town. Mark knew she planned to study to be a molecular scientist after high school. Maybe it was unfair of him to put her in a box the way he did, but being as intelligent as she was made him trust her more easily. While she'd proven to be trustworthy, she hadn't watched the girls for this long before—two hours each way, plus however long he'd be at the hospital. Previously, she'd stayed in the house while the girls slept for a few hours while Mark and Rachel went out. It didn't happen much these days. With the extenuating circumstances in front of him, he had no choice but to trust her today.

He hugged the girls with one arm and pulled them each in close, the way dads sometimes did that seemed halfhearted but was anything but. Abagail let him, but she didn't like it; she squirmed. For Mark, it was good enough. Another step in the right direction. After, he thanked Hannah again and headed out. She had his number if an emergency arose, though he wouldn't be able to do much about it. He crossed his fingers that there weren't any problems.

Evansville State Hospital was a two-hour drive from their home in Brooklyn, Indiana, which gave Mark a lot of uninterrupted time to focus on his thoughts. He turned the radio off and drove in silence, the evenness of the open road smooth beneath his tires. He was relaxed. More relaxed than he would have thought. Missing Rachel the last couple of days told him all he needed to know about where he stood; he was going to have her back and support her however he could, whatever that future looked like.

The time he spent with the girls was precious. That wasn't something anyone could ever take away from him. He cherished it. Mostly. At least, he thought he did. But the truth was, he didn't think he could handle it all the time. How long did it take Abagail to be angry with him? Not very. He wasn't cut out for it. Between his professional obligations and logistically working in the city with the girls' school being forty or forty-five minutes away, how would that work? If there was an incident during the day—an upset stomach, bloody nose, scratchy throat, or a genuine emergency—would he be able to drop everything on a whim and attend to that situation? The answer to that was an easy no. His clients were on-demand at times too, sometimes scheduling same-day appointments if something urgent, in their eyes, came up. His lifestyle wasn't set up to be a full-time dad and a full-time working professional. It just wouldn't work.

Alternatively, he could hire a nanny to pick up the girls and give them snacks after school and maybe even prepare dinner. Someone who could pick up around the house and throw in some laundry. Run a vacuum. But was that the life he wanted for himself, or for his girls? Another easy no. His girls wanted their mom back, and Mark wanted his wife. Which made what he had to do very simple.

Whatever it took. He'd have to battle through it, for as long as he and his girls needed.

The footage from Indy Guns and Ammo still ran through his head on a loop. There was no question to him or to Tom or to anyone, except Rachel, about what they saw. Rachel was in the gun shop. She leaped over the counter when the employee snuck out back, grabbed a box of 9mm ammunition, and left the store with it. She shoplifted. No doubt about it. Not the end of the world, considering, but still against the law. He kept going back to, what for?

He played out a new approach in his mind. Rather than another confrontation demanding answers, he'd take a gentler, calmer, more understanding approach. He'd shoulder some of the blame, if he could, to make himself seem more sympathetic. None of this was to manipulate or deceive her, though; he just wanted answers. Needed them. And he thought trying a different approach was worth a shot. He had to know what was going on with Rachel and what, if anything, he could do about it.

Evansville was a grand brick structure nestled behind a charming pond. The buildings were elegant with historic features—large windows, observation towers, steeply pitched roofs—and spread across an expanse of lush greenery. It could have been a photograph torn from an album of historical Oxford or Cambridge buildings. More of a college campus feel than a hospital, he thought. Not at all what Mark was expecting.

Inside, he gave a nicely-dressed woman behind the desk in reception his name and said he was there to see Rachel Starr. She asked him to wait in the seating area while she made a phone call. She tenderly smiled at him, quite unlike the reception he received from Lawanda.

Shortly thereafter, a thin man with long legs and an even longer stride appeared from around the corner. A white lab coat covered a collared shirt with a necktie—in a comfortable, relaxed, unstuffy way. Mark felt the man's warmth immediately.

"Are you Mark Starr?" the man asked. The doctor, Mark assumed.

Mark stood. "I am."

"Hello, Mark. My name is Doctor Jonathan James. I'm one of the board-certified psychiatrists here at Evansville."

Mark shook his hand.

"You can call me Doctor Jonathan, Doctor James, or just JJ." The doctor smiled. "Whatever you feel most comfortable with is fine with me."

"Thank you, Doctor." Mark anxiously wanted the tedious but necessary housekeeping details out of the way. All he cared about was how Rachel was doing and when she could come home.

"Come along," Doctor JJ said. "Let's sit down."

Mark followed him back the way he came. The walls, floor, and ceiling were off-white. No artwork hung. The overhead lighting was bright and warm, and made the corridor even whiter. Mark's vision spun.

Inside Doctor JJ's office, they sat. A single window behind the doctor's desk invited in some welcomed natural light, and some much-needed color. Outside the window, a dove landed on an overhanging tree branch but didn't stay long; it chirped and flew away right after, off to find a more comfortable spot somewhere else, giving the humans some privacy.

Doctor JJ shuffled through a stack of manila folders on his desk and pulled one out. He opened it, glanced at the contents, and closed it again. He found what he was looking for, it seemed. "So, Rachel," he said.

"Yes, Rachel. How is she?"

"She's doing well. After some initial resistance, she's responding well to the treatment and has been more open to our analysis."

"What exactly is the treatment?"

"We've given her some mood stabilizers to help calm her. When she arrived, she was, shall I say, irritable."

"She was bombarded with all of this. She wasn't expecting it. I can't say I blame her."

"I can understand that. Has anyone explained to you what we're looking for in a psychiatric evaluation?"

"No, actually."

"The reason these things take time, a couple of days in this case, is that we run a lot of tests. Diagnostics, blood tests, behavioral assessments. We don't like to overwhelm the patient, so we try to be cognizant of how much we can or should do at one time. It all depends on the patient. With Rachel, we started with a physical exam, looking for any disorders. As part of that exam, we took blood from her and ran several tests. From the physical examination and with the results of the blood tests, we found nothing abnormal."

"That's good, right?"

"Well, sure. It's good to rule out some of these factors in the beginning. So, we learned there's nothing physical going on. After giving Rachel some time to calm her nerves, our team spent yesterday engaged in extensive dialogue with her. On a basic level, we discussed her family history when it comes to mental health or psychological disorders, as well as her personal history with those things. Nothing noteworthy came up.

"From there, we moved on to more comprehensive mental and cognitive evaluations. We discussed her thoughts and feelings. Her behavior. Then she partook in different examinations that evaluated her ability to think clearly, recall information, use sound reasoning. All common practices."

"How'd she do?"

"Well, Mr. Starr, it's not a pass–fail type of examination. Everyone is different, so all results should be taken into consideration when making a diagnosis."

"Understood."

Doctor JJ opened the folder again and looked inside as if needing to verify the facts before sharing them. He closed the folder and gave his attention back to Mark. "We had a team of three doctors spend time with Rachel in various capacities, myself included, in order to get a comprehensive evaluation. After discussing as a group, our consensus opinion is that while Rachel shows depressive and addictive tendencies, there isn't any evidence of any acute or underlying psychiatric conditions present."

Relief flooded through Mark. There wasn't anything wrong with Rachel. That was a good thing. But, the more he thought about it, it was also a bad thing. If there wasn't something psychologically wrong with Rachel, then what was going on?

From relief to defeat. Mark was no closer to answers, even after all this.

"I can see you're experiencing a lot of emotions right now," Doctor JJ said. "That's normal in a situation like this. I know you haven't had much time to process this yet, but do you have any initial questions I can answer for you?"

Did he? What did he want to know? So many thoughts ran through his mind, he had trouble keeping them all straight. "What happens now?"

"From the hospital's perspective, we see no medical reason to keep her any longer."

"She can go home?"

Doctor JJ didn't smile, but Mark felt like he did. "I'll ask Amy to prepare the discharge paperwork."

•   •   •   •   •

The moment Mark saw Rachel was unexpectedly emotional. Whether it was guilt for the part he played in sending her there or some form of angst by osmosis for seeing his wife going through this alone, he felt it in his bones. Whatever it was, he felt it, and it hurt. He bit onto the inside of his cheek to distract himself from thinking too much.

A woman in the same style of overcoat Doctor JJ wore escorted Rachel toward him. Rachel's head sagged. She walked slowly, tiredly, dragging her feet as if they were too heavy. Her hair hung straight down, well beyond her shoulders.

"Rachel," Mark said when she was close enough to hear. His voice was unsteady.

She looked up in acknowledgement and showed off her barely recognizable face. The pain Mark experienced before intensified, his chest aching. Black rings swallowed her eyes beneath a pale complexion. Her cheeks drooped, and she looked malnourished. He'd never seen her look like this before—so exhausted, so beat down. So weak.

What the hell happened to her in here?

"Come here," Mark said. He spread out his arms and stepped forward. She ambled toward him and fell against his chest. He breathed her in and she smelled nothing like herself. Stale. He wrapped his arms around her and lightly squeezed, not wanting to fracture the fragile woman before him. "I'm so sorry," he whispered. Tears welled in his eyes. Against his back, he felt her hands.

"Get me out of this place," she said to him. "Take me home."

CHAPTER 23

They didn't talk much on the way home. Mark didn't know what to say or what to ask, and Rachel looked exhausted. She drifted in and out of sleep, once frantically jolting herself awake and digging her nails into Mark's thigh. He nearly screamed out in pain. Rachel was on edge. Whatever happened inside Evansville seemed to have traumatized her.

Which made Mark feel even worse.

Rain started falling during the drive. Saturday had turned gloomy in a hurry, both inside and outside. The squelching of the windshield wipers against the glass was the only sound for quite a while. Traffic was surprisingly light.

At home, Mark maneuvered around Hannah's car in the driveway and pulled into the garage and killed the ignition, closing the garage door behind them. Rachel was asleep, her lips twitching. He leaned over to wake her, but only after glancing around the chaos that was his junk in every crevice of the garage. He couldn't help but wondering, still, if Rachel had hidden a 9mm handgun somewhere in the mess. Inside one of the old coffee tins that now held a bevy of nails and screws, or tucked under a pile of lumber scraps, or maybe somewhere right in plain sight. He tried to put himself in Rachel's shoes. Where would a logical place be? Somewhere Mark wouldn't think to look but also somewhere that gave her easy access. He didn't know. Blankness filled his mind.

It was hopeless. He'd need to be alone for a while, several hours, to dig for it, but that wouldn't happen anytime soon. He made a mental note to prioritize organizing the garage—something that had been on his to-do list for months now, maybe longer, and he'd been avoiding. Now, it seemed more important than ever. Not quite urgent, but definitely something he should make time to do sooner rather than later. Just like the faucet in the kitchen—it was only a slow drip, and not all the time, but if he let it go without attention for too long, one day he'd wake up with a basement full of water. He didn't want a basement full of water—or a bullet in his back.

Mark's fingers gently caressed Rachel's shoulder, slightly pressing into the fabric of her blouse—the same clothes she had on a few days ago, when they went to see Tom. The hospital's stench lingered. "Rachel?"

She stirred but didn't wake. She tried rolling over but was constricted by the belt across her chest. Mark called her name again. Rachel's eyes shot open and she gasped as she lunged forward, flailing her arms in desperation.

"Hey, it's okay," Mark said, dropping a hand on her forearm. "It's just me. You're home."

Rachel's breaths were heavy, her chest bouncing up and down. After a few seconds, she regained control of herself and looked around—at her hands, out the window to her right, eventually at Mark.

"You're home," he said again.

Rachel didn't acknowledge him. She leaned over, unclipped the seat belt, and opened her door. Mark didn't try to stop her as she stepped out and retreated into the house. It took less than thirty seconds before a jubilant screech ricocheted off the walls; the girls had their mother back.

He should have felt happy and relieved about Rachel being home, but he didn't. Something was off. Rachel clearly wasn't herself. While it wasn't surprising, he'd expected more. He thought she'd be thrilled to see him, maybe even apologetic for allowing it to get this far. Maybe that was foolish of him. She remained insistent that it wasn't her in the video, even though it was, so she probably held some anger toward him for not believing in her.

Mark wasn't sure how they were going to get past this. It seemed a bridge too far to gap—she, adamant of her innocence; he, certain of her guilt. But he'd leave that for another day. For now, his duty was to make Rachel feel comfortable and to get her whatever she needed. After what she went through, she at least deserved some comfort.

Inside, he heard the shower running upstairs. That was fast. Rachel must have been desperate to rinse all the filth of the last couple of days off her. It wasn't hard to understand why.

"Daddy, Mommy's home!" Maureen said as she ran up to him.

"I know, sweetheart."

Abagail stepped out from the kitchen and stood at the end of the hallway. She looked at Mark as if she knew something was wrong, as if her mom wasn't quite the same as she remembered her. He couldn't tell if she was still mad at him.

"Girls, Mommy still doesn't feel very well, so let's give her some space, okay?"

Maureen enthusiastically nodded. Abagail didn't but Mark could tell by her flat expression that she understood and would obey. She most often did. While she had a curious, mature mind, she was eager to please. That was something he had going in his favor right now. He needed and wanted Abagail on his side.

With that, Mark and the girls left Rachel alone for a while. He figured she'd take a long, steamy shower, and that was exactly what she did. Mark paid Hannah double like he promised, profusely thanked her, and closed the door behind her. In the kitchen, he prepared a snack for the girls. He joined them on the sofa and watched a Disney movie about a princess—always a princess. They split a bag of buttered popcorn and wiped their greasy fingers on their shirts. Better than the sofa, he supposed. Abagail sat next to him, which he thought was a good sign.

Mark couldn't focus. The sounds of the running water and the whir of the fan upstairs stole his attention. That was all he heard. He didn't have a clue what was unfolding on the TV in front of him, seeing it but not at all watching. He needed to think about how he should approach things with Rachel. Should he ask her what happened at the hospital? How many details should he demand? Or should he wait and ask her nothing, not to pretend it didn't happen but rather to wait for her to come to him when she was ready to talk about it? The decision felt too important to screw up. His approach could permanently change everything between them.

The shower stopped. The girls were too engrossed in the movie to notice. An anxious lump formed in his throat. A minute passed. The stairs squeaked under each step Rachel descended. Mark sensed her presence behind him but he didn't turn to look at her. He waited for her to place a hand on his shoulder or loosely run her fingers through his hair like she often did, but she did neither of those things. It seemed she wanted nothing to do with him, at least right now. Not yet. He told himself to brush it off, to give her space to recover from the trauma she went through, but it wasn't easy. He craved her touch and affection. For as much as he felt like he had let her down—and still was—he wanted nothing more than her forgiveness. Perhaps that was selfish of him, considering the circumstances, but it was the truth.

"This movie again?" Rachel asked, startling them all.

"It's my favorite!" Maureen said without turning away from it.

Rachel walked around the sofa, her loose hair damp, and found a seat. She sat as far away from Mark as possible, on the opposite end without looking at him. Maureen snuggled in against her.

Rachel was home, but it felt like anything but. Physically, she was present. But mentally, psychologically, emotionally, she might as well have been in a different universe.

•   •   •   •   •

By the end the weekend, Rachel had reacclimated to her life, to their normal routine. Mark let her sleep in as late as her body needed on Sunday. The girls had each eaten two breakfasts and a morning snack and were anxious by the time she finally rolled out of bed and joined them downstairs. The extra rest seemed to help. The color in her face was livelier and more radiant. She hugged both girls and at least looked at Mark. Not great, but at least she knew he existed. Abagail had gotten over Mark's dad fail and gave him a hug out of the blue, making that part of his world all better.

In the afternoon, they played Candy Land as a family. Abagail won. Maureen cried about it. Although without passion, Rachel was kind to Mark. She thanked him when he retrieved a glass of water for her, asked him what he wanted for dinner and about the logistics for the week that was to come. In some ways, everything felt normal, as if nothing had ever happened. In another, an unsaid tension existed that forged a wedge between them he knew wouldn't be removed by talking alone.

They ate dinner together. The meal Rachel prepared was hot and as delicious as usual. She convinced the girls to eat all the vegetables on their plates by bribing them with extra screen time afterward. Classic mom move. Unbelievably, Mark hadn't thought of it a few days ago, which said a lot more about him than it did about Rachel.

"Can I clean up in here?" Mark asked Rachel after dinner was complete and the girls were off to cash in.

"No, thank you. I'm fine."

"Are you sure?"

"I'm sure."

Hesitation aside, Mark took her hand and spun her toward him. She let him. "Hey, are you okay? Do you want to talk about what happened?"

"I'm fine," she said with a quick smile. "I'm exhausted, though, so I'm going to go to bed early tonight." She gave him another quick smile and turned away, gave her attention to the dishes. Maybe she just wanted a task that was mundane and normal, to help bring her back.

Mark knew she wasn't fine. Fine never meant fine. But he also knew when he should and shouldn't push it. This was one of those moments where letting it be was the only option, so that was what he did.

Rachel went to bed early, just as she said. As soon as the girls were down, she changed into one of her oversized T-shirts and went to bed. Mark sat alone downstairs, hoping Rachel might change her mind and join him for a glass of wine or at least come and say goodnight, but neither happened.

The last thing Mark needed was to postpone more client appointments tomorrow, but it was necessary. Stanley Lyons had been talked off the ledge, so that wasn't a concern anymore. His other clients, while important, weren't anything like the priority Stanley was. They'd understand. They were all small fish, like him.

Mark needed one more day to clear his mind and get into the right headspace to service his clients the way they deserved. He texted Carly and let her know. Tomorrow, life took priority.

While Rachel said she was okay, he couldn't take her at her word yet. She needed to prove it to him. He needed to ensure the girls were safe tomorrow, and in a good place themselves. While deep in his being he knew Rachel wouldn't ever hurt them, Tom's words still rang true.

She'll always love them. No matter what.

No matter what.

The words were chilling. The insinuation behind them was enough to raise the hairs on the back of Mark's neck.

After all Rachel had been through personally, and all of them as a family, he wasn't yet ready to go back to how things were before. He needed to speak with Rachel without distractions first, to find out where she was at with it all. And he needed to connect with Tom too. He hadn't heard from Tom at all since Rachel's admission to the hospital, which Mark found strange. He would have thought Tom would have at least checked in, as a friend. Mark needed to know what was next for Rachel. After being released and essentially cleared psychologically by the doctors at Evansville, what did that mean? Would Rachel be officially charged and arrested next?

He had so many questions, and he thought he deserved answers from both of them. Tomorrow, it was time to figure out what the hell was really going on.

Rachel didn't stir when Mark's alarm went off. He didn't bother waking her. Since he wasn't going into the office today, he skipped a shower. He allowed himself to close his eyes for twenty extra minutes. It was something he never did, and it felt so good. His life was always sped up, rushing from one thing to the next. He got to enjoy the comfort of being half-awake and half-asleep, and the deep state of relaxation it offered him. Rachel dozing peacefully next to him made it even better.

Or at least it would have been, if his wife wanted him there.

It was the third day of getting the girls up, ready, and out the door in time for school. By now, he felt like an old pro. He knew what Maureen would protest against and what to do about it. He knew he'd need to remind Abagail three times to shut the lights off when she left a room, and it was fifty-fifty if she'd actually do it. And he knew he'd leave the girls with cheeky smiles and promises to see each other later.

The line at school didn't seem as congested, though it could have just been that not needing to rush to get to the office offered a sense of calm Mark desperately needed. Especially on a day like today. The principal, whose name he still didn't know and conceded he likely wouldn't ever at this point, waved and greeted him by name. He'd become quite the regular in the drop-off line, right along with the minivan-driving PTA moms and helpful but overeager grandparents. It was amazing how quickly he'd adopted this new way of life.

The girls were off. Mark waved out the window and they both waved back. Maureen blew him a kiss. He caught it and clenched his fingers around it, forever cherishing it. She and Abagail disappeared into the sea of hundreds of other backpacks and jackets, and Mark drove away.

He was unusually relaxed. Those extra twenty minutes in bed made a huge difference in his mindset. Which was good. A relaxed state of mind was exactly what he needed right now, because there was a phone call he had to make. He didn't care what time it was; he'd waited long enough.

Mark dialed the Indianapolis Metropolitan Police Department and asked for Tom Wilde. Apparently, it wasn't too early; he was patched through right away by a woman who sounded like his new friend Lawanda, but he wasn't positive.

"Tom Wilde," Tom said when the line connected.

"Tom, it's Mark Starr."

"Mark! You've been on my mind all weekend. I'm glad you called."

"I think we need to talk. Have you heard about Rachel?"

"I have. I was notified of her release on Saturday."

"I thought I might hear from you over the weekend."

"I wanted to give you some space. Both you and Rachel."

Mark supposed he understood that.

"How is she?" Tom asked.

"Honestly? I don't really know. She says she's fine, but something's not right. She's being reclusive. Sleeping a lot. Not paying much attention to me or the girls. I'm concerned, Tom. What did they do to her in there?"

"I'm sorry to hear that. Trust me when I tell you this, Evansville has an amazing reputation. We wouldn't have reached out to them if we thought otherwise. She'll bounce back. Just give her time."

Time? That was one thing they didn't seem to have.

Mark flicked his directional and merged into traffic. He pressed the pedal toward the floor and picked up speed, changing gears. "Well, that's the thing. I don't know if we have much time. What happens next is unclear."

"I understand. What I can tell you is that as of right now, the shop owner still hasn't pressed any charges. That could change at any time, you need to be aware of that, but as of right now, nothing is imminent."

That was a relief. Mark thought he knew what that meant, but he had to be sure. He couldn't be left wondering. "Just to be clear, does this mean you won't be pressing any charges?"

"It's not me. It has nothing to do with me. But that's correct; the way things stand right now, you can expect that no charges will be filed."

Right now.

Mark hated the uncertainty of how that sounded. It felt like a ticking time bomb that could explode at any moment. Whether that was tomorrow or next week or next month, who knew? Was there a statute of limitations on theft? He didn't have a clue. He couldn't live with this hanging over their heads like this. He knew what he had to do.

"Mark? Did you hear what I said?"

He hadn't. He'd zoned out. "Say it again."

"I asked if you'd give Rachel my best. Please assure her it was nothing personal and I couldn't be more thrilled with the results. That's the truth. Will you tell her?"

"I'll tell her. Thank you."

"Listen, Mark, I have a call on the other line I need to take. Can I call you back?"

"No need. I've got somewhere to be, actually. Unless there's anything else?"

"No, there isn't."

"Well, I guess that's it then."

"Stay in touch, Mark. I'll see you at your office in three weeks."

Mark hung up. Not long after, he pulled into the driveway. He parked and went inside to check on Rachel. She was still sound asleep upstairs in the dark, the blinds untouched, the sheets next to her crumpled. Her face-down phone was plugged in on the nightstand next to her. For a second, he thought about going for it. He knew her password. If he took a quick peek, maybe he'd get some answers …

No, he couldn't do that. Looking at her phone would be a major breach of trust. He wouldn't be that guy. If she woke up and caught him scrolling through her phone, how would he explain himself? Just no. He moved on.

All signs pointed to Rachel not getting up anytime soon, so he let her be. She must have needed the rest. He backed out of the room, slowly closing the door behind him so it wouldn't make a sound. Downstairs, he found a piece of scrap paper in the drawer. He jotted a note on it, telling Rachel he was running an errand and would be back later, after he picked the girls up from school. He told her to relax and enjoy some time to herself, and that she deserved it. He went back upstairs and slipped the note under her phone. He could have texted her, but he didn't want to wake her; he didn't know if her phone's notifications were turned on.

Back in his car, he did a quick search on his phone. First to verify the hours, then to get directions. Turned out, he knew exactly where the place was. He'd driven past it thousands of times without noticing it. That was just how those things went sometimes. Unless someone was looking for it, it was easy to miss. Now that he knew, he closed his browser and tossed his phone in the cup holder. Directions weren't necessary.

He started the car, stepped on the clutch, and reversed into the street. One of the neighbors waved and he waved back because that was what neighbors did. Then he pressed the clutch again, shifted into gear, and headed for the city.

CHAPTER 25

There was a surrealism about being inside the establishment. He'd physically never been, but with how many times he saw it loop in his head, it was like he had. The bell chime over the door surprised him when he walked in. A man behind the counter looked up when the bell sounded, and he nodded a hello to Mark.

Everything looked so familiar. Based on the camera's location—a bird's-eye view from the corner to the left of the door—the angle made sense. The lens pointed directly at the counter and the cash register. The third of the shop directly underneath the camera was a blind spot, but it didn't matter; there wasn't any product there anyway. A decal that read Indy Guns and Ammo stuck to one of the glass-front cases.

Another customer, an older man wearing a Vietnam baseball cap, spoke to the man behind the counter. About what, Mark wasn't listening. He wandered around the shop instead, trying to look like he might consider buying something. Maybe in a way, he would, if it all went to plan.

The older gentleman in the hat left without purchasing anything, leaving Mark alone in the shop with the employee.

The door chimed as the man and his hat walked through it. Mark lingered for a few seconds before making his way over to the counter to speak with the employee.

"I help you?" the man behind the counter asked. Up close, his belly was enormous. His navel protruded out, pressing against his shirt.

"I'm looking for the owner," Mark said. "Is he around?"

"You're looking at him."

"Oh, hi. My name's Mark."

"Woody."

"Hi, Woody."

Woody stared.

"I'm here to ask you about something that happened last week. I heard somebody walked out with a box of ammunition."

"Stole is more like it."

"Right, well … that's why I'm here."

"How did you hear about that?"

"From a friend."

"You a cop?"

"I'm not."

"Who are you then?"

Mark took a deep breath. He wasn't sure how his next statement would land with Woody, who seemed anything but welcoming. "I'm the husband of the woman who took the ammunition."

Woody looked at him sideways. "Is this some kind of sick joke?"

"Not at all. I came here to apologize on behalf of my wife. She's experiencing a bit of an identity crisis right now and she made a horrible decision." Mark told Woody the story — about the footage he saw, Rachel's denial, briefly about her mental health evaluation. Woody listened, saying nothing, resting his folded arms on his belly. They both ignored the door when it chimed. "So, I guess what I'm trying to say is, I'm struggling to wrap my mind around all this, as her husband. Are you married?"

"I am."

"You understand then. Well, maybe not understand exactly what I'm dealing with … but you know what I mean."

"What is it you want?"

Mark reached into his pocket and grabbed his phone. He waited the two seconds it took his phone to recognize his eyes before swiping it unlocked and navigating to the gallery. He pulled up the most recent photo he had of Rachel and showed the screen to Woody. "Is this her? Is this the woman who stole from you?"

Woody stepped forward, leaning over the glass as far as his extra weight would allow, and squinted at the screen. It didn't take long, less than ten seconds, for him to step back. "That's her."

Mark pulled his phone back and pocketed it. "I thought so."

"I'll be right with you," Woody shouted to the potential paying customer who'd entered the store a few moments before.

"My understanding is that you're not pressing charges," Mark said. Not a question.

"I never said that."

"But you haven't yet."

Woody shrugged.

"What I'm really here for is to find out what it'll take to make this all go away."

"Are you trying to bribe me?"

"No, not a bribe. Not at all. I want to pay you for what my wife took, so we can pretend like this never happened. No harm, no foul."

Woody's arms were still folded. He scrunched his eyes as if in deep thought. A good sign, Mark thought. He was at least considering it.

"Plus a little extra, for what you've been through," Mark added. It never hurt to sweeten the deal if somebody was teetering.

Woody took a few more seconds. He unfolded his arms. "You think it's going to be that easy?"

"I was hoping so. Name your price."

"The stolen inventory was fifty bucks. But the emotional trauma I was put through, the nightmares." Woody grinned. "It's been terrible."

"Name it."

"A grand."

"Fine." Mark reached behind him and snagged his wallet. He pulled out the first credit card he saw and slapped it on the glass.

"Cash."

"I don't have that much cash on me."

Woody folded his arms again.

Mark thought he remembered seeing an ATM across the street. He told Woody to hold on, then he grabbed his card and left the gun shop. At the ATM, he agreed to pay to the three-dollar fee for using an ATM that wasn't associated with his bank, and he asked for a thousand dollars. It hurt, but he didn't care. Whatever it took — he had to keep reminding himself of that. He used his body to shield the screen and the cash dispenser; he didn't want a random passerby to see what he was doing and try to catch him off guard. The machine made a loud noise like the gears needed to be greased and the dispenser door opened. Mark grabbed the stack of hundreds without counting and made his way back across the street and into the gun store.

He pushed past the customer, moving in front of him, and slammed one thousand dollars in cash on the counter in front of Woody. He was pissed off about everything — at Rachel, for what she did; at Woody, for being an ass about it; at the ATM, for charging him a fee to withdraw his own money; at the world, for existing.

"Uh, excuse me?" the customer said, a man with a gray goatee and a smoker's rasp.

Mark ignored him. He couldn't have cared less about what goatee guy had to say. "Here. A thousand bucks. Cash."

Woody grabbed the stack, thumbed through it, and pocketed it.

"Are we square?" Mark asked when Woody looked at him.

"We're good."

"I won't be hearing from you ever again?"

"Not if you and your psycho wife stay the hell out of my shop."

Mark could have punched Woody in the jaw, but he let it go. He bit his tongue. He just needed this over with. "Fine."

"Then we're done here."

Mark held out his hand. It wasn't a signed agreement, but a handshake to seal a deal meant something. Especially, he suspected, to a guy in Woody's line of business.

Woody grabbed it and squeezed, stared Mark in the face. Woody let go and Mark turned his back to him and the goateed man. He walked out of the gun shop he knew he'd never step foot in again. He didn't even care that the security camera saw everything.

Mark took the drive to try to calm down. The confrontation with Woody left him fired up, his adrenaline still pumping. He still had a few hours before he could pick the girls up, but he didn't want to go home. Plus, he hadn't heard from Rachel. No thank you for handling the girls this morning or for letting her rest, no wondering where he was or when he'd be home. None of that while he was out there covering for her, cleaning up her mess, protecting their family.

He was close to snapping.

He needed to blow off some steam before he was ready to deal with any more of this today. He remembered he hadn't eaten yet, even though he wasn't hungry. The traffic was backed up, signs for road work up ahead, so he was still in the city. He hadn't made it far. The light turned green, but nobody moved. Horns blared. Some guy angrier than Mark rolled his window down and yelled at someone to move their ass. The only response was more horns.

Screw this, Mark thought. He didn't have the patience for this crap today.

A single on-street parking spot was open to his right, so he whipped the wheel toward it and thrust himself into it. He'd walk to where he was going. And by the looks of the nonmoving traffic, he'd make better time too. Johnny's was only a few blocks away. He could use the fresh air to reset himself anyway.

The walk helped. The sun shone bright against his face. A cool breeze countered it and kept the sweat away. By the time he made it to Johnny's, hunger pangs had revealed themselves as cramps underneath his ribcage and his stomach growled. He ignored the pangs and the growling and pushed inside, where he sat at the bar. He didn't bother scoping out the place to see who else was there this time; he didn't care in the least. He grabbed a menu from the rack and scoured it for something that struck him.

"Hello, stranger."

Mark looked up. He smiled when he saw Sarah, the bartender, and her pussycat neck tattoo. The flesh tunnels hanging from her earlobes were bigger than he remembered.

"Day drinking your new thing?" she asked with a smile.

"Hi, Sarah."

Sarah faked flattery. "You remembered my name."

"You're hard to forget."

"I'll take that as a compliment."

He smiled at her.

"Let me know when you want to order."

He gave it a few, let his eyes settle to the darkness that was Johnny's in the middle of the day. Part of him felt guilty for being there, like he was doing something he shouldn't, but it was just a beer. Adults drank a beer with their lunch all the time.

Sarah came back over after what she deemed had been enough time for him to decide. She leaned over and rested her forearms on the counter. "So, what will it be?"

"I'll take a beer, please."

"Bud again?"

"No, not a Bud. Michelob this time."

"Coming right up." Sarah spun, did her thing, and returned with a full glass. She set it in front of him.

"Can I grab a chicken sandwich to go with this?"

"Fries okay?"

"Fries are perfect."

Mark sipped on the beer and waited for his food. The Michelob, he found, went down a lot smoother than the Budweiser had the last time he was there. The bar wasn't busy, Mark realized, so it wasn't a surprise when Sarah brought him a basket of food in short order. The guys in the back must have been eager to do something.

"Anything else?" she asked.

"No, thank you."

Sarah nodded and started walking away.

"Actually, wait," he said.

She turned back.

"Do you remember what you said to me the last time I was in here?"

She cocked her head. "Should I?"

"We were talking about truth. I asked you how you know when someone's lying to you and you said—"

"It's all in the eyes."

"That's right."

"I remember."

"What did you mean by that?" Mark grabbed the sandwich with two hands and took a huge, mouth-filling bite. There was so much chicken and bread and sauce in his mouth that he could hardly chew. He imagined he looked as ridiculous as Todd had when they were at Tony's, but he didn't care; he wasn't trying to impress anybody. He instantly felt his body refueling.

"People say that the eyes are the windows to our souls, right? I admit, it's a little cliché and maybe even a bit corny, but there's a lot of truth in it. You can see a lot by looking into someone's eyes. Emotions, fears, motivations. You just have to look close enough."

Mark finished chewing and swallowed. The bite was so big, it hurt going down. "That's pretty deep."

Sarah smirked. "I'm getting my master's in philosophy."

"You're just full of surprises, aren't you?"

"You have no idea."

Mark finished his sandwich in the quiet, then he washed it down with the Michelob. It might have been his new favorite beer, he decided. When he was finished, he gave Sarah his credit card and signed over a massive tip.

"Is this a mistake?" Sarah asked when she saw it. She picked up the receipt and showed it to him.

"Not a mistake. You're impressive. I enjoy talking to you."

"And I enjoy talking to you."

"Good luck in school."

She smiled. Blushed, maybe, but it was hard to tell because of the darkness.

Mark wiped his mouth and stood up. Now that he was satiated, he felt so much better. He was ready to tackle the rest of the afternoon.

"Hey, Mark," Sarah called as he started leaving.

He turned back to her. "You remembered."

She laughed. "Busted. I saw it on your credit card. I just wanted to say thank you, Mark."

He nodded and smiled. "You're welcome." Then he left.

•　　　•　　　•　　　•　　　•

He made it on time to pick up the girls. He went through the usual routine, except this time he led the line, so he was in and out quickly. He waved to the principal, who lit up with delight at the gesture.

"Girls, what's the principal's name?" Mark asked once they were in the car and appropriately buckled.

"Miss Campbell," Abagail answered.

"Is that her first name or last name?"

"Dunno."

Miss Campbell. Mark was determined to remember that for next time. "So, girls, how was school today?"

"Good," Abagail said.

Mark peeked in the rearview at Maureen, who was unusually quiet. "What about you, Maureen?"

She shrugged. Her torso faced the window.

"What's the matter?" Mark was still looking in the mirror, his eyes darting between it and the road.

Maureen seemed to sigh, then she turned her body so she was facing forward. "I saw Mommy today."

Rachel had been asleep this morning, but it was possible Maureen had snuck in to say goodbye at some point without Mark noticing. He wasn't sure when, though. "This morning, you mean?"

"No, at school."

Mark's chest pounded.

"She came to see me at recess," Maureen added.

"What? But how?"

"She told me not to tell you." Her bottom lip quivered. "Is Mommy going to be mad at me? Am I going to get in trouble?"

Mark's heart raced so fast, he was afraid he might pass out. He had to roll the window down to get some air. He didn't know how to answer Maureen's questions.

Why would Rachel go to the school? And for what?

"You're not in trouble," Mark said. He watched as Abagail took Maureen's hand and held it.

The girls snuggled together, their heads meeting in the middle of the backseat. Some other time, Mark would have found it adorable, the way they came together in times of need.

But now, today, it was anything but. What was most striking to him was the expressions on their faces. Neither girl looked happy nor excited that Rachel had made a surprise visit to the school today. Both of them looked upset. Definitely sad. Possibly a little afraid.

But of what? Their mother?

It made little sense, but Mark understood why. Whatever it was, whatever that peculiar, eerie energy was between Rachel and the rest of them, he felt it too. He thought the girls were sheltered from it, but he couldn't have been more wrong about that. Knowing that made his skin crawl. He had the feeling this was about to get a lot worse before it got better.

This wasn't possible. Rachel couldn't have gone to the girls' school today. No way. And in secret? Not plausible.

Except, it was.

Mark was gone all day. Rachel had been sleeping still when he got home, but he'd gone into the city and was gone for hours. He had no way of knowing what Rachel did today or any day. Something he'd gathered, based on Maureen's reaction, was that this hadn't happened before. One of the girls would have told him about it. The big question was, why today? And why in secret?

Rachel better have a good explanation, he thought.

Rachel's SUV was in the garage, in the same place as always. It looked the same as it did earlier, but it was impossible to tell if it had been moved. The tires looked dry, but everything was dry today; it hadn't rained since Saturday.

The girls grabbed their backpacks and retreated into the house. Their energy was lower than normal, more subdued. Mark didn't spend any time lingering behind them. Trying to spot the hidden gun in the garage wasn't important today. What was more important was following his girls inside and trying to figure out what was going on with their mother, his wife.

The smell hit his nose as soon as he crossed the threshold. It was one of those smells that went immediately to his brain then took a beeline to his stomach. It didn't matter when or where; the smell brought him feelings of euphoria.

Cookies.

"Mommy made cookies!" Maureen shouted when Mark rounded the corner.

"I smell them," he said.

"Hi, honey," Rachel said with a smile.

Honey? After not looking at him for a day and a half, he was honey again.

"Want a chocolate chip cookie?" she asked from behind her favorite disgusting apron. "Your favorite."

"Uh, thanks," he said. He accepted the napkin with a warm, gooey cookie on it. If she was trying to drug him, this would be the way to do it—with cookies. His weakness. He smelled it up close and visually inspected it. It looked normal. His mouth watered.

"These are so yummy, Mummy!" Maureen said with a full mouth.

Abagail laughed. "You rhymed!"

"Don't chew with food in your mouth, sweetie," Rachel said.

What was going on?

Rachel looked wonderful. Radiant. She'd done up her makeup and gotten dressed. Her hair was tied up above her head, a stick through the center of the bun. Either she'd made the most miraculous recovery mankind had ever seen, or she was full of shit.

Mark's money was on the latter.

"How are you feeling?" he asked her.

"I feel great," she said. "Thanks for letting me sleep in."

He was glad she acknowledged it. Maybe that's all it was. Between yesterday and the extended sleep today, maybe she just needed a reset after the psychological trauma she experienced at Evansville.

The girls shoved the rest of their cookies in their mouths and ran off to play, laughing.

The oven beeped.

"Oh! The next batch is ready!" Rachel said.

Mark watched her. He didn't offer to help. She slipped an oversized oven glove on each hand and bent down in front of the oven, returning with another tray of fresh cookies.

"You've been busy today," Mark said.

"Yeah, I woke up feeling refreshed and fully energized, so I thought I should take advantage of it."

"Uh-huh. What else did you do today?"

Rachel placed the tray on the stovetop and started moving the older cookies from the cooling rack into a plastic container. "The usual, really."

"Like what?"

"I read for a while when I got up, took a shower, started meal prep for the week." She turned and faced him. "Chicken casserole sound okay for dinner?"

He wouldn't tell her he had chicken for lunch. "Sounds great."

She smiled and turned back to her cookies. "It was really nice, actually. Thanks again for letting me sleep in. I must have needed it. How was your day?"

"Fine. Ran an errand in the city."

"That's nice." The cookie tray was empty now, so Rachel scooped more batter onto it for the next batch.

"Did you leave the house today?"

"No." Rachel kept scooping and dropping, scooping and dropping. "Why?"

Mark waited. He wanted to look her in the face. It wouldn't take her long to turn around if he didn't answer her.

It's all in the eyes.

Rachel put down the scoop and turned to face Mark. "Why do you want to know if I left the house today?"

"I know you did. And I know where you went."

Rachel sighed. "What are you talking about now?"

"Rachel—"

"Actually, you know what, never mind. I don't want to talk about this. I'm in too good a mood for you to ruin it."

"You can't keep—"

"Mark, stop! Enough."

"Are you guys fighting?"

Mark whipped his head toward the voice. It was Abagail's. She stood in the entryway to the kitchen, one of the saloon doors swinging on its hinges.

"No, sweetie, we're not fighting," Rachel said.

"It sounds like you're fighting."

"We're not. We're just talking," Rachel said.

Abagail looked at Mark with a confused expression. He had a hard time meeting her gaze. He didn't want to lie to her.

"Do you want to come help me finish making these cookies?" Rachel asked.

Abagail kept her attention on Mark, as if asking for permission. He subtly nodded once, and she started toward her mother.

Rachel spread out an arm and wrapped it around Abagail's shoulder. They turned toward the stovetop. As they did, Mark caught Rachel's gaze, and she caught his. There was an undeniable tension in her eyes. Whatever façade she was trying to put forth was just a show, and he knew it—and he was certain she knew that he knew. It might have been enough to fool the girls, but not him. But considering what happened in the car earlier, he wondered if they knew more than she thought.

He didn't trust Rachel right now. Not for a second. He left his uneaten cookie on the counter and walked out of the kitchen.

•   •   •   •   •

They followed the typical weeknight routine. Playtime, dinner, more playtime. Mark did the dishes while Rachel packed lunches for the next day, then she went to spend some time with the girls in their playroom. Mark joined them once he was done. He and Rachel didn't speak, only watched. Maureen looked upset, but he figured it was something Abagail said to her.

Later, the girls had an after-dinner snack — a no longer warm but just as delicious chocolate chip cookie each, they said, and a couple for Mark. By then, he figured he was being paranoid, and he couldn't restrain himself any longer. Hoping he didn't make a lethal mistake, he wiped the crumbs off the table and the countertop and scooped them into the trash. Before bed, Mark and Rachel joined the girls on the sofa for a half-hour of screen time. They sat on opposite ends, their daughters sandwiched between them.

Thirty minutes felt like three hours.

The girls took turns using the bathroom, then brushed their teeth together. During, they argued about whose timer would go off first. The answer was neither; they shared a timer, so they were both done when it went off. It seemed simple enough to understand, but Mark hadn't been a kid in a while. He wouldn't try to pretend to understand their logic.

In Maureen's room, Rachel read the girls a bedtime story. She made silly voices as she read, giving each character something unique. Mark found it delightful on most days, but today it felt like a stall tactic. The faster the girls went to bed, the faster he could confront Rachel. Again. Although he figured it wouldn't get anywhere, he still had to try.

"Goodnight, girls," he said from hallway once the story was done, in the spot where he could see both beds at once. Their bedrooms were adjacent to one another, so the right angle made all the difference. "Love you."

"Daddy?" he heard Maureen say as he started for the stairs.

He told Rachel he'd handle it, and she obliged by heading downstairs. He kept the light off but went into Maureen's room and sat on her bed. "What is it?"

Maureen started crying.

"Is it Mommy?"

She nodded.

"Want to tell me what happened at recess today?"

Maureen shrugged.

"It's important."

"Okay. I was playing Hopscotch with Libby and Violet. My turn was over, so I waited. I looked around and saw Mommy. I ran over to her and gave her a hug."

"What did Mommy say?"

"She said I was beautiful and she couldn't wait to see me."

"What do you think she meant by that?"

"Dunno. But then"—Maureen started crying again—"at home, she didn't say anything, like she forgot what she said."

"What do you mean?"

"At school"—Maureen sniffled—"Mommy said she'd come visit me again tomorrow."

"She said that?"

"Yes. Then when I asked her if she was still coming tomorrow when me and Abby were playing, she asked me what I was talking about." More tears fell. "I think she forgot about me."

Mark sat her up and squeezed her. As his little girl wrapped her arms around his neck, desperate for his protection, he had to fight his own tears back. "Mommy didn't forget about you. I promise."

"I saw it too."

Mark spun toward the voice. It was Abagail again, who'd apparently formed a habit of creepily sneaking into people's conversations. She stood a few steps into Maureen's bedroom.

"I saw it," Abagail repeated.

"What did you see?" he asked.

"At recess. I saw Maureen talking to someone. My recess was over so my class was going inside. I was too far away to see who it was, but I saw it."

Mark didn't doubt Maureen was telling the truth, but the validation from another source took it to a whole other level.

Rachel wasn't just lying to him. She was lying to their daughters, too.

"The thing I thought was weird," Abagail said, "was that when we got home, Mom had different clothes on. So maybe it was someone else."

"It was Mommy," Maureen said. "I swear it was Mommy. Pinky promise."

The girls looked at each other, but not in a confrontational way; they were still afraid of whatever was going on with their mom. Mark knew what he had to do.

"Sweetheart, did you say Mommy said she was going to visit you at recess again tomorrow?"

"Yes," Maureen said.

"If I put a note in your lunchbox tomorrow, will you give it to Mommy for me?"

"Okay."

"But you can't give it to Mommy in the morning, okay? Just at recess. Can you do that for me?"

"I think so."

By now, Abagail started crying too. "Daddy, I'm scared," she said.

He couldn't remember the last time she'd called him daddy. Hearing her say it, he felt the way he did when those songs about dads and their daughters came on the radio—weak. "Come here."

Abagail walked toward them and sat on the bed next to Mark. He hugged them both, hard, and they hugged him back. He was thankful for the darkness in the room so his girls didn't have to see him cry. He couldn't think of a time when they had.

"It's okay," he said as calmly as he could. "You don't have to be scared. Daddy's got you."

The truth was, and the girls would never know this, he was freaked out too. Had Rachel gone to the girls' school then came home and changed? He couldn't fathom why that would make any sense. What would be the reason for doing something like that? Something strange was going with her; that wasn't even debatable anymore. He didn't know what he was looking for, but all he could do was hope that he'd figure out what it was before it was too late.

Morning came in a hurry, and with it, a stiff neck. Mark had fallen asleep in Maureen's bed after comforting her. The battery on his phone was in the red, just about dead. He awoke four minutes before his alarm was scheduled to go off, which couldn't have been any more perfect. Rachel would be up soon too.

Mark slowly swung his legs out of Maureen's bed, careful not to disturb her. It took her longer to fall asleep than normal, so she didn't get as much sleep as she should have. He wanted her to get every extra minute she could today. She'd need it for the big day ahead. The floor creaked when his foot hit the ground, then again when the other one did. He tiptoed out of the room.

Downstairs, the house was silent. Peaceful. The sun had risen, leaving a kaleidoscope of colors dancing on the horizon. But there wasn't any time to stand in the kitchen and admire it through the window; there was something he needed to do. And fast.

The miscellaneous items that weren't valuable enough to give them a permanent home but too valuable to discard were kept in the cabinet drawer next to the refrigerator. He opened it. It was the same drawer where he'd found the scrap paper the day before. Inside, on top of all the junk—the bottle opener, corkscrew, box of matches, old magnets missing the magnetic parts, button cell batteries—was a stack of sticky notes. A household staple. Where were those yesterday? Mark grabbed a pen and jotted a note on it, just like he said he would. The note was simple, not really even a note. A number. Seven digits.

His phone number.

Under it, he wrote his first name with the words "call me." That was it. He folded the adhesive on itself and slipped the note into Maureen's lunchbox. After, he filled it with the prepared lunch from the fridge and zipped it—that way, Rachel wouldn't have any reason to open it again and stumble upon the note intended for her later. He had to keep this from Rachel if it was going to work.

The good thing about falling asleep in Maureen's bed last night—or maybe the avoidance it created was a bad thing, though it sure felt like a good thing—was that Mark didn't have another argument with Rachel. Her showing up at the school unannounced was yet another issue they needed to discuss head-on, but he thought both of them were better off for not having the argument yesterday. His mind desperately needed a break from the arguing. He imagined Rachel's did too. It was exhausting.

Which was why he decided he wouldn't ask her about her visit to school. Everything about it bothered him—how she wanted Maureen to keep it a secret, the quick change of clothes when she got home, why she was even there in the first place; what couldn't wait for three hours until the girls got home from school?—but he'd hold on to that burden, at least in the short term. He had to see where this went, what doors would open if she showed up at school again and called him, like his note asked.

Why did he leave his number? If it was indeed Rachel who'd shown up and would again today, or so she told Maureen, she obviously had Mark's number. But what if it wasn't her? It was plausible—more than that, really, more like probable—that the girls were wrong. It must have been someone who looked like their mom, dressed like her, talked like her. Maureen was only five years old, so it wasn't difficult to imagine such a mistake. At eight years old, Abagail would be less likely to make a mistake like that—but she'd said that she was too far away to see much detail, so that easily explained that away.

If it wasn't Rachel, then who was it? And what did she want with Maureen?

No clue. That was why he needed to find out.

The more Mark thought about the possibilities of what could happen to Maureen, the more he doubted if he could go through with this. The logical, fatherly thing to do would be to tell Rachel and call the school to give them a heads up about what Maureen said. How did they allow a stranger on school grounds during the school day in the first place? They wouldn't want that information getting out to the other parents. People would be rightfully pissed. It might cause an uproar. To avoid that, the school would do all they could to put the kibosh on any of this, then Mark would never find out who it was.

But what if something went wrong? What if the woman was indeed a stranger and not Rachel, and what if she had sinister motives? What if—he didn't even want to think about it, but it was hard to ignore—what if this woman took Maureen? Mark would never be able to live with himself. And if someone found out about the note he left for this unknown person, this kidnapper, it'd make him look either complicit or like the worst father who'd ever lived.

Or both.

He wasn't sure which would be worse.

He had to stop this. These thoughts were unhealthy, and unhelpful. He'd decided what he was going to do and would live with the results. The worst-case scenario mindset wasn't how he lived his life. Bad things happened every day; he could only control what he could control. Right now, taking control of the situation was precisely what he was trying to do.

Rachel brought the girls to school. It was an immense sense of relief for him. The pressure of being the sole caregiver had been weighing on him. Some people weren't cut out for it all the time, and he, it turned out, was one of them. He didn't know that about himself until he was forced to go through it. He wouldn't beat himself up about it, though. Spending a few days trying to juggle the girls' needs with his clients' needs, and his own, gave him a whole new perspective on Rachel and others like her. Full-time mothers and homemakers truly had the most difficult and underappreciated job in the world.

Mark rolled into the office early. It'd been a while since that'd happened. He was the first one in. He left the lights off, except for in his office. He closed the door so he could catch up on work without distractions, but then he realized how stupid that was; he felt like a creep sitting behind a closed door when he was alone. He reopened it.

It was close to an hour before the next person came in and lit up the office. By then, Mark was so absorbed in his work that he hardly noticed; he left his office door open, ignoring the noise. At some point, Carly popped her head in to say hello, but that was all. She left him to his work. Another one of her strengths was that she was an excellent room reader. Today, that strength paid immediate dividends.

By late-morning, he needed a coffee refill, and also to stretch his legs. He was making a significant dent in the backlog of work, so he was confident he could finish what he needed to in the next hour, before his first client of the day was scheduled to arrive.

He took a stroll through the office, popping in to the breakroom to get a refill, then back out to continue his journey. There was something else he needed to do today too. Something that had been bothering him that needed fixing. He found Todd in his office with the phone against his face and his feet on the desk. Todd held up a finger when he spotted Mark. Mark leaned against the door frame and waited, sipping his coffee.

"Look who the cat dragged in," Todd said as he hung up the phone. "You look … human."

Mark chuckled. "I feel human. I just came by to apologize, Todd."

"For what?"

"For the way I treated you the last time we spoke. I was rude to you, and I'm sorry."

"No sweat off by balls, man. I didn't even notice."

Mark doubted that, but he appreciated the sentiment. "You free for lunch?"

Todd smirked. "Tony's?"

"Of course."

"Hell yes. Markster is back!" Todd clapped his hands, the momentum nearly toppling him over backward in his chair. "Whoa!"

"Easy there, killer."

"Noon-thirty?"

"Come get me if I'm running behind."

"You got it."

With that, Mark left and headed back to his office. Todd was a man-child, but he was Mark's closest friend in the office. Come to think of it, Mark spent most of his time at the office, so Todd may have been one of his only friends at this point in his life. It felt good to reconcile. Mark needed a friend right now. Especially one who wasn't a police officer. He was even looking forward to ordering something at Tony's this time.

Back in his office, he settled into the rest of the backlog with his coffee. It felt so good to be back in the zone. He felt alive in a way he hadn't in several days. He hadn't realized how much he missed having a busy mind and feeling productive.

He met with his first client, who showed up on time, and left with marching orders. His second client of the day was a half-hour early, but Mark was in a good mood so he saw her right after his first. It took until he felt the vibration in his pocket while he shook his client's hand to remind him of the predicament at home.

It had to have been recess time by now, or close to it. Truthfully, he wasn't certain of the girls' schedules during the day. He said goodbye to his client, trying his hardest to ignore the vibration against his thigh. As soon as he could, he spun and hurried back into his office, where he pulled out the phone and glanced at the screen.

An unrecognizable number.

Not Rachel's.

Indianapolis zip code.

His first reaction was wondering if it was the same number he'd called from the Doctor Lisa Show call log, when he'd spoken with Rachel and she hung up on him. He'd have to check later, though. There was no time now. He pressed on the green icon and swiped, then pushed the phone to his ear.

"Hello?"

"Hello, Mark."

His breath caught. Two simple words, yet so heavy with significance. Despite knowing it all along, he was still shocked to her hear voice. "Rachel?"

Sometimes, when you want something, you have to go for it. Which is why I went for it. The wheels were officially in motion. I hadn't quite felt myself in recent days, for obvious reasons. There was a lot going on inside my head.

I did something I shouldn't have. But the timing felt right and there was an unexpected window of time to make it happen, so I did it. I walked through that open window. My husband was gone, doing whatever it was he needed to do, and I was alone, left with my thoughts and an empty house. Again. The emptiness of the days ran into my mind sometimes. It was hard not to. And my mind had been fragile recently, so the two were a bad combination.

It doesn't mean I'm crazy, though. Everyone gets into a funk sometimes. That's all it was; I was in a weird funk.

I'd thought it out ahead of time. This wasn't something I did on a whim. I was fully prepared and knew what I was doing. But I was still nervous because there wasn't any way to know how it'd go.

I went to the girls' school. In the middle of the day. Unannounced. As far as I knew, I wasn't spotted by a staff member. That would have led to too many questions I wasn't prepared to answer. I got lucky in that way. I parked in the visitor's parking lot and walked toward the back of the building, as if I belonged. Looking the part was half the battle. I was just a regular mom visiting the kids' school for one of many possible reasons. It happened every day at every school in America.

I stood behind the chain-link fence and leaned my forearms in between the grooves. I waited. Watched. A group of kids—had to have been fifteen or twenty of them—ran and screamed and chased one another. Two staff members chatted by the back entrance to the school, apparently oblivious to the extra adult on the playground.

She saw me before I saw her. My everything fluttered with anticipation.

After hopping on one foot, then two, then one again, she stopped and turned in my direction, as if she knew I was there. Her eyes lit up and her jaw dropped open. She ran straight toward me. I stepped around the fence and crouched down, getting to her level. She leaped into my arms and I caught her, and I squeezed.

"Mommy!" she said.

I kept squeezing, lost for words. She was so precious. She pulled back and looked at me, a huge smile on her face. I had one on too.

"You are so beautiful," I told her.

She glowed. "Why are you here?"

"I couldn't wait to see you! That's why."

She smiled and wrapped her arms around me again.

"Looks like you were having fun over there," I said after she pulled away again.

"Do you want to play?"

"No, thank you. I like watching."

"Please, Mommy!"

I beamed and almost said I would. She made it so hard to say no. "I'd love that, but I can't. I need to go now."

"Mommy, no!"

"It's okay. You need to get going soon too. But don't worry, I'll visit again soon."

"When?"

I quickly thought about it. "How about tomorrow?"

"Really? Yay!"

We hugged again.

"Will you do something for me?" I asked her.

She enthusiastically nodded.

"Can we keep this our little secret? Just for a little while?"

She looked at me curiously.

"Can you do that?"

"Will I get in trouble?"

"Of course not! I'll tell Daddy later, so you don't need to tell him anything, okay?"

She nodded.

"Good girl. You should get back now, okay? See you later."

She waved and ran off, back to her friends. Before anyone noticed me, I spun back around the fence and disappeared.

The next day, I went back, just like I promised I would. How could I break my promise to that precious little girl? No way I could do that to her. I stood in the same spot behind the fence at the same time as the day before, waiting. I scanned the group of kids, looking for her. They all looked the same from that distance, with their puffy jackets and short legs and loud voices.

Finally, I saw her among the others. She skipped around the yard, holding hands with another girl, both laughing. The two on-duty staff members were spread out this time, both wandering casually around the perimeter of the playground, their watchful eyes overlooking the children. Which posed a problem. It wouldn't be long before the staff member with the long brunette hair, her curls bouncing down around her neck, came upon me.

"Maureen!" I yelled out, but she didn't hear me. On the second try, she did.

She stopped skipping and looked around her, for the sound of my voice. Her gaze landed on the same spot it did the day before, and we locked eyes. I raised my hand and waved to her, and she ran over. There was noticeably less enthusiasm in her step than there was the first time. I didn't like that. Something was up. I tried not to overthink it, though. There wasn't any time for that, not with the brunette closing in on me.

"Hi, beautiful!" I said when she was close.

"Hi," she somberly answered.

"Are you okay?"

She nodded.

I looked down and noticed something clenched in her hand. "What's that in your hand?"

She pushed her arm forward and handed it to me. I took it. It was a folded sticky note.

"Daddy wanted me to give you this."

I was shocked—in a good way, I thought, though the jury was still out at the time—and unsure how to react. I hadn't expected it in a million years. He shouldn't even have known about this.

"He did?" I asked her.

She nodded again and said, "I gotta go."

I was confused, unsure what was happening. Why was this so different than the last time, so awkward? I thought she would have been happy to see me. I asked her if she was sure.

"Yes," she said, then said she said goodbye.

I watched as she scampered off, back toward her friends. I stood up straight and fingered the note in my hand, watching the kids. I was just about to move on and read the note when I heard a voice.

"Mrs. Starr?"

I looked up and found the voice. It was the woman with the curly hair. The brunette.

"What are you doing here?" she asked.

There was a lump in my throat. I was caught. I needed to come up with something, and fast. "Oh, hi, there. Nice to see you again."

She folded her arms and waited for me to explain what I was doing.

"Sorry to just drop in like this," I said with a laugh, trying to lighten the mood. "I forgot to give Maureen something this morning, so I thought I'd drop it off."

"There's a procedure for that, Mrs. Starr."

"You're right. I'm sorry. I shouldn't have done it like this."

The woman's arms were still folded, but her face had softened.

"I'm leaving right now," I said. "I'll stop into the office on my way out and let them know what happened."

The woman nodded, seemingly accepting my explanation.

"Bye, sweetie," I yelled out to Maureen, knowing she wouldn't hear me. "See you later!" Then I gave my attention back to the curly-haired woman and smiled. "Sorry about this. Won't happen again." I turned my back to her and walked away before she had the chance to respond.

I didn't stop into the office. Instead, I walked back to my SUV and got in, and finally pulled apart the sticky note. It was a phone number with a name—Mark's—along with a suggestion to call him. That's what I did. I called him.

The phone rang through the Bluetooth of my SUV's speakers. I anxiously waited for him to pick up. It rang more times than I liked.

Eventually, he answered with, "Hello?"

"Hello, Mark," I said back with some force in my voice.

"Rachel?"

I cringed. "Can we meet?"

He didn't hesitate. "Where?"

Where? I hadn't planned for this, so I hadn't thought about it. "The park. Thirty minutes."

"Which park, Rachel? That's not helpful." There was an edge to his tone. Frustration.

"Which one is closest to you?"

"Southwestway is closest to *you*. Let's meet there."

"Fine."

"And Rachel?"

I waited.

"I hope you have a damn good reason for showing up at the girls' school unannounced two days in a row."

My breath caught.

"Maureen told me."

I had no words.

"See you in thirty minutes. You better be there."

CHAPTER 30

Mark was so pissed that he threw his phone onto his desk. It was Rachel all along, just like he knew it was. How could she? How could she try to manipulate their daughter like that, by showing up at school and telling her not to tell Mark about it and … and what? Something wasn't quite adding up. What was Rachel's endgame? Something was off with her; anybody could have seen it. But what did that mean? What was she up to?

Maureen crossed his mind. Was she okay? She must have been. If Rachel called him from a different phone number—it must have been the second phone she had, like the one she called the Doctor Lisa Show on, or a burner—then that meant she must have received the note he left in Maureen's lunchbox. Right? He supposed she could have called from her own number, though. Why didn't she?

He must have been missing something. There was a piece to this puzzle he wasn't seeing yet. How had he not known she had a second phone?

"Carly?" he called out.

She popped her head into his office. "What's up?"

"How long until my next appointment?"

"An hour."

He did some quick math. Almost thirty minutes to Southwestway Park to meet Rachel, almost thirty minutes back. That didn't give him long, but he had to make it work—and he would.

"Why?" Carly asked. "Is everything okay?"

"Yes, fine. I need to run out for a bit. I'll be gone an hour, an hour and ten max. Who's coming in?"

"Sally Meadows."

Sally. Sixtysomething. Recent divorcee. Serious about planning for her life after divorce. She was friendly enough. Understanding.

"Will you stall her for a few minutes if I'm not back? Tell her I'm running behind and ask if she'll mind waiting."

"Of course."

"Thank you." Mark grabbed his bag but changed his mind. He'd be back. He needed some normalcy back in his life, so this would force him to come back. No more excuses. "I really appreciate it. Oh, and I almost forgot. Would you mind letting Todd know that I'll need a raincheck on lunch? Tell him something important has come up that I need to attend to."

"No problem."

Mark dropped a hand on Carly's shoulder as he walked past her. He gently squeezed it. "Thank you for this. I know I've been flaky lately. There's something going on with Rachel, and the girls, they need—"

"You don't need to explain it to me. Honest." She smiled to show her sincerity.

He tried to return one but struggled to. He thanked her again and took off.

Southwestway Park was ten miles southwest of the city and almost exactly the center point between work and home. It had athletic fields and equestrian trails, bike and walking paths, and was nestled up against a golf course. All of which meant the parking lot was jammed, even in the middle of the day, and there were active people everywhere. Lots of thin, sweaty, shirtless men, but not enough women. Mark pulled into the lot and drove through it, both looking for a parking spot and for Rachel's SUV. He found a spot with ease, but didn't find the SUV.

He got out and walked over to one of the trailheads overlooking the parking lot. From there, he could see anyone who drove in and anyone who left. He twisted his torso and leaned against a post. His back was to the forest. He kept his head on a swivel.

He waited. A trio of bicyclists pedaled past and waved. He waved back. What appeared to be a mother's group walked by with their strollers in tow, black yoga pants everywhere, talking among themselves. None of them waved or even acknowledged his presence. Somewhere in the distance, somebody laughed. The park was alive.

"Mark?"

He spun in every direction, trying to find the voice that called his name. It was so subtle, he wondered if he imagined it. But then he heard it again, louder this time, and his senses heightened.

"There you are," the voice said. Her voice.

Rachel's voice.

Hearing it in this setting made him stiffen. There was no doubt in his mind that it was her. He turned to her voice. "Rachel? How did you …"

"I parked in the south lot," she said, as if reading his mind.

That explained how he missed her.

"Hi," she said, gazing at him, smiling. "It's so nice to see you."

He thought he saw lust in her eyes, but that wouldn't make sense; they were hardly on speaking terms. He stood back and took her in. All of her. From face to feet. Incredible. It was her—

the same curves in the same spots, the same white teeth behind the smile he missed so much, the same face. It was so her.

Rachel. His Rachel.

"Rachel?"

"Hi, Mark."

He wanted to be angry with her—because he was, he really was—but for some unexplained reason, he was lost for words. His wife was like a beautiful stranger.

"The girls are beautiful," Rachel said.

Mark snapped back to reality. "Excuse me?"

"Especially Maureen. She's such a doll, isn't she?"

He agreed, of course, but that seemed like a bizarre thing to say. "Rachel, what the hell is going on? Why were you at the girls' school? And what's up with the second phone?"

She reached for his hand. "Can we go sit down somewhere? There's so much I want to say to you."

He snatched it away. He had to fight through her charm. Whatever she was up to, he'd force himself to see through it. "I don't want to sit. I want to talk right here, right now. No more pushing it off. No more denials."

Rachel sighed.

"Spill it. It's time to put everything out on the table. What's going on with you?"

"Fine, Mark. If that's what you want. Will you make me a promise first?"

"What?"

"Please listen. You might hear some things you've never heard, but I need you to know it's the truth. Can you promise me that?"

What was she talking about? She was talking crazy. But whatever; he'd play along. "Fine. I'll listen."

"Are you happy, Mark?"

The question took him by surprise. "Am I happy? Right this second, not particularly. In general, yes, very. Why, aren't you?"

"When I was a kid, something happened to me, Mark. Something that would change the entire trajectory of my life. It could have gone either way, an actual flip of the coin. I guess I was the unlucky one, right? Do you know how often I think about that? How many times I've wondered what would happen if things went differently? Do you?"

"I don't—"

"Every day, Mark! Every single day."

Mark noticed a hand-holding couple walking past who turned and looked at him and Rachel as she said that, with judging eyes.

"Why her?" Rachel said. "Why not me? What made her so special and me so ... so unworthy?"

"I don't understand what you're talking about. Who's her?"

"Come on, Mark. Her. Stop playing around."

"I seriously don't know who her is."

"That's the thing about women. There's always competition, right? Even when there shouldn't be. Even when it has nothing to do with the other person. But it still exists. It does. And when the other person has everything you've ever wanted, you'll do just about whatever it takes to get it too. Do you know what I mean?"

"I really don't," Mark said. Rachel was rambling, talking nonsense. He realized she'd answered none of his questions, either. "Why were you at the girls' school the last couple of days?"

"I had to see them. It's a shame I missed Abagail, but Maureen ... she's so special."

"I know that, Rachel. But why? What was so important that you had to go to the school in the middle of the day for?"

"I just told you! Are you not listening to me?" Rachel was angry. Furious. Her face was as red as he'd ever seen.

Mark took a step back.

"All I asked is that you listen to me, Mark! Why can't you just listen?"

Mark sensed people watching them and the scene that was unfolding.

"The girls are beautiful. I had to see it for myself."

Rachel had gone completely nuts. That, Mark was certain of now. She'd lost it. She had to be having a psychotic episode; that was the only explanation he could come up with right now. At least that would have offered some semblance of logic about what was happening.

"I love you, Mark. I know it sounds crazy, but I do." She laughed. "I really do. You're everything I've ever wanted, and the way you—"

"Please stop, Rachel. Just stop. I love you too, but come on, this is crazy. You're not making any sense. Honestly, you're scaring me a little."

Tears filled Rachel's eyes. He watched as she let them fall, then wiped her cheeks once they were gone. A smile lit up her face.

"You do? You love me?"

"Of course, I do. I know it's been rough recently, but that doesn't change how I feel about you. But Rachel, this has to stop. Maybe if I call Doctor James at Evansville and we talk to him together, we can explain—"

"Evansville State Hospital? I'm not going there. Who do you think you are, my father?" If Rachel was angry before, she was furious now. A vein exploded out from her forehead. Mark was unsure what she meant by her last comment, though. "How dare you—"

"I can't do this right now," he said. "Not in public like this. We can talk later."

Before she could respond, he turned his back to her and walked away. His steps were faster than normal. The truth was, he downplayed to Rachel how he felt. She wasn't scaring him a little; he was legitimately afraid. Not of her, exactly, but of who this version of her was. He'd never seen this side of her before. She needed some serious help that he couldn't provide.

He tensed with each step, half-expecting her to chase after him or hit him with many would-be weapons at her disposal. Not looking behind him took all the willpower he could muster, but he didn't. He got to his car, unlocked it, and practically leaped inside. He managed a glance in the direction he came from as he cranked the engine, but Rachel was already gone. Before he could figure out where she went, he stepped on it and sped out of the parking lot. He had to get the hell out of there.

CHAPTER 31

Sucking wind, Mark ran into the office. He was about thirty minutes behind schedule; the traffic heading back into Indianapolis was horrible. He should have known better.

"Miss Meadows," he said, walking up to Sally with his hand extended. "I'm so sorry to keep you waiting."

Sally Meadows stood up and shook his hand, a sour look on her face. She followed him into his office. Before he closed the door, he glanced at Carly's desk and caught her attention. He mouthed a thank you. She smiled in return. He closed the door behind him and Sally.

Mark spent the rest of the day trying to catch up. With him being late for his appointment with Sally, that made him run late for Genevieve, then Peter, then Mary and Jack. By four o'clock, he was exhausted, had a new stack of paperwork—albeit, a much smaller pile of assignments then before—and was as concerned about his girls as he'd ever been in his life. His focus was being tugged in every direction, challenging his fortitude to keep it all together.

His meeting with Rachel at the park had to have been the most bizarre, disturbing interaction he'd ever had with anybody — not just Rachel. She spoke with so much passion, yet, none of the words made much sense to him. The way she spoke, it was as if she didn't know the girls at all, like they were strangers. While unquestionably uncomfortable, the moment seemed significant. He jotted down a few bullets about Rachel's behavior so he wouldn't forget the details. Not that he could, but just to be safe. He needed a full arsenal of information when he called Doctor JJ at Evansville tomorrow, which would be the first thing he did when he got to the office. Based on what he saw and what he experienced with his interaction with Rachel earlier today, he was officially worried about her. And for the girls, and himself. The doctors must have missed something when they evaluated her.

Mark left the office early, but not too early. He'd been out so much lately, he thought it would benefit him professionally to be seen as close to five o'clock as possible. The last thing he needed was to become the gossip of the office and have that make its way to Marty Joyce's ear.

Traffic was horrible again. Horns blared. Walkers made more progress than the drivers did. Today of all days, Mark could have used a break — green lights, slow vehicles driving in the right-hand lane, no speed traps. He anxiously strummed his fingers on the steering wheel, his mind spinning with visions of Maureen and Abagail.

How did Maureen react to seeing her mom at school again today? How did she feel when Rachel picked she and Abagail up from school, in all likelihood pretending like she hadn't seen her since the morning? Did Abagail see anything again today, like she did yesterday? Mark was struggling to wrap his mind around it all, so he could only imagine how confused the girls must have felt. He'd do whatever it took to keep them safe. If that meant protecting them from their mother while she was dealing with whatever psychological issues she was dealing with, so be it. He'd just have to do it subtly, so to not trigger Rachel.

After crawling past a collision, the traffic opened up. Mark merged onto the interstate and found a comfortable speed to cruise at in the left lane. His eyelids were getting heavy. He'd been restless lately and it was catching up to him. The weekend was chaotic. Last night's sleep was iffy at best. He still had a twinge in his neck from where he slept awkwardly on Maureen's bed. Friday couldn't come soon enough.

He flipped through the radio stations but couldn't find a song he was in the mood for. Too poppy; too loud; too sad. Nothing was connecting. Keeping both eyes on the road and on the moving but congested roadway, he turned the radio's seek knob. He stopped when he heard the voice.

"How can I help?"

"Hi, Doctor Lisa. Thanks for taking my call."

"Sure."

He cringed. He couldn't do it. He just couldn't. Too soon. He gave up and turned the radio off.

By the time he got home, the sun was setting. The automatic lights shone against the back wall of the garage as he pulled in, then died out when he killed the engine. Rachel's SUV was in its customary spot, which was a complete relief. The girls, he assumed at this point, were safe and sound.

Inside, he dropped his bag in the laundry room but kept his shoes on. He made his way down the hallway. Soft music and laughter filled the air.

"Hi, Dad," Abagail said when he rounded the corner.

He took it all in. Maureen stood on one of the chairs in front of the sink, a tiny apron tied around her front, like her mom, her sleeves rolled up above her elbows. Abagail sat at the table with a box of colored pencils and a drawing pad. Rachel held a large pot with two hands. Steam billowed above it.

"Daddy!" Maureen said.

"Hi, everyone," he said, trying to process the scene in front of him. "Looks like a busy place."

"Dinner will be on the table in five minutes," Rachel said.

She looked normal. Sounded normal. Was acting normal. Nothing like she was at the park. The girls looked content too. Happy. Everything seemed … fine.

"I'm going to change out of these clothes," Mark said. "I'll be back."

Rachel smiled her acknowledgment.

More laughter rang out when he ascended the stairs. He sat on the bed and allowed himself a moment to rest. And to think. The scene downstairs should have released some of the tension he held, but it didn't. Quite the opposite. The girls seemed settled, which was great, but it wouldn't last. They were young and adaptable; not like him, who held grudges and resentment with the best of them. How could Rachel have acted so irrationally earlier in the day, only now to seem so domesticated and completely normal?

One moment, Jekyll. The next, Hyde. It was infuriating.

Rachel called up the stairs. Dinner was ready. Had it been five minutes already? He hurriedly changed out of his stuffy work clothes and slipped into something with far more room around his waistline. He tossed his shoes in the closet. Downstairs, he joined his family for dinner.

The girls were chatty. A little silly at times. Lots of laughter. It worked out because he didn't feel like talking much tonight; he wouldn't have gotten a word in edgewise even if he wanted to. He tried to avoid looking at Rachel, instead focusing on the homemade mashed potatoes on his plate. How Rachel found time to make fresh potatoes today was yet another thing he couldn't quite wrap his mind around. There were a lot of those things lately.

After dinner, Mark cleaned up the kitchen while Rachel made lunches. The usual. He forced himself to make small talk with her if only to avoid having a real conversation, but also because he didn't want her to ask him what was wrong. He didn't want to have to lie to her when he told her nothing was wrong, that he was just tired.

Later, after the girls went to bed, he was ready for bed himself — at least enough to say he was — and he made it an early night. Rachel told him she wasn't quite ready and would stay up and read for a while. That happened sometimes. But what didn't usually happen — never, really — was what happened next.

He lied to his wife.

"Hey, are we okay?" Rachel asked him.

Mark stopped in his tracks. There were two ways he could have handled this. The first was to sit down with Rachel and have a candid conversation, to tell her all that was bothering him. The second was to say anything to avoid the conversation she was opening the door to having. The problem was, they'd had this conversation so many times over the last week that he had nothing new to say to her. Different times and places, but the same old story. He, being honest; her, not.

He didn't have it in him tonight.

"Everything's fine," he said. "I've got a busy day tomorrow, that's all."

"Promise?"

He tried to smile, but just couldn't. "I promise."

At the office the next morning, Mark wasted no time in dialing the hospital. Rachel's behavior last night didn't sway his opinion on this matter. If anything, it validated his concerns. Rachel needed help.

He asked for Doctor Jonathan James and was asked to wait on the line. The hold music tried its best to be relaxing, but Mark was too impatient to let himself enjoy it. He hardly slept at all, too wired thinking about Rachel's behavior, so he was irritable. He was tired of waiting.

"Doctor James here," Doctor JJ finally said, cutting off the relaxing music that wasn't doing its job.

"Doctor JJ, hi. This is Mark Starr. My wife Rachel was recently a patient of yours."

"Hello, Mr. Starr."

"Do you remember Rachel?"

"Of course. How's she doing?"

"Honestly? Not so good. That's actually why I'm calling."

"I'm sorry to hear that. What's going on?"

Mark had his bulleted list ready to go. Each bullet served as a reminder, a talking point, as Mark told the doctor about her mood swings since she'd been home. The exhaustion and the detachment; the mysteriousness and the intense anger; showing up at the girls' school without an explanation; the tearfulness with illogical stories Mark had never heard before; then being completely normal but just as uncomfortable as any of her other moods.

"Is there anything else?" Doctor JJ asked when Mark was finished, the first time he'd spoken since Mark began his spiel.

"I think that covers it. Give me a week and I can only imagine what else there might be. So, what do you think?"

"I think your concerns are justified."

Hearing that was a relief. The vindication from a medical professional who had some background knowledge about Rachel and her situation was an important step. It was another notch in Mark's belt. Yet another person who saw the same things he did.

"What do you want to do?" Doctor JJ asked.

"I want her to be admitted again. Maybe you could run more tests or keep her for observation a little longer. Something isn't right."

"No problem. We have room. Our team would be happy to reanalyze her. When do you want to bring her in?"

"Oh, well, great." He wasn't prepared for this part. He didn't think it was going to be this easy. "I'm not sure. I mean, as soon as possible, but logistically it's challenging."

"I can understand that. Maybe there's someone who can drive her, or she could even drive herself."

"I don't think that's an option."

"What do you mean?"

"Well, I haven't spoken to Rachel about this. I can't imagine she'd agree to it."

"I see. Mr. Starr, without Rachel's cooperation, I'm not sure what you're asking is going to be possible."

"I don't understand. Last week, she was ... the police, they ..."

"Those were entirely different circumstances. The police felt she was potentially a danger to herself or others. That was involuntary. The state has a right to do that."

"She still is. A danger to herself or others, I mean. Clearly."

"The problem is, our team here has already cleared her medically. It would be a hard sell to reverse our conclusions in such a short time. And frankly, I don't think I'd be comfortable signing off on it at this point. There simply isn't enough evidence that she's a threat. The data we have doesn't agree with that assessment."

"Not enough evidence? With everything I just told you ... you just told me you agreed that something's wrong."

"What I said was your concerns are justified. Those are different things. Suspicion isn't evidence, I'm afraid."

Mark wanted to throw the phone across the room. This conversation was going nowhere. He thought Doctor JJ would be on his side. "What do you suggest I do then?"

"If Rachel won't agree to voluntarily admit herself, it'll take some time for another involuntary admission. You could see if she'll meet with a therapist. In a month or two, maybe then—"

"A month or two? You've got to be kidding me. I don't have a month or two. I'm not sure I have a day or two."

"I understand this is frustrating, but by the letter of the law, my hands are tied. I'm sorry."

Mark sighed. He didn't like it, but he guessed he understood. The system was what the system was. There was nothing he, Doctor JJ, or anyone else at Evansville State Hospital could do about it. "I understand, Doctor. I wouldn't want you to do something that might put you in jeopardy."

"I appreciate that."

"Thank you for your time this morning."

"Of course, Mr. Starr. If there's anything we can do for you, please don't hesitate to reach back out."

"Thank you."

"Please give Rachel our best. Good luck to the both of you."

Doctor JJ hung up. Mark sunk into his chair. Now what? Rachel would never agree to go back. And he'd have to be a fool to even suggest it, especially after what she went through the first time, just a few days ago. It was a dead end. He'd have to come up with something else.

But what?

The situation felt urgent. Last night seemed like the calm before the storm, as if something wicked was brewing on the horizon. What that storm was, he couldn't say. But he felt it. And the possibility of the storm touching down at any time without warning terrified him.

•   •   •   •   •

Despite not being in the mood, he needed to cash in his raincheck with Todd. A promise was a promise, and Mark needed a distraction. It was a light afternoon, so he had plenty of time after cleaning up the paperwork he needed to. He walked down to Todd's office and rapped on the door. "Hey, Todd."

Todd looked up from his desk. "Markster!"

"You busy?"

"Nah, just looking busy. What's up?"

"You in the mood for Tony's?"

Todd's face lit up. "I'm always in the mood for Tony's."

They went. At Tony's, Mark stared at the menu. Everything sounded the same to him. A chalupa versus a tostada versus an enchilada, what was the difference? Hell if he knew. A burrito, he was familiar with, so he ordered one of those, plus a water. He wasn't even hungry.

They found a table and sat. Mark's back faced the window. Todd sat across from him. Todd's plate was just as full as it was the last time they were there, but Mark wasn't as repulsed this time. As horrible as the thought was, he was relieved to have some company that wasn't Rachel. Sometimes he just needed to clear his mind and get away from it all.

"Thanks for joining me, Todd. Sorry I had to bail out on you yesterday."

Todd's mouth was full, but it didn't stop him from answering. "No sweat, man. What's been going on with you lately?" Partially chewed up beans fell from Todd's mouth. "Oops." He picked them up and shoved them back in. "You've been out a lot."

"You've noticed, huh?"

"Everyone's noticed."

That's what he was afraid of. "There's just some stuff going on with Rachel that I've had to deal with."

"Same shit?"

"Different day."

"I'm sorry, man."

"I don't want to talk about it, though. Like, I really don't want to talk about it. Can we talk about something else? Anything else."

"Like what?"

"Not me. You. Let's talk about you."

Todd took another bite. "Me?"

"Yeah. What's new with you?"

"What's new with me? Oh, right! Remember that chick at The Pony I told you about? Charity."

Mark only vaguely remembered the name, but that was good enough. "What about her?"

"I hit it, bro." Todd grinned. "Finally. The best part? It was because she wanted to. I was at The Pony, right, having a drink …"

Mark tuned the rest out. He took a bite of the burrito and nodded, watching Todd's lips move but not hearing any of the words that slipped out between them. He took another bite. Then another. The next thing he knew, the burrito was gone. Turned out, it wasn't bad. Spicier than he thought.

"I also found one of the hats I've been missing," Todd said.

"What's that?"

"The trucker hats. You know, the ones I collect."

"Yeah, right. What about them?"

"I walked in to this consignment store the other day, just for shits and giggles, and you won't believe what I found, bro. A green trucker hat, a little dirty but that's okay, with a bottle of maple syrup on it." Todd laughed. "Maple syrup! I don't even like maple syrup. On the bottom of the hat, right under the syrup, it says established in Vermont, then a year. I forget what year. But that gives me forty-three different states now. Seven left." Todd smiled. Legitimately smiled. He was genuinely happy about this.

"Good for you, Todd. That's great, man."

Todd smiled again and took another bite of whatever he was eating.

Just then, Mark's leg vibrated. He reached into his pocket and pulled out his phone. Rachel's number popped up on the screen. His eyes bulged. Why was Rachel calling him right now?

"Rachel?" he said when he answered.

"Mark! Oh my God, Mark!" Panic filled her voice.

"What's going on?"

"She's gone, Mark! She's not here!"

"Who's not there? Where are you?" Mark pulled the phone away from his ear and glanced at the time. It was after two o'clock. Later than he thought.

"I'm at school! I'm in the pickup line getting the girls, but Maureen's not here! She's gone!" Chaos ensued in the background. Loud, frantic voices. A horn or two. Squeaking air brakes.

The vortex of the storm had landed, sending Mark's entire existence into a tailspin. Just like he knew it would. Even though he was sitting, his knees felt weak. "Are you sure she's not there?"

"Of course, I'm sure! She's not here, Mark."

Mark was on his feet now, frantically feeling for his wallet and his balance. He found the wallet and threw twenty bucks on the table. He flexed his quads to keep himself upright. "I'm leaving right now. Bring Abagail home and stay there. I'm calling Tom."

The police were already there when Mark got home. Tom was there too. The street in front of their house was lined with police cars, the driveway too. Mark parked on the street, behind one of the cruisers, and ran toward the house. He could only imagine what the neighbors were thinking. Right now, he didn't care. There was only one thing, one person, on his mind. The front door was unlocked. He pushed inside.

"Mark!" Rachel exclaimed when she saw him. She ran toward him, her cheeks damp with torment.

He hugged her. "What's going on? What's the latest?"

"No news," Rachel said. "Nothing new."

"Where's Abagail?"

"I called my mother and told her what's going on. She came and picked Abagail up. I didn't think she should be here."

Mark nodded. He agreed with her logic.

"Mark."

Mark looked for the voice. Tom walked toward him.

"I'm so sorry, Mark," Tom said. "We'll find her."

"Thank you."

"Should we talk?"

Mark nodded and followed Tom into the kitchen. Rachel joined them. They all sat at the table—Mark next to Rachel, Tom across from them. Other police officers wandered past them, looking for who knew what. Walkie-talkies crackled.

"Tell me what happened," Mark said to whomever. He didn't care who answered; he just needed answers.

Rachel spoke. "I did the same thing I always do. I drove to school and waited in line. I said hello to Kim Campbell and she radioed for the girls. I pulled up in the line and Abagail came out. Other kids were coming out of the building and leaving with their parents behind us. Maybe five minutes in, I asked Abagail if she saw Maureen today. She said she did, at recess. Not after that, but she said she doesn't usually. Their grades are separated in the building."

"Did she say anything else about recess?" Mark asked.

"No. Like what?"

Mark looked into her eyes, hoping to find something, anything.

It's all in the eyes.

"You tell me."

"What are you insinuating?" Rachel asked.

"I'm not insinuating anything. I'm asking a question."

"No, she didn't say anything else about recess." It looked like she rolled her eyes afterward, but it could have just been the angle in which he sat. "Anyway, I lost my train of thought. Where was I?"

"You were in the pickup line," Tom offered.

"Yes, right. So, as other kids filed out, I started worrying. It was taking too long. It never took that long. I flagged down Kim and asked her to radio for Maureen again. She did, but whatever she was told on the other end seemed to bother her. Her expression changed. I saw fear in her eyes. No mother should have to see that.

"I asked her what was wrong, and she said there must have been some mistake, that Maureen was already picked up earlier. At that point, I panicked. I asked Kim who picked Maureen up. She had to check with the office, so she ran into the building to do that in private. When she came back out, she looked …"

"She looked what?" Mark asked.

"She looked … confused."

"How so? What did she say?"

Rachel looked away, as if trying to make sense of what she was about to say. "She said Maureen was dismissed about a half-hour earlier … by me."

The room collectively gasped. By now, a few other police officers, aside from Tom, were standing around and listening. Mark looked over at Tom, who sat up abruptly. The tension was so tight in his chest, Mark was short of breath.

"But I didn't dismiss her," Rachel said through tears.

"Are there cameras that would show the entrance?" Tom asked a fellow officer. All of them in the room looked at one another, but nobody answered.

"I'm on it," one of them said, then he left the room.

"What did you do today, Rachel?" Tom asked Rachel.

He took the words right out of Mark's mouth.

"Tell me everything. Even the mundane things."

"Well," Rachel began, now looking uncomfortable, redistributing her weight, "I got up, had coffee, made the girls breakfast, got them off to school. When I got home, I had a bowl of oatmeal and took a shower. After, I'm a little embarrassed to say this because I don't usually do this, but I haven't been sleeping well lately and I've been so tired, so …"

"It's okay," Tom said.

"I took a nap for a while."

"Until when?" Tom asked.

"I'm not sure. I didn't look at the clock."

Mark wasn't buying it. He hoped Tom wasn't either.

"Your best guess," Tom said.

"Let me think. It had to have been sometime between twelve and twelve-thirty. I say that because I was reading after I woke up and I remember being starving around one o'clock, so I took a break and made myself a sandwich."

Tom jotted something on a small pad he pulled from his breast pocket. "Then what?"

"Then I pulled out some ground beef to thaw for dinner and started chopping some vegetables. Look." She pointed to the kitchen behind her.

Mark looked and saw the package of ground beef on the stovetop, along with a wooden cutting board with a chopping knife sitting next to the sink. It didn't mean much. That wouldn't have been hard to stage.

"What after that?" Tom asked.

"After that, I left to get the girls, just like normal. And you know the rest."

They all sat in silence for a minute after that, each of them processing.

"Can you excuse me for a minute?" Rachel asked. "I need to use the bathroom."

"Of course," Tom said.

Once Rachel was out of earshot, Mark filled Tom in. "Something's not right here, Tom. Yesterday and the day before, Rachel showed up at the girls' school during recess and spoke to Maureen."

"About what?"

"Nothing important, that's the thing. I don't understand why she'd do that. Rachel told Maureen not to tell me about it."

Tom leaned in. Mark told him about the lunchbox note and his meeting with Rachel in the park.

"The girls are a bit freaked out. Frankly, so am I. To make things even weirder, when I got home from work yesterday, everything was normal. Like we didn't have that bizarre meeting in the park. Maureen was helping Rachel make dinner. Abagail was sitting here at the table, coloring. They were all laughing and smiling like nothing had ever happened. How do you explain that?"

"Why didn't you tell me this?"

"What was I going to say? Rachel's acting like herself again and the kids are happy. She wasn't doing anything wrong. She was in a great mood, actually."

"Fair."

"But I didn't buy it. So, this morning, when I got to the office, I called Evansville."

"What for?"

"I spoke to one of the doctors who analyzed her."

"Jesus, Mark."

"I told him what's been going on and he agreed it was strange. He said they'd see her again if I could get her to agree to be admitted."

"Which she won't."

"Exactly. I didn't even ask."

Down the hall, the toilet flushed.

"The point is, this is all bullshit. She's up to something, Tom, but I don't know what the hell it is."

The energy changed when Rachel entered the room. Darkened. She walked toward Mark and sat down in the same seat as before. He cringed when she rested her head on his shoulder.

"I'm worried sick about her," Rachel said. "I wish there was something I could do."

At least that was something they could all agree on.

Rachel popped up with a startle. The phone in her hand lit up. "Look." She showed the phone to Mark. "It's the school."

Mark sat up.

"Answer it," Tom said. "Put it on speaker."

They all leaned in.

"Hello?" Rachel said after she answered and did what Tom asked.

"Mrs. Starr, this is Meghan from Brooklyn Elementary. We have Maureen."

Mark almost fell out of the chair with relief. But he was just as confused as ever. If Rachel was here and Maureen was there … what did that mean?

"Oh, goodness!" Rachel said. "Thank God."

"Where was she?" Mark asked. "This is Mark Starr."

"I don't know," Meghan said. "She won't say."

"Is she all right?" Mark asked.

"She seems fine. She's asking for you."

Mark didn't hesitate getting to his feet. "Tell her I'll be there in fifteen minutes."

CHAPTER 34

The whole crew went to the school—Mark, Rachel, Tom, and two other officers. With the police escort, fifteen minutes was more like nine. Mark parked in the no-parking school bus pickup zone—screw that, he thought—and he and Rachel sprinted toward the school. The door buzzed as they approached it, as if somebody inside was waiting for them and watching the door. Mark yanked the door open and ran through it, Rachel on his heels.

"Daddy!" Maureen cried out when he rushed into the room. Tears gushed from her eyes. She looked unhurt physically—no scrapes, no bruises, no tears in her clothing. Just innocent and tiny and vulnerable.

Mark wrapped his arms around her and squeezed, tried to catch his breath. Soon, Rachel's arms were around them both.

"Where's Abby?" Maureen asked.

"She's with Grammy," Rachel said. "She's fine."

Maureen cowered away from Rachel and leaned into Mark.

"What's wrong, honey?" Rachel asked with hurt in her voice.

Maureen didn't answer, just buried herself deeper into Mark's chest.

Rachel looked at Mark now. "What's going on?"

He didn't have it in him to tell her. Not like this. Not now. "Just give her a minute."

Rachel backed away, looking close to tears, and hugged herself. She left the room, her shoes clanking on the tile.

"Thank you, Meghan," he said to the receptionist, ushering Maureen into one of the chairs to sit. "What happened?"

"Not really sure, to tell you the truth," Meghan said. "I was sitting here frantically trying to remember anything I could about what happened earlier, when the door buzzed. I looked into the camera and almost screamed. Your little Maureen was standing there by herself, backpack on, like nothing had ever happened."

"Did you see where she came from?"

"No, sorry."

"Miss, what happened earlier today?" Tom asked her, jumping in. Mark hadn't heard him enter. "When Maureen was dismissed, I mean."

"Nothing unusual. Mrs. Starr came in and said hello, told me she was getting Maureen early."

"Are you certain it was her?"

"Positive. She's around here all the time."

That much was true. Rachel spent a lot of time at the school, helping with the PTA and volunteering as much as she could.

"She signed her out in the logbook," Meghan added. "Take a look."

Tom walked toward the desk. Mark followed.

"1:58," Tom said, reading the logbook.

"School's dismissed at 2:19, so it wasn't even a big deal," Meghan said.

Mark noticed the reason for dismissal column was left blank.

"Do you recognize her handwriting?" Tom asked him.

Mark studied it. There wasn't much there. "I'm not really sure."

"Do you have anything else with Rachel's signature on it?" Tom asked Meghan.

"Already ahead of you." She tossed a form Mark didn't recognize in front of them. Rachel's signature was on it.

Mark looked at both signatures, quickly trying to compare. They looked similar enough, he supposed. Not perfect, but did anyone really sign the exact same way every time? He'd never paid much attention to it.

"Deputy?"

Simultaneously, Mark and Tom turned. An officer stood before them.

"What is it?" Tom asked.

"I just got off the phone with the school's superintendent," he said. "He'll be sending a file with the video footage from the front camera over to a Meghan Burnett any minute now."

"That's me," Meghan said from behind her desk. "Let me check."

"Thank you, Officer," Tom said, and the officer left.

"Got it," Meghan said.

Tom and Mark walked around the desk.

"Can you play it?" Tom asked.

Meghan double-clicked on the file and a video player popped up.

"Fast-forward to 1:45," Tom instructed.

Meghan did. They watched.

At 1:51, a woman somewhat resembling Rachel approached the door and waited. But to be fair, the camera angle was such where they couldn't see the woman's face straight-on. It wasn't a clear shot. A few seconds later, the woman entered the school and disappeared from the camera.

"There's no camera inside the school," Meghan told them.

"Is that who dismissed Maureen? Is that Rachel?" Tom asked.

"Yes, that's her," Meghan said.

"What's going on?" Rachel asked, appearing in the office.

Mark looked at Tom, who looked back at him.

"Why don't you come look at this, Rachel," Tom said.

Mark didn't like the idea, but it wasn't his call. Maybe he was afraid at what was about to happen.

Rachel joined them behind the desk. Meghan restarted the video upon Tom's request. Nobody said anything as they watched it through. At the 1:59 timestamp, the woman appeared back outside the office, holding Maureen's hand. In the video, the woman's face wasn't clear, but the physical attributes were similar, if not identical.

"At 1:58, Maureen was dismissed from school," Tom told Rachel. "By you. You signed the logbook."

Rachel gasped. Tom reached over and grabbed the logbook. He handed it to her. Rachel looked at it and gasped again.

"Miss Burnett here confirms it was you," Tom said.

Rachel's mouth was agape. She was lost for words.

"And here you are, holding your daughter's hand, walking out of the school. Is that your signature?"

"I … it looks like my signature, but it wasn't me. I didn't sign it. Look at the woman's clothes. I'm wearing a different outfit. I don't even own a blouse like that. You can go check my closet if you don't believe me."

Mark didn't know if she was being honest about that or not. He paid little attention to those types of details.

"Rachel, Miss Burnett confirmed—"

"Mommy?"

Everyone's heads snapped. Maureen stood on the other side of the desk, staring up at them.

"Maureen, sweetheart," Tom said in a soothing, fatherly voice. "Who picked you up from school today?"

Mark's hands shook with worry. He clenched his fingers, using his thumbnails to pinch the loose skin, offering a distraction. He wanted nothing more than to reach out and comfort Maureen, but he didn't want to influence her response. She needed to say it, in her own words.

Maureen looked between them, not answering.

"Go ahead," Mark urged. "It's okay."

"Who picked you up from school today?" Tom repeated.

Tears filled Maureen's eyes. She looked between the adults, looking unsure of who she could trust. "Mommy."

•   •   •   •   •

Everyone gathered in a meeting room. There were no desks, which told Mark it was usually a room meant for adults only. Mark was there with Rachel and Maureen, who insisted on sitting on Mark's lap, and the police. Meghan Burnett was sent home once the superintendent arrived. He was behind a closed door somewhere else with principal Kim Campbell.

"Tell us what happened this afternoon after you left school with Mom," Tom said to Maureen.

Mark slowly, gently rubbed Maureen's back to try to help soothe her. Rachel sat tensely next to them, her foot tapping.

"Mommy asked if I wanted to get ice cream," Maureen said. "I love ice cream."

"What's your favorite flavor?"

"Vanilla."

Tom smiled at her. "Vanilla's my favorite too. What happened next?"

"She said we could walk because she had a different car and didn't have a seat for me."

Mark and Tom looked at each other, then at Rachel, their antennas up. Rachel gave them a look as if what Maureen just said proved her point that it wasn't her.

"It was a long walk," Maureen said. "My feet hurt."

"Did you get ice cream?" Tom asked.

"Yes."

"What did you do after that?"

"We went to the park. She pushed me on the swing."

"Did Mommy say anything to you?"

"She said it was fun spending time with me."

"Anything else?"

"She asked me if I wanted to have a girl's day soon. Just us."

Mark tensed at this. Tom flinched.

"Doing what?" Tom asked.

Maureen shrugged.

"After the park, where did Mommy bring you?"

"Back to school. She said she had to go home. But Mommy's home is my home."

"Did you see the car Mommy drove home?"

Maureen nodded.

"What do you remember?"

"It was red."

Mark's breath caught. Rachel's SUV was white.

"I'm hungry," Maureen said. "Can I have a snack?"

"Of course. Officer Kevin will bring you to get a snack, okay?"

Maureen spun and looked at Mark. He nodded his approval. Maureen leaped off his lap and followed Officer Kevin out of the room, off to find something to munch on. Mark was so proud at how great she was doing, at how brave she was.

"My SUV is white," Rachel said as soon as the door closed.

Tom looked at Mark, who nodded his confirmation.

"See, it wasn't me," she said.

Mark felt sick, wondering if it possible he was wrong about everything from the start.

"I'm telling you, it wasn't me. How could it have been? I was at home with both of you when she was brought back. Someone must be pretending to be me."

Mark started believing her. He got the feeling Tom was too. All the evidence was pointing in that direction now. A silent moment passed, then Rachel made a sound approaching a yelp and everything changed.

Rachel appeared spooked.

Mark was about to ask what was going on, but then something hit him. A realization. It popped into his mind with a flash, pounding against his skull, begging to be heard.

During his meeting with Rachel in the park yesterday, she said something. It didn't stick with him at the time because she was talking crazy, but now, it explained all of this. Could it really be?

At the park, when Rachel broke down in tears, Mark looked into her eyes. He didn't notice it then, but now he saw it with perfect clarity.

It's all in the eyes.

"Rachel?" he said, nearly choking on it. "Do you have a sister?"

Rachel gasped. The gasp told him everything he needed to know.

Just like how he'd know Rachel's voice anywhere, he'd know her eyes anywhere too. They were blue. A deep, sea blue. He was mesmerized by them when he first met her, when he crashed into her in the library at their college and she dropped all the books she was carrying. He practically drowned in them when he fell to one knee, shaking like a nervous teenager overwhelmed by the feelings of having his first crush. Then when he asked her to marry him two years later. Then again when they committed to each other for life a year after that. He felt those first-time feelings all over again on the day Abagail was born, then when Maureen was. He lost count how many days he woke up to those blue eyes being the first things he saw.

It's all in the eyes.

Those teary eyes at the park weren't blue. As beautiful as they were, they were green.

It wasn't Rachel, he realized.

"Oh my God," Rachel said. Her complexion was as white as a ghost's.

By then, Mark already had his answer. Numbness crawled all over his body. "I think I know who took Maureen."

Rachel looked at him wide-eyed. She knew it now too.

CHAPTER 35

I regret losing my cool with Mark, but I can't take it back. He didn't understand what I was saying to him, and that frustrated me. Why are men so difficult to talk to?

Don't say anything.

I forgive him. I threw a lot at him, and I thought he handled it well. Confused, sure, but he didn't deny anything. Maybe he already knew. Unlikely. Honestly, at the time, I didn't know how much she even knew herself. She had to know, though, right? Right?

My parents—my adoptive parents—made my life a living hell. We've established that. I don't want to talk about that anymore. Is that cool? What I want to talk about today is what happened before that.

When I was fifteen, I learned I was adopted. I could have strangled my mother. I didn't, of course, so relax. It's just a figure of speech. It was three weeks before my sixteenth birthday. My dad was out of town for work, doing whatever it was he did when he was out of town. I never asked and he never offered. On a Saturday, my mom asked me if I'd join her for breakfast at the diner in town. That should have been my first hint that something was wrong. We never went out. Never. And she never wanted to talk to me about anything that mattered. Begrudgingly, I accepted.

I remember ordering a Belgian waffle. There was something about significant moments in my life that I can associate with meals. Is that weird? Must be the fat kid in me, that I've somehow kept hidden for all these years. It doesn't happen by mistake, you know. Anyway, I ordered a Belgian waffle with powdered sugar and real maple syrup — never the fake shit. My mom ordered scrambled eggs and white toast. Who ordered white toast at a restaurant, by the way? It fit my mother's personality to perfection. Vanilla and boring. Bland.

She took one sip of her coffee and just said it. "Holly, you're adopted."

I almost shit a brick right there in the booth. "Excuse me?"

"You're almost sixteen years old. I thought you were old enough to handle this like an adult."

"Mom, what the hell?"

She told me the story. My biological parents weren't teenagers when I was conceived, but they were still very young. They couldn't handle the situation they'd inadvertently gotten themselves into. The truth is, I understood and respected it. I wasn't even mad; just surprised. Their intentions were pure. Offering their child the chance at a better life with a couple who could provide it. It wasn't their fault my adopted parents turned out to be overbearing assholes.

What my mother told me next set me over the edge.

"They had to make a choice," she said. "It was nothing personal — you have to know that. You were a newborn. There was no way to differentiate the two of you."

"What are you talking about?"

"Your birth parents, they weren't able to financially to care for two babies."

"Two?"

"No one is prepared for multiples, but when you're young, it must be overwhelming."

"Multiples? Mom, what are you saying?"

"You're a twin, Holly. Your sister was born three minutes before you. Your birth parents decided ahead of time that they were going to take home the firstborn. It could have been you, Holly. You must know it has nothing to do with you. It was simply a numbers game. You weren't unwanted. They just couldn't afford both of you."

I admit, I may have lost my cool then. I recall a plate being shattered and the diner manager asking us to leave, but the specific details are fuzzy. You remember what you want to remember sometimes, you know?

We went home and I stayed in my room for the entire weekend. My mother didn't bother checking on me. That summarizes our relationship. She dropped a bomb on me that shattered everything I thought I knew about my existence, then left me alone with my thoughts for almost two full days. What kind of mother does that?

I spiraled a little. That's normal, though, right? My whole life was ripped out from underneath me; I had the right to process it in my own way.

I was angry at my mother. Obviously. Not for telling me—I was thankful to learn about my true identity, and it explained a lot about my strangely detached parents at times—but for the aftermath. In the weeks that followed, she didn't once bring it up again. She didn't ask me how I was doing or if I wanted to talk about it or if I had any questions. She just went about her business as if the revelation never happened, as if she didn't send her almost-sixteen-year-old daughter into an identity crisis. A tailspin. I was already having body image issues. My boobs were too small, my ass too fat. When I looked in the mirror, cellulite the size of craters stared back at me. Why not add an identity crisis on top of it?

As the months went on, the separation between me and my parents grew. We hardly communicated at all. I saw them only at dinner, and even then, my father was so distracted talking about himself that I might as well not even have existed. My mother was too focused on him to give two shits about me and what I was going through. Sometimes I think she was incapable, for whatever reason.

I tried to forget that I was unwanted and unchosen. For years, I did. I finished high school, went to college, and tried my best to avoid my parents. Turned out, it wasn't that difficult. With a degree in hand, I found a job and moved into the city with some girlfriends. I met a man I could see myself making a life with, convinced him he wanted to marry me, then happily had his children. And then I met a man at work, Jimmy, and all my old insecurities resurfaced. After he died, those feelings were twofold.

I questioned everything. My marriage, who I was, who our firstborn son's father was. So, I started trying to find out the answers to some of those questions. I did research and called around to some adoption agencies in the area—my mother told me years before which hospital I was born at; it was even in my baby book—and I was able to narrow it down. From there, people in my situation—known to be an identical twin where only one was adopted—was quite rare. And by quite rare, I mean for identical twins ages thirty to forty in the state of Indiana, there was one match. One. Us.

It wasn't easy—privacy laws are a bitch—but I figured it out. I had plenty of time on my hands while everyone was at school and work during the day. Turned out, my biological twin sister still lived in Indiana too, like me, so I started looking into her. Not stalking her in the traditional sense, at least not physically. Social media enabled me to do all the stalking I needed. One unique advantage I had was that I knew I was an identical twin. One afternoon, I uploaded a photo of myself and did a reverse image search on Google, and voila—in a matter of minutes, I found her.

Rachel Starr from Brooklyn, Indiana. Married to the handsome Mark Starr. The mother of two beautiful daughters—Abagail, eight, and Maureen, five. Her family was picturesque.

I envied her.

I created a fake Instagram account and followed her. Watched her Stories and obsessed over her Reels of her family. I became infatuated with her screen-shy husband, Mark. He seemed like everything my husband wasn't, and everything I ever wanted. His girls adored him.

He was perfect.

I couldn't get over them, over him. I'd check Instagram every hour to see if any of my favorite accounts posted new content. I even enabled the notification so I'd be alerted when Rachel posted, so I wouldn't miss anything.

It was ridiculous. I know that. I had my own family. My husband was who he was; we've been there. My kids were my life. Which is what makes my current situation so difficult for me. Do the first nine and seven years of their lives mean nothing? That's not a hypothetical question.

It all goes back to wanting what you can't have. Rachel got the parents who actually loved her—and wanted her. Mine tolerated me. She got the perfect husband. I got the C-plus version. She got the idealistic life, I got the secret dead lover I never completely got over and never could, since my firstborn looked just like him, down to the widow's peak. How did my husband not see that and question where it came from? Seriously. Come on.

While most people would see a therapist and talk about this, I couldn't. Not after what my parents put me through as a kid. So, I did the next best thing. I called one on the phone using a fake name instead of owning my truth. But I'm such a disaster, I couldn't even lie my way into the truth. Even hiding behind the façade of the radio and a fake name, I couldn't say what I really wanted to. I couldn't anonymously say what had been eating at me for nine years, ever since the day my first son was born. I couldn't say out loud that my son wasn't my husband's. It was a blockage of sorts, like I was physically incapable of speaking the words. I was bound to live with that burden for the rest of my life.

But I've come a long way. Obviously. Look at me now. I've broken through the wall I had, and now there are two people on the planet who know my truth: me, and now you. Don't you feel special?

"Why didn't you tell me?" That was the question Mark asked Rachel when she confirmed she had a sister. This was the first he'd heard of it. He couldn't fathom how that hadn't ever come up in all their years together. It felt like a betrayal.

They were at Rachel's parents' house, picking up Abagail. Mark had told the police everything he realized he knew, and Tom told them there was nothing else that could be done tonight. They'd reconvene in the next day or two, he said, once someone at the department could meet with a judge and gather the paperwork. It wouldn't be too long. Rachel was useless and offered nothing additional. She seemed in shock, left physically speechless by the revelation.

Sandy and Harold Pearson. Those were Rachel's parents' names. Rachel spoke with her mom regularly, her dad less so although there weren't any issues between them. If she needed something, she could call Harold at any time, for any reason. She knew that. He just wasn't the chitchatty type, so they didn't call each other to chitchat. Made sense.

Mark was close with them in the way a son-in-law was close with their in-laws. He was their daughter's husband, so they liked him just fine. If, for whatever reason, he wasn't Rachel's husband anymore, he imagined his relationships with Sandy and Harold would be no more as well. That was just the way it was, and he was okay with it. He liked them both just fine too. They were amazing with the girls, and that was all that mattered in the end. Mark's parents lived in some small town in Arizona and didn't check in much. He couldn't have cared less. He was fine being a phone call away rather than a town line away.

Rachel sat next to Sandy, their knees touching. Harold was somewhere in the other room, but Mark had the feeling he was within earshot; he always seemed to be. Maureen and Abagail were in the back bedroom together, hopefully unwinding with a mindless show that could distract them from the realities of what their day was.

"It didn't even cross my mind," Rachel said with tears in her eyes. "She's not a part of my life, so I didn't even think about it. I feel so stupid. How could I not have made the connection?"

"You haven't mentioned anything about her," Mark said. "Never." He wasn't in the mood to feed into her mother's guilt right now. He needed real answers about how she could have let something like this happen without mentioning she had a twin sister.

"What was there to mention? I don't even know her."

"How about her existence?" Mark snapped with more bite than he meant to, especially in front of her parents.

"This is just horrible," Sandy said in the way grandmothers did. Mark could tell she meant it, but the lack of emotion behind it didn't quite match the words or the gravity of the situation.

"What a relief it is that everybody is okay," Harold said, reentering the room and the conversation. He handed a glass of water to Rachel, who took it and cradled it between her hands.

It wasn't lost on Mark that Rachel sat in between her parents on the couch with him in the chair next to it. There was an obvious divide that had been set up, a not-so-invisible line. Mark could only wonder what Rachel told her mom about what he'd been putting her through in recent days. He imagined her parents were especially upset about what transpired with her involuntary admission to Evansville, which was fair. But the truth was, it was out of Mark's hands. He had nothing to do with that. He guessed they wouldn't see it that way. He wasn't about to explain to them everything that had been going on.

Nobody had to know about his follow-up call to the hospital for readmittance. The way things were shaking out now, Mark might have been completely wrong about everything anyway, so it could have been all for naught. At the time, it seemed like his only option. Rachel wasn't crazy; she was just a liar. Which was worse? Maybe that was too strong, but he was angry.

Unprompted further, Rachel cried. It wasn't difficult to understand why. She'd been through so much. First with Mark accusing her of trying to manipulate him, then being asked to turn herself in and forcefully held against her will at Evansville. But again, if she at any time had said something about her sister …

Instead, she had to live with the burden of feeling like nobody believed her, and that nobody was on her side. Not even the one person on the planet who should have been: Mark. And now her daughters were feeling tense around her and didn't know what or who they could believe. As much as he tried, Mark couldn't understand how she let it get this far. What was he still missing?

Sandy's arms were wrapped around Rachel as if she were a child in need of protecting. Mark wanted nothing more than to reach over and grab Rachel's hand, to show her he was still on her side, despite everything, but something stopped him. He felt for her, but he was pissed. How could she not tell him she had a sister? After all these years? For as angry as he was, they'd work to repair the damage that had been done to their marriage, and to their trust, later on. For now, he had to see this through.

"I know this isn't what anyone wants to do right now, but can you please tell me what you know about Rachel's sister?" Mark asked. They all looked at him. None pleasantly. "Please. It's important."

Rachel leaned into her mother. If what she said was true—which Mark was willing to give her the benefit of the doubt about—she knew very little about her sister beyond her existence. Which meant he needed to hear the details from her parents.

"Mindy, is it?" he asked.

"Mindy?" Sandy said. "No, the name her adoptive parents gave her is Holly. Where did Mindy come from?"

"Oh, it's just … there was this radio caller, Mindy from Indy."

"Mindy from where? Who?"

Rachel glared at him.

"Never mind that. So, Holly, what's the deal with her? What happened?"

Harold leaned back, physically detaching. Rachel tucked her head, Sandy stroking her hair. Sandy was the one who kept her eyes in Mark's general vicinity. She would tell him what happened.

"It's my fault," Sandy said, turning to Rachel now as if Mark were no longer present. "Our fault. Me and your father. We should have told you, Rachel."

Rachel sat up. "Told me what?" she asked, her voice tinged with confusion.

"We told you what happened at the beginning, right? How we got pregnant sooner than expected. And how there were two babies and not one."

"And how you could only afford to keep one," Rachel added. "Yes, I know."

"Right. Abortion wasn't an option. Never. We were put in an impossible situation. We did what we thought was best for us, for you, for your sister. Isn't that right, Harold?"

"That's right," he confirmed.

"We made our decision, and we had to live with it," Sandy said, "as unorthodox as the decision may have seemed. Trust me, we heard about it. Everyone had their opinion. But it wasn't up to them, and we'd made our decision. To make things as easy as possible, we decided that no matter what—if something went wrong or worse—we'd keep and raise the firstborn. We weren't going to pick and choose which baby we'd bring home based on how delivery went, or by seeing you both. We made that agreement with the adoptive parents ahead of time."

Mark listened intently and tried to process the information. He'd heard none of this before. Obviously.

"That was what we did," Sandy went on. "To make it easier on ourselves—maybe it was selfish, I don't know—we chose not to see baby number two. The nurse brought her to her new parents straight away, who were waiting in the other room. We never even saw her, Rachel, we didn't. The adoption was mostly closed. We gave them our information and told them they could reach out if they wanted to, but they didn't have to. We didn't get their information. On Holly's first birthday—that's when we learned her name—they sent us a photo of her. And we couldn't believe it, Rachel. I swear. We didn't know the two of you were identical until then."

That confirmed what Mark had figured out on his own. Rachel didn't just have a sister; she had a sister who looked exactly like her, except the eye color. An identical twin. It explained everything.

"We were stunned," Sandy explained. "Shocked. In retrospect, we should have considered the possibility of the twins being identical. But for whatever reason, we didn't. We had so many other things going on, I guess. Holly's parents would send us photographs from time to time. That was all we heard from them. Many years after the adoption, when Holly was twelve or thirteen—I don't recall which—her mother called me out of the blue. I almost didn't believe it at first. I called for your father to come over so he could listen with me. Remember that, Harold?"

"I remember," he said, finally contributing to the conversation.

"Her mother said Holly was showing signs of psychological distress," Sandy said.

Mark watched Rachel stiffen.

"She was angry and defiant, acting out. She wanted to know if we'd been experiencing any similar issues with you. Which, of course, we hadn't. The truth was, I didn't like the feeling I got from talking to her mother. There was something off about the woman. I hadn't noticed it years before when we first met her, but that was so long ago and we were all young. Maybe she'd changed. But I, we, wanted to stay out of it. We were busy with our own lives and with raising you." Unexpectedly, tears slid down Sandy's cheeks.

Mark was too stunned to react. All he could do was listen.

Sandy leaned across Rachel and toward Harold, where she buried her face into his neck. He embraced her and whispered something in her ear. She nodded.

"What did you do, Mom?" Rachel asked when too much time had passed. She almost sounded angry now too.

Sandy pulled herself away and wiped her face. "We asked Holly's mother not to contact us anymore. It was cruel, I know, but legally, she wasn't our responsibility. You were a great kid, smart and happy, so we had nothing to worry about. I've always been more in the camp of nurture over nature, so that was how I justified it." She sniffled. "I figured if there was something off with Holly, it was because her mother didn't do a good enough job of raising her."

"Mom, you don't think this is something I should have known? Not only did I not know I was an identical twin, but you withheld a possible mental illness from me too? What if I'm predisposed to something that just hasn't manifested itself yet? We're identical, Mom! The same!"

"Now I do!" Sandy was a mess. The tears had fallen onto her collar and soaked it. Mascara left a black smudge on her face. "I didn't think twice about it. We stopped receiving photos on her birthday, both of your birthdays, so she wasn't top of mind. A mother never forgets, believe me, but we'd given up the chance to be her parents, so I tried to let it go."

"And now?" Rachel asked.

"And now, after what happened tonight, I feel like if I would have told you sooner, all of this could have been avoided."

You've got that right.

"I'm so sorry, Rachel," Sandy said, grabbing for Rachel's hand. "Can you ever forgive me?"

Rachel sighed. "I understand what you're saying, I do. But it's a lot to process right now. I need some time."

"I understand."

"But Mom, you should have told me about this. I had the right to know if I might be predisposed to something, and my girls."

"You're right. I'm sorry, Rachel. I'm so, so sorry."

●　　　●　　　●　　　●　　　●

Mark, Rachel, and the girls left after that. Both girls had fallen asleep in front of the TV, so Mark and Rachel each carried one of them into the car and buckled them in, trying not to wake them.

"I can't believe this," Rachel said to him on the drive home. Her mouth remained open as if she wanted to say something else, but nothing came out.

Mark reached for her hand. He found it and squeezed it.

"I should have told you I have a sister, but it really didn't matter. Not to me. We didn't grow up together. I was happy with my life as a kid and honestly, I enjoyed being an only child and having my parents' attention all to myself."

"When did you find out?"

"My parents told me the story when I was fourteen, maybe. Or fifteen. Something like that. They never told me we were identical, though, I swear! Just that we were twins."

Mark nodded. He believed that. He thought Sandy's story was believable too. "Did you ever try to find her?"

Rachel hesitated. "No. I mean, to me, it was what it was. They explained their reasoning for what happened, and I understood it, even then. The three of us were happy as we were, so there was no point in trying to disturb that. They certainly didn't give me any indication they wanted to try to meet her, so I didn't either. I saw no reason to."

Mark tried to understand. How could he judge her? Nobody knew how they'd react to learning they had a sister out there somewhere. For him to say he would have done something differently if the roles were reversed would have been unfair.

"I'm sorry it never came up," Rachel said. "She's not a part of my identity. Never has been. I never thought to put the pieces together, that it could have been her all along. But maybe if I would have told you, you could have seen the situation for what it was and ..." She shook her head. She was clearly beating herself up about not mentioning her sister.

"It's okay, Rachel. We're past that now." Mark held on to her hand. Her grip softened, the tension falling away. They rode that way for a while, holding hands in the quiet. "What are you going to do about your mother? I can't believe she withheld that information from you."

"I don't know. I really don't. I'll deal with that later. I'm just glad our baby's back home."

"Me too."

More quiet came. The darkness was making Mark tired.

"So—"

"What happens—"

"Sorry," Mark said. "You go."

"I was going to ask what happens next."

"I guess I don't really know. Tom said he'll reach out with a plan, once there is one. At least now they know who they're looking for. We should have your mother call him, to let him know what she knows about Holly. Could help with trying to locate her."

"You're right. I'll text her now." She pulled out her phone and did.

"I'll call Tom first thing in the morning and see where things stand."

She nodded.

"Rachel?"

"Yeah?"

"Holly's going down for this, even if she is your sister. How do you feel about that?"

"We may be related by blood, but we're not family. Not by a long shot."

"Are you sure?"

"I'm positive. Whatever it takes to bring that bitch down, let's take her down. No one walks into my life like that and tries to turn my family against me. She could have taken Maureen, Mark! Like, really taken her."

Mark cringed at that. It hurt, because it was true. Holly had almost destroyed their family. They were fortunate she didn't abduct Maureen and take her away for good. Maureen wouldn't have known any better; Holly had them all fooled. He suspected they wouldn't be that lucky a second time. She'd proven herself to be dangerous and willing to go to great lengths to get what she wanted. Although Mark still didn't know what that was.

"I'm glad to hear you say that," he said, and he was. Rachel turned and looked at him. He did the same, switching between Rachel and the road. "Because I have an idea."

The evening had a settled feeling to it. Not in the sense that everything was past them — because it clearly wasn't — but rather that Mark had come to an understanding with Rachel, which he had. She made a mistake and owned up to it. A big one, at that, but it was what it was. Nobody was perfect. He didn't have to understand or approve of every decision she made or didn't make. He tried to accept it for what it was and move on to more important things.

Like putting an end to Holly's assault on their marriage.

They weren't at the end by any means, but the finish line was in sight. It was so close, Mark could feel the relief bubbling in his gut. The problem was, he still didn't know what he was looking for. He couldn't figure out Holly's endgame.

When they arrived home to a dark house, they each grabbed a girl and carried them upstairs and tucked them in their beds. Neither girl stirred, clearly exhausted from such a hectic day. Mark was exhausted too. He was sure that Rachel was as well. Once the girls were down, they both got ready for and climbed into bed themselves, paying no mind to what the clock on his nightstand said.

Rachel snuggled up against him. As pathetic as it was, it was enough to crank up his libido. It hadn't been too long since they'd touched one another — a week or two — but it seemed like a lifetime. Rachel was usually a touchy-feely person, so going without her affection for even a handful of days was enough to make him feel disconnected from her. His body craved hers. They held hands under the top sheet — yes, they were proud top sheet people — and it felt like it was the right thing at that moment. Sometimes, the not doing was better than the doing. This was one of those times.

As they lay there in the dark, fingers intertwined, his manhood swelling, his eyes grew heavy. The weight of the day and all it brought overpowered him. He didn't have long left before he'd succumb to the exhaustion. His regular alarm was set for the morning. For as mentally exhausted as they were, the girls included, carrying out a normal day tomorrow was necessary. It wouldn't do anyone any good to keep the girls home from school and make them worry even more than they already did. Maintaining a normal routine was important. The same went for Mark. He'd go to work, do what he had to do, and wait to hear from Tom on the next steps.

In the morning, Rachel hugged him before she left with the girls. They held it longer than they had in a while. His eyes closed during it as a warming sensation flooded through his entire body. It was another step toward rebuilding their marriage, and their lives.

"Stay by the phone," he told her.

"You too."

Mark drove into the city. The traffic was heavy, but it didn't bother him as much as it had been recently. A weight had been lifted off his chest, and with it, the tension he'd been holding.

He was the first one into the office again. He had the feeling he'd need to cut out early again today, so he tried to focus and get as much work done as he could while he was there. By the time the office filled up and the noise level raised, Mark still hadn't heard from Tom, so he sent him a text asking for an update.

He met with a client. No phone call or returned text.

He met with another client, then another. Nothing from Tom.

At lunchtime, he gave Rachel a quick ring to check on her and to find out if anyone had reached out to her. Fine, she was, and no, they hadn't. Todd swung by to make a crude joke, but Mark suspected the real reason was that he wanted to check in on him, to see that everything was okay after Mark had unexpectedly cut their lunch short the day before. For everything Todd was, and he was a lot, he was becoming a good friend to Mark.

After another client meeting came and went without a word from Tom, Mark couldn't wait any longer. The waiting wasn't just making him anxious; it was irritating. He had forty-five minutes before his next meeting, so he went into his office and closed his door and made a phone call. If Tom wouldn't call him, he was going to force the issue.

The phone operator—not Lawanda today—patched Mark through without asking for his name. He waited for Tom to pick up.

"Mark, thanks for calling," Tom said when he did. "I saw your message earlier and I wanted to reply, but I wasn't able to. Sorry. It's been a day here."

"Do you have anything for me?" Mark wasn't in the mood to waste any more time with small talk. They were past that.

"Based on the information you provided me last night, I had my team take another look at the footage we have. The gun store and now the school. You're right, Mark. The woman's eyes are most definitely green, not blue. There's one still shot, especially in the gun shop when she's walking out, where it's clear as day."

"That's good to hear. Sounds like Rachel's officially off the hook then."

"The new evidence is pointing in that direction."

Mark's cheeks widened.

"I've got to be honest with you, Mark, and I shouldn't be saying this, but I feel awful. I don't know how I missed this. The face detection software has some flex in it to account for skin tone changes based on lighting and shadows, that type of thing. Eye color must be the same. I didn't know that. Until the images are blown up, it's tough to see that level of detail. Even then, the quality isn't great."

"It's all right, Tom. We all missed it. Rachel included. I don't blame you. If I would have known … if Rachel would have told me she had a sister …"

"I heard. Rachel's mother called me last night and told me."

"I can't believe it. I honestly can't. After all these years."

"I was surprised myself when I heard. You just never know what to expect sometimes, you know? Just when you think you know everything there is to know about someone, something pops up and surprises you. Happens all the time."

"But she's my wife. How did she not tell me? How did her parents not tell her?"

"I wish I could answer that."

Mark sighed. This would bother him for some time. Maybe forever. "So, now what, Tom? Where do we go from here?"

"The team is gathering intel on the subject as we speak. The additional information from Mrs. Pearson last night has been extremely helpful. We're still waiting on a warrant from the judge, though. There have been some unexpected challenges with it. Most of what we have is circumstantial at this point. Technically, a crime hasn't even been committed. We spoke with the owner of the gun shop, and he remains committed to not pressing charges. Without that, we're struggling a bit."

Mark cringed. His visit to Indy Guns and Ammo couldn't have backfired any worse. "What about what happened with Maureen? Holly abducted her."

"Listen, I'm on your side here. You know that. But there isn't much legal precedent for a situation like this. We've engaged the county prosecutor, but it's going to take more time. There seems to be an aspect of the law involving fraud — in this case, identity fraud — that may give us a legal leg to stand on, but we're still working through it. We're trying to make sure we have a solid case so she can't just walk out the door once we have her."

This wasn't what Mark was expecting. Quite the opposite. To him, it seemed like an open-and-shut case. Holly impersonated someone, Rachel, and dismissed his daughter from school without permission. Whether Maureen was physically unharmed was irrelevant. Emotional and psychological trauma were real too, even if more difficult to measure. Even so, he understood knowing the truth often wasn't enough when it came to the legal system; you had to prove it.

"I'm sorry if that's not what you want to hear," Tom added.

"What are we supposed to do?"

"Sit tight. Go about your normal daily lives. Let us handle it."

That answer didn't quite seem good enough. "I've been thinking about this, Tom, and I have an idea. A way to get us in front of Holly, maybe even get a confession out of her."

"Is it legal?"

"Absolutely."

Tom didn't respond, as if trying to decide if he believed Mark.

"Do you want to hear it?" Mark asked.

"I don't see any harm in listening. No promises, though."

"Fair enough. So, this is what I was thinking."

• • • • •

Tom said he thought Mark's plan could work. It was worth a shot, anyway. Seemed foolproof. Mark called Rachel to tell her the good news, but she didn't answer. He tried again right after on the landline, but got the same response. Nothing. He sent her a text asking her to call him and waited ten minutes. She didn't call.

He had a bad feeling. Something was wrong.

He'd completed all the work he needed to for the day and as if it were a sign from the universe, his last scheduled client of the day called to cancel with a family emergency. So, Mark left.

He hurried home, weaving in and out of open lanes, laying off the gas with every median he passed. At home, the garage was open and Rachel's SUV was inside. She was home, which was a relief, but it didn't explain why she didn't answer her phone or respond to his text. Maybe she fell asleep, he thought.

"Rach?" he called when he walked into the kitchen.

No response.

No sign of activity. The counters were bare, the sink empty. Nothing in the oven.

He pushed through the saloon doors and climbed the stairs. "Rach?" he called out again toward the closed bathroom door at the end of the hallway. Light crept out from underneath, where there was a tiny gap between the bottom of the door and the floor. He walked to the door and stopped. Listened. The shower was running. He reached for the handle and turned, pushed inside. "Rachel?"

Rachel gasped and spun toward him, throwing a hand over her chest. She was fully clothed except for her pants, which were piled on the floor in front of the toilet. Her blouse was just short enough where he saw the bottom of her underwear peeking out.

"Jesus, Mark! You scared me."

"I called you. Twice. And I texted you. You didn't respond."

Rachel turned toward the vanity and picked up her phone. "Really? Nothing came through. The Wi-Fi's been spotty in the house lately. Have you noticed that?" She fumbled with the phone and a noise alerted her of a new message. "Now it comes.

I switched off the Wi-Fi and it came through. Maybe we should get one of those network extenders for upstairs."

Mark didn't respond.

"Is everything all right? Your text message looked important."

Mark was too distracted to answer. He couldn't take his eyes off her pants on the floor. "Rachel, what the hell is that?" He looked at her to gauge her reaction, then he saw something else. Two things.

Behind her, next to the sink, sat a small container. It could have been a pill organizer, except there were only two dispensers. And unlike the pill organizers he'd seen, which were typically square or rectangle, this one was round. Both of them. Grooves surrounded the sides, to help with grip when opening. Rachel didn't take any daily medication outside of some vitamins.

"Mark, uh …"

He looked at Rachel's face. At her eyes.

It's all in the eyes.

He fell backward against the door as his breath caught. His chest was tight, his heart thumping.

The iris of Rachel's right eye wasn't the sea blue it should have been. Mark rapidly blinked, trying to clear whatever he thought he saw. It must have been a mistake. But even after his vision cleared, it was still there. Rachel's once blue right eye was now as green as an emerald, and there was no mistaking it.

"Rachel. Your eye."

Rachel's eyes popped as if the realization hit her. She quickly spun and faced the mirror, and she gasped. A hand shot up to her face and she stuck a finger in her eye. When she pulled it back, a u-shaped saucer rested on her fingertip. She removed the cap from the right side of the small container and slipped the saucer inside, then closed it back up. She faced Mark again. Both of her eyes were blue.

"Rachel?"

"Mark, I can explain."

"What's on the floor over there?"

"Um …"

Mark walked over to it and bent down. Wrapped up in Rachel's pants, the butt end sticking out like a sore thumb, was a handgun. Black all around, scuffed up and faded in spots. Clearly used. Mark grabbed the handle and picked it up.

"I can explain—"

"What the hell is going on here? Where did you get this?"

"If we can just talk about it, I can—"

"I'm about two seconds away from calling Tom and—"

"No, don't! Wait. It's not what you think." Rachel walked over to him, grabbed the gun with two hands, and set it gingerly on the vanity. "I'm going to put my pants on, okay? Then I'm going to turn off the shower, then we're going to go downstairs and talk. Okay?"

"What about the girls?"

"I asked my mom to pick them up after school. She'll bring them to do something fun this afternoon, then she'll drop them off before dinner. Something to distract them."

Mark was hot, his adrenaline pounding, but he owed it to Rachel to hear her out. "What kind of gun is this?"

"You know I don't—"

"Enough!" he snapped. Rachel's shoulders sank. He took a few seconds to settle, to calm himself down. "Please tell me what kind of gun it is."

"It's a 9mm."

Exactly what he thought. Just like the ammunition stolen from Indy Guns and Ammo.

Rachel put her pants on, keeping her eyes on Mark, then went to shut the water off. She moved around the bathroom slowly, cautiously, as if trying to avoid a landmine on the battlefield. She grabbed his hand, held on to it loosely, and led him out of the bathroom. For some reason, he let her.

Oh, how the tides had turned.

Maybe he hadn't been so wrong about her after all.

CHAPTER 38

The first time I met my sister, I knew I didn't like her. I hadn't planned to arrange a meeting; it just happened. I'd been following her online. Closely. Maybe too closely, I don't know. Some might call it cyberstalking, I call it research. I couldn't help being curious about my sister's life.

Rachel posted a Story with a photo of where she was one afternoon — typical of the phone-obsessed generation, am I right? — and it was nearby. I was at home, loathing my life, when the notification popped up on my phone. Rachel was at some boutique in Indianapolis, shopping for who knew what. In the middle of the day. Spoiled, entitled bitch.

My house was just on the outskirts of the city, less than ten minutes to the boutique. I had to see her in person, and this was my chance. It was the opportunity I didn't know I was waiting for. Was she thinner than me? How big was her wedding ring? Did she walk around with the same piss-poor handbag I did? I had a feeling I knew the answer to the last one already.

When I arrived at the boutique, I hesitated before going inside. Did I really want to do this? I didn't know. How weird would it be to see your doppelganger in real life, even for me, who knew it was coming? Rachel could have passed out with the shock of it. I didn't know what she knew, if anything. I entered the store, ignoring the chime and the employee who tried to greet me, and walked right up to her.

The ring on her finger was massive. Of course, it was. So much larger than the puny one I had on. Which, to me, meant her husband loved her more than mine loved me. Which tracked. Her waist was thin, her blouse tucked in comfortably without pinching at the seams. I saw the conjoined reverse Cs on her handbag and wanted to puke. Chanel, of course. I was left slumming with Coach. My blood boiled with jealousy.

From behind, I tapped her on the shoulder as adrenaline flooded my system. Startled, she swiveled her neck to look behind her. I felt immense pleasure in the way her eyes crept wider and her mouth fell open. Her complexion whitened.

"Hi," I said. "I'm sorry to bother you, but I just wanted to tell you how much I adore your bag." Which was a lie. I hated it. I kept my expression flat as I watched her struggle to speak.

"Oh my God," she managed. "What the? You're me, I mean you. You must be my … How did you …"

"Should we get some coffee?"

She nodded and we left the boutique without buying anything. Sorry, not sorry.

Being downtown, there was a coffee shop practically every fifty feet. The closest one was three doors down. Inside, we sat at the small table for two near the door. Neither of us ordered anything.

"This must be weird for you, right?" I asked her. I tried hard to smile, to make myself seem welcoming.

"Weird would be an understatement." Her eyes were still huge. She looked me up and down, down and up.

I'd already planned what I was going to say ahead of time, so I went for it. "When I was fifteen, my mom told me I was adopted. I had no idea. It was hard at first, I admit, but I got over it. Took a while, but I did. Six months ago, I started thinking about it again. Thinking about you, Rachel. I was curious where my sister was, what her life was like. I'm embarrassed to admit this, but I searched for you online."

"Hold on, wait. How do you know my name?"

"Like I said, I started searching for you online. I found your Instagram. I feel like I almost know you now, you know?"

She looked disgusted. "Is that how you found me at the boutique? Are you stalking me?" She shot up from her chair, clutching her Chanel bag in her fingers like she was afraid I was going to steal it.

"No, it's not like that! I promise. Please, sit."

Except, it was like that. It was exactly like that. But I had an agenda.

For whatever reason—either I was a good liar or Rachel was a complete idiot—she believed me. She still looked and acted cautiously—she sat slowly, methodically—but she sat back down. And she listened to what I had to say. She must have been curious. If it were me, I would have been.

"The truth is, I wanted to reach out so many times," I said to her. "I wanted to know my sister. But I didn't know how much you knew or didn't know, so I didn't say anything. Until today."

Rachel sat there, pondering, the whites in her fingers slowly turning back to peach as her grip on the Chanel bag loosened.

"I know this is a lot. It's a lot for me too. I mean, look at us. We're … the same." I laughed.

She didn't. She held out a hand toward me, toward my face. "May I?"

I nodded. I knew I had her. Right then, in that moment, I knew I'd won.

I have to admit, the sensation of a stranger touching my face so tenderly was magical. I hadn't been touched like that—or at all, really—in quite some time. My husband barely looked at me anymore at that time. I felt her soul through her fingertips, and it warmed my whole body. Honestly, that was how it felt. I think my eyes might have shut, but I'm not positive. It was nice.

"I can't believe this," Rachel said then.

"Did you know?"

"My parents told me I had a twin when I was a teenager, but I didn't know we were identical. They never said anything about that."

"Wow."

"I can't believe this." Tears pooled in Rachel's eyes. "I really can't."

We agreed to stay in touch. Just us. For now. Which was fine. We met at the same coffee shop once a week for a few weeks, a month tops. We even ordered coffee and stayed awhile.

Turned out, we had quite a lot in common. Some of it I knew — like how we were each married with two children about the same age — but others I didn't. Like me, Rachel hadn't ever told a soul about having a sister. Not her best friend, not her husband, not the therapist she denied having. Ha, yeah, okay. She tried to forget about it, she said, since having a sister wasn't ever part of her life. That, I understood. I wasn't offended. I felt the same way for a long time.

What was unexpected was that I grew to like Rachel. Despite the façade of her fancy lifestyle, I learned she and her husband lived rather modestly. I respected that. She told me about her girls, Abagail and Maureen, and I told her about my boys, except for that one thing about my oldest; she didn't need to know that. She'd only judge me for it. Maybe someday. She gushed about her husband and how wonderful he was. He was such a great dad, she said, and he was too good to her. I smiled and nodded and pretended like I understood because mine was the same. All the while, my jealousy had risen to another level, and I wanted Mark Starr, despite never having met him, more than ever.

"Do you ever feel like less than because you're a woman?" I asked her one afternoon during one of our meetings.

"What do you mean?"

"With Mark, I mean. Does he ever … put you down without actually putting you down? Do you know what I mean?"

"Sorry, I don't."

"It's like how Kevin talks to me sometimes. I don't know if he does it consciously, or if he's just a dick." I laughed to try to mask the hurt. "He'll talk to me like I'm stupid. Like I'm not good enough sometimes. Like if it wasn't for him, I'd be nothing."

Rachel reached out and grabbed my hand. "I'm so sorry, Holly. That's horrible."

"Does Mark ever do that to you?"

"I can't say that he does."

Of course, he didn't. Why would he? That was only how my life worked.

"He seems really great," I said.

"He is."

"I've seen photos. He's so handsome."

Rachel pulled her hand away. "Yes, I think so."

"In some of the videos you've shared, the way he plays with the girls, it's amazing. You're so lucky."

Rachel squinted her eyes and cocked her head.

"Are you happy, Rachel?"

"Of course. Why would you ask me that?"

"You know, seeing how we look the same, do you think he could tell the difference between us?"

Rachel's jaw flexed under her skin.

"A surprise visit at work one day from his wife to spice things up a bit. A little dangerous with all those people around. You think he'd be into it?"

Rachel stood up so fast, her chair fell over backward. Every customer in the coffee shop looked at us. The employees too.

"You stay away from him," she said. "Stay away from him and stay away from me. Never contact my family again. Do you hear me?" She sized me up with her eyes, glaring. Then she made a noise that sounded like it hurt, as if it described how she felt about me. "Look at you. Now I see it. You're pathetic and ungrateful. It all makes sense now." Rachel picked up the chair and turned to leave.

"Hey, Rachel," I said before she got to the door.

She turned back and looked at me. She was seething.

"The thing about mini revolvers is that they're so small they can fit in your hand with no one noticing. You wouldn't even know it if someone had one right next to you."

Rachel turned white.

"But the damage they inflict," I went on, "is anything but mini. Isn't that interesting?"

Rachel's chest bounced up and down. Panic was setting in.

"I just thought you'd find that interesting. Sister."

Without another word, Rachel pushed the door and walked out, disappearing into the city.

That was the last time we had coffee together.

At the time, I thought it was mission accomplished. Rachel knew my intentions, and she was too weak to do anything about it. That's what I thought. Turns out, I couldn't have been more wrong about her. I almost respect her for it.

Almost.

Next time, I want to talk about Mark Starr. If it wasn't for him, none of this would have ever happened and I wouldn't be here. I don't think I would have gone through with what I was planning. I mean that. Meeting Mark face-to-face that day in the park, it shook my world in a way I didn't think it would. If I was obsessed before, I became haunted by my desire to have him. I dreamed about him. Fantasized about him. Touched myself thinking about him. Sorry to be crude, but it's the truth.

The plan that had been in motion before went into high gear after what he said to me. I got sloppy. Careless. And now, I'll be left wondering what if for the rest of my life. Tough break, huh?

CHAPTER 39

Mark sat across from Rachel so he could see her face. After what he just learned, he felt a chill run up his spine. Rachel had green contacts, which meant all signs were pointing to him having been right the whole time; it was Rachel all along. Add that to the fact she had a 9mm handgun, the same type of gun the stolen ammunition would go in to, and the outlook was bleak. What was she going to tell him next, that she was the one who visited Maureen at school and dismissed her? How, though? Rachel was at home, with him, when the call came in from school saying Maureen had returned. He was so confused, he wanted to scream. He didn't trust her.

The idea of the gun being upstairs and out of his sight didn't make him feel at ease; it made him even more anxious. Having a gun in the house at all freaked him out. He thought Rachel agreed with him on that. Although, as he was learning, perhaps he didn't know Rachel very well at all.

"Explain yourself, Rachel."

"Okay. I will. It's not what you think. I tried to tell you, Mark. Several times. I did. I just couldn't find the right words or the right time." She took a deep breath and let out a heavy sigh. "I met my sister."

He was disgusted already. "Holly?"

"Yes."

"Or is it Mindy from Indy?"

"I don't know who that is, Mark. You keep bringing her up, but my answer hasn't changed. Maybe it was her, but I don't know anything about that."

"Well, it's not like you've been honest with me."

Rachel lifted her hands and rubbed her eyes. They were bloodshot. She didn't require corrective lenses, so Mark wondered if her eyes were sore having not been used to wearing contacts.

"You know what, you're right. That's fair," she said. "I want you to ask me anything you want. I'll give you a straight answer. I promise."

Mark looked away. She made it so difficult to believe her, especially when she kept lying.

"I swear it on our girls' lives."

He looked back at her. "Don't do that."

"I'm just saying. I want you to know that everything I say right now is the truth. Every word. Okay?"

He had no choice but to accept her at her word, even if he had doubts. "Fine."

"I met Holly at a boutique about six months ago. She came up to me and started a conversation. She knew who I was, apparently."

"So, last night, you lied to your mother when you said you didn't know."

"I'm not sure I said I didn't know."

"You sure acted like you didn't know."

"You're right, I did. That's true."

"Why? You had me convinced."

"If I told her I knew, then you would have asked me how. And then you would have pressed me for more information. Which is fair. I didn't want to do that in front of her. Not like that. And to be honest, she should have told me a long time ago, so I wanted her to feel that guilt. Is that bad?"

Mark wanted to smile at that but he held it back.

"I had to act surprised when she told me. Do you have any idea how weird it was to turn around and see someone who looks just like you staring back at you?"

"I can only imagine."

"It was like being in the twilight zone, some alternative universe. Some sci-fi shit. Seriously."

Mark felt himself softening.

"I thought my mom deserved to feel that burden, for putting me through that. At least if I knew, I could have prepared myself if we ever ran into each other."

"I get it, I guess. I understand what you're saying. It's a little twisted, maybe, but I get it. What about Maureen? It wasn't you, right? Please tell me it wasn't you."

"Of course not! I was right here with you the whole time."

"Did you suspect Holly?"

"Honestly, I don't know. I haven't spoken to her in months. I cut off all communication with her. I tried to put her out of my mind for good, after what happened."

Unexpected. "Why? What happened?"

"She's crazy, Mark. Actually crazy."

"How so?"

"Do you know how she found me? She saw where I was on Instagram and she followed me there. That's messed up."

Messed up, sure. Crazy? Proved nothing. Maybe if Rachel stopped posting her every move online …

"But it's not just that," she went on, sensing his doubt. "We got to know each other a little, and there's something off about her. The way she carries herself. She gets this look in her eyes, this coldness. It's creepy. I get the sense she's a very unhappy person. She thinks the world of you, though."

"Me?"

"Apparently. Like I said, she's been stalking me. She's taken quite the liking to you. Honestly, I think she's obsessed."

Mark thought back to his meeting with Rachel at the park—or, as he'd figured out, his meeting with Holly. Her erratic behavior. The way she went from zero to one hundred in a flash. Their conversation.

The girls are beautiful ... That Maureen especially ... She's such a doll, isn't she?

I love you, Mark. I know it sounds crazy, but I do ...

You're everything I've ever wanted ...

Oh, no. What had he done? Rachel still didn't know about that meeting.

"Actually, there's something I should tell you too," he said, even though it pained him to do it.

"Oh ... kay."

"I know why the girls have been off with you recently. Why they've seemed ... different."

"You're scaring me, Mark. What happened?"

He told Rachel about the school visits. About how Holly showed up and talked to Maureen two days in a row; about how he slipped a note in Maureen's lunchbox; about his meeting with Holly in the park.

Rachel threw her hands over her mouth. "How could you not tell me that?"

"I thought it was you! I'm sorry, but I did. It was the only way to make sure for myself."

"No, no, no."

"I obviously didn't know it at the time, Rach, but I see it now. She was nuts. Your mother said it last night too, remember? About how Holly's own mother had to question her mental stability."

"Right, yes, that's right."

"If I would have known … I never would have—"

"I understand. I do."

Tears trickled from all four eyes.

"She threatened me," Rachel said. "During our last meeting. She told me something about how mini revolvers are small, but they can still inflict a lot of damage."

"What?"

"I know. I don't know. It was weird. Nothing happened, obviously. I thought it was over with, that she'd gotten the message. But then, a few weeks ago, I started getting these messages—"

"I thought you said you stopped communicating with her."

"I did. That's the point. These random accounts started following me on Instagram and commenting on my photos. Nothing weird at first. 'Nice family.' 'Happy couple.' 'Beautiful girls.' Stuff like that. But then it got weirder. 'You don't know how lucky you are.' 'He should have picked me.' 'Cool neighborhood.' Then I got a DM and it was nasty. Sexual and nasty. After that, I blocked all the accounts I didn't know. I didn't know it was her."

Mark wanted to ask why she didn't tell him, but he didn't bother. At this point, did the why even matter?

"I realized it could have been her," Rachel continued. "Obviously. But I tried to forget about it, about her. But I couldn't get the messages out of my mind. They freaked me out. I'm home all day by myself and … I was scared. I panicked." Her cheeks were drenched now.

"I could have helped you. If you would have told me—"

"I know, Mark! It was stupid, okay! I get it."

"What happened? What did you do?"

"I got a gun. And I kept it hidden."

"How? Where? How did …"

"There are these chatrooms. You can go there and ask for advice or get recommendations. Stuff you can't just ask your mother's group."

"Oh, Christ."

"I found this guy in Indianapolis who said he'd meet me. He said he had a gun that was untraceable, so I met him."

"Are you kidding me? You could have been killed!"

"I know that. I wasn't thinking. I'm sorry. But nothing happened. He was a little creepy, but I tried to be smart about it. Met him in a public place, paid in cash."

"Holy shit, Rachel. You don't have any idea where that gun's been, who its killed! Please tell me you haven't shot it. For the love of God, tell me you haven't."

"No, I haven't. I swear. It's been in the basement this whole time. The girls never go in the basement, I was safe. I put it on top of one of the crossbeams. Nobody would have found it."

"What were you planning on doing with it?"

"I don't know. I really don't. I didn't even have bullets for it until recently."

Indy Guns and Ammo.

"Was that you? In the video."

She nodded. "That's why I got the green contacts. I bought a new outfit, something I wouldn't usually wear. I put in the contacts."

Mark thought about that for a few seconds, considered what she was saying. "You wanted to be caught?"

"I was hoping there was a working security camera. Lucky me, I guess."

Mark tried to put all the pieces together. He thought he had it, but there were still some things he couldn't figure out. "So, then what?"

"Then … I don't know. I'd have bullets for a gun I had. Either for protection, in case she tried to attack me, or for something else."

"Like what?"

"Frame Holly, maybe. Don't ask me how, I don't know. I hadn't gotten that far. If she was seen on camera, even if she denied it, there would be evidence. And if she had the bullets and an unregistered gun, that might be enough to put her away for a while." She dropped her head. "It sounds so stupid when I say it out loud."

"What about just now, before? What were you planning on doing with it?"

"Just what I said. My mom is taking the girls, so I was going to head to Holly's house and leave the bullets somewhere. Maybe call in an anonymous tip. I couldn't say anything to Tom. You get that, right? If I confessed to stealing the bullets, that would lead to questions about a gun. Maybe they'd search the house, I don't know. It would have spiraled out of control. After I planted them at Holly's house and called in the tip, everyone would have realized we were twins and figured out the identity switch up. She had the bullets, so I'd be in the clear."

Mark tried to process it. It didn't sound like a horrible plan. It might have worked.

"I was in too deep, Mark. I couldn't say anything to anybody. Not even you. I just had to keep denying and wait for someone to figure it all out. I'm sorry I put you through that."

Now would have been a good time to tell Rachel about how he paid off the gun shop owner, but it didn't seem relevant anymore. There was no need to get into it.

"You don't know how badly I wanted to tell you about Holly," Rachel said. "I wanted to every single day. But she made me question everything. She's not a good person. We're twins; am I like her? I was confused and a little ashamed. I was going through an identity crisis. It was a lot to take in. I'm sorry."

"You're not a bad person. You're the best person I know."

She scoffed. "Yeah, I doubt that."

"We all make mistakes. I've made plenty too. You were just trying to do what you thought was right. Just like I was."

Rachel nodded at that.

"I think I have a way out of this," he said. He already ran the idea by Tom before. The general concept was still the same, so Mark was confident Tom would go for it, despite the minor detail swap.

"You do?"

"You're going to have to trust me, okay? Do you trust me?"

Rachel looked at him. Really looked at him with those blues. "With my entire being."

"Good. The first thing we have to do is get rid of the gun."

She exhaled with relief. "Deal."

He stood. "Come on. The girls will be home in a couple hours and I want this out of the house before they get back."

The first order of business was disposing of any evidence that could have tied Rachel back to any of this. Maybe it was wrong of him to want to help her, but Mark didn't care. He was on Rachel's side. No matter what, he would have her back. In this case, having her back meant helping to cover her tracks. Whatever it took, like he kept telling himself. It wasn't like she killed someone.

In the bathroom upstairs, Rachel twisted off the caps to the contact lens case. She flipped it upside down over the toilet, sending both the green contacts and the liquid solution into the bowl. With a flush, they were gone. Piece of cake. Mark snapped the case in half and threw it in the trash. One issue, gone. Next, he grabbed the handgun and held it loosely.

"It's not loaded," Rachel told him.

That was a relief, but did she even know how to check? Mark didn't. He wouldn't take any chances. "Where's the box of ammunition?"

She motioned for him to follow, which he did. They walked through their bedroom and into Rachel's closet. It wasn't a full walk-in, but it was large enough to hold every piece of clothing

Mark had ever owned, plus some. It was just barely enough space for Rachel. The shelves were piled high with totes filled with seasonal wear, one for each season. Rachel reached above her head, standing on her toes, and grabbed one of the totes. She pulled it down and dropped it on the floor. Inside were neatly folded sweatshirts and lounge pants. She grabbed the top sweatshirt and left it aside, revealing a box of 9mm ammo underneath. She grabbed it and handed it to Mark. The box was still sealed. He helped her put the tote back up.

"Now what?" she asked.

"Now we get rid of it."

"White Lick?"

White Lick Creek was his first instinct too, but he didn't think it was the best idea. The creek was too narrow and shallow. It wouldn't be long before the gun washed up on an embankment. As much as he wanted it out of their house, he wanted it in the hands of an innocent, curious kid less. The creek wasn't an option. He considered Cox Lake. That checked off more boxes. It was deeper than White Lick and the gun could easily sink to the bottom and stay there. But it was too close to their house—the connection would be too easy to make if something ever happened—and the boat traffic on the water was too high. Someone might see them tossing something into the water and call it in. Getting deep enough where it would disappear would require a water vessel too, which they neither had access to nor were able to deal with in short order. Mark considered a more unorthodox solution.

In the garage, he popped the trunk and loaded two shovels in the back. They'd bury the evidence. He drove them out to Brooklyn Cemetery on the less populated east side of town. A forest surrounded the cemetery, which offered the perfect cover. People were unlikely to be hanging out in and around the cemetery. If they were, seeing someone digging a hole might be the one place nobody would think twice about it.

Mark followed the paved path and drove to the edge of the cemetery, as far as he could. He parked the car and they got out, leaving the trunk open and facing the dense forest. Rachel shoved the handgun with the box of stolen ammunition inside a small tote bag decorated with a rainbow and some message about saving the planet. Mark hoisted both shovels over his shoulder and led the way.

A couple of hundred feet into the forest, when the cemetery was out of sight and all they could see was a canopy of trees in every direction, they found a spot. Mark stabbed the earth with the shovel, searching for a soft enough place to dig a hole. He found one at the base of a towering oak tree. With Rachel's help, they dug a hole at least three feet deep and dropped the gun inside, sweat pouring off their faces and necks. They filled in the hole and spread some leaves over it. They found another spot a few hundred feet away and buried the box of ammunition as well.

Easy. Gone. Like it never happened. Mark made a mental note to have Rachel clear her search history from all her devices, in case they were linked, just to be safe. He wasn't confident she searched for and chatted in that chatroom securely. Probably unlikely.

They made it back home with twelve minutes to spare before the girls arrived. Neither Mark nor Rachel was in the mood to cook, so they ordered in. It wasn't something they did often, so the girls were excited. They agreed Maureen would open the door for the pizza delivery driver while Abagail accepted the pizza box. It was quite an exciting moment for them.

After bedtime, Rachel joined Mark in front of the fireplace. They sat and enjoyed each other's company, both too exhausted to talk much, and listened to the sounds of the house. The subfloors creaking, the furnace clanking as it burned oil, and the heaters clicking. Wine wasn't in the cards tonight. Clear heads were needed. Mark checked his phone, hoping for a message from Tom, but there wasn't one. He dialed him quickly, to see if he'd pick up.

"Sorry, Mark, can't talk," Tom answered. Sirens rang out in the background. Voices were busy.

"What's going on?" Mark asked.

"There's been a shooting. We're en route now."

Mark sat up and looked at Rachel. "A shooting? Where?"

Rachel sat up too, her attention sharp.

"Can't talk, sorry."

Tom hung up.

"That's scary," Rachel said. "I have an idea." She pulled out her phone and pressed on the screen. Two minutes later, she spun the screen and showed it to Mark. She had downloaded a police scanner app, which was now running.

"A new hobby?"

"I just downloaded it. We can listen in."

Together, they fumbled through the app, trying to figure out how to use it. It didn't take long before they heard the radios crackling.

"Calling all units en route to the crime scene. ETA?" voice one said, a woman.

"One minute," a man said, voice two.

"Three minutes," a second man said, voice three.

Voice one: "Over."

Listening felt like an intrusion, but it was riveting, even through the phone. Mark was on the edge of his seat with anticipation.

Voice two: "Pulling up now. The house is dark. Can you confirm the address?"

Voice one: "17 Smith Street, Beech Grove."

Voice two: "Confirmed."

Voice one: "Unit, you're requested to hold for backup."

Voice two: "Waiting."

Voice three: "Ninety seconds."

The radios crackled, the signal weak.

Voice three: "Pulling in behind you."

Voice one: "Approach with caution."

Voice two: "Confirmed. Over."

Voice three: "Over."

It was like riding along in the front seat. Who knew listening to a live call would be so thrilling? Mark glanced at Rachel, whose chin rested on her hands. She was locked in too, like he was.

Voice two: "House is clear. Victim is on the kitchen floor, bleeding profusely but still alive."

Voice one: "An ambulance is on the way."

Voice three: "The victim is trying to speak. He's holding up two fingers. Two what?" Fifteen, maybe twenty seconds passed. "Children! Two children!"

Voice two: "House is clear. There's nobody else here. I think we have two missing children."

Voice one: "Stay alert. More help is on the way."

The signal weakened further. It became inaudible.

"This is crazy," Mark said, settling back into the chair.

Rachel closed the app and frantically scrolled through her phone, looking for something unknown. "What was that address?"

"Smith Street. Beech Grove. I don't remember the number."

Rachel kept scrolling. "17? Was it 17?"

"Could have been."

Rachel gasped. "Oh my God, Mark."

"What is it?"

Rachel's head snapped and she looked at him with shock on her face. "17 Smith Street in Beech Grove. That's Holly's address."

•   •   •   •   •

After what they witnessed on the police scanner, they were too wired to sleep. This was either a mammoth-sized coincidence, or something more sinister was going on.

Mark didn't think he believed in coincidences.

Hours passed with no word from Tom. Rachel was pacing around, anxiously mumbling to herself. Mark remained seated, fidgeting. His head spun with the possibilities.

"We have to do something, Mark," Rachel said. "We have to."

"Like what? What can we do?"

"I don't know, but we need to do something. First Maureen, now these boys. She's taken them. I know it."

Mark had the feeling she was right. The evidence pointed in that direction. But to him, the situations weren't the same. Holly was the boys' mother, not Maureen's. He kept his thoughts to himself. Sometimes it was best to say nothing at all.

"I know I don't know them, but they're my nephews. Even if they weren't, they're just kids."

"I know, Rachel. I know."

Shortly after midnight, Rachel had fallen asleep in the chair. Mark's eyes were tired, but he couldn't shut his mind off and do the same. His phone was plugged in next to him, the charging cable barely long enough to reach the table.

Just when he finally gave in and closed his eyes, the table vibrated. He shot up, startled, and grabbed his phone before it woke Rachel. He separated the phone from its charging cable and left the room, slipping into the darkness of the kitchen before answering. The saloon doors creaked as they swung open.

"Tom?"

"Did I wake you?"

"No, no. I'm up."

"Sorry about earlier."

"Don't worry about it. We heard it all on the police scanner."

"You did?"

"Rachel downloaded an app."

"I see. So, you know then?"

"Some of it. The signal wasn't great. Was it Holly?" Mark felt his way toward the microwave, where he flipped on the dim light underneath it.

Tom sighed. "I think so."

"What happened?"

"Apparently there was a domestic dispute at the residence. According to Mr. White—that's Holly's husband—his wife pulled out a weapon and shot him in the knee, leaving him disabled. She shot him a second time, this time in the shoulder, then she took the children and left. That's what his story is."

"Jesus."

"All indications are, he's going to make it. There was a lot of blood, but the officers who arrived on the scene were able to stop the bleeding enough until the paramedics arrived."

"That's great. I'm happy to hear that."

"Yes, we all are. Nobody wanted this to happen, obviously, but this only helps our case, Mark. She's proven herself to be dangerous."

A rush of adrenaline overtook the exhaustion.

"We're still looking for her," Tom said. "And the children. We have an APB on her vehicle and troopers waiting at every exit fifty miles in each direction. We're not that far behind her. We'll get her."

"What if she's not on the freeway?"

"We'll handle it."

Mark wanted to protest but he knew better. His opinion didn't matter. But if he could help, why not offer the chance? "Hey, Tom, remember what we talked about before? About what I suggested?"

"I do. But considering the new circumstances, I don't think it's going to work. The level of danger has increased too much."

Mark's original plan had been to use Rachel as bait to draw Holly out, to play the sister card and try to pull on her heart strings. A long-lost sister desperate to connect with the sister she didn't know she had. That was before Mark knew Rachel and Holly had met — and certainly before he knew the true extent of their relationship. And also before he knew Holly's true motivations, her true desires.

"I agree," Mark said. "But I know what she wants now. I know what will bring her out of hiding."

"I'm listening."

"Me."

CHAPTER 41

Tom wanted to wait forty-eight hours to see if his team could track down Holly on their own. As Mark had suspected, Holly was either smart enough to avoid the interstate, or the police were too late in setting up barricades; she went uncaught. Mark had no way of knowing, but he suspected she was somewhere close, under their noses. Just a feeling.

The call came from Tom during the forty-fourth hour. Sometime around 8 p.m. The girls were asleep upstairs. Rachel joined Mark in front of the fire, two wine glasses half-full.

"We're a go," Tom said, avoiding pleasantries. "You can initiate contact."

"Just like that?"

"Do what we discussed, and yes."

"Okay."

"And Mark?"

"Yes?"

"Is there anything else I should know? Anything you need to tell me first?"

Mark's mouth dried out. Did Tom know about the gun or the truth about what happened at Indy Guns and Ammo? Was he giving Mark the opportunity to come clean, before it was too late? Even if he was, it was much too late for that. For as deep as Rachel was in this, Mark was right there with her. If something went bad, he'd be next to her, holding her hand on the way down. He was all in.

"Mark?"

"No. You know everything." He hated having to lie to Tom, but his family came first. Always. Tom would do the same thing if the roles were reversed.

"That's what I thought, but I had to ask. All right then. Talk soon."

They disconnected.

"Go time?" Rachel asked.

"Go time."

Of all the steps in this plan, the first might have been the most difficult. Mark was confident in the phone number — the number Holly called him from matched the one he'd found in the call log from the Doctor Lisa Show, and it was the same one Rachel had from the short time she and Holly were regularly communicating — but less confident that Holly still had it. If he were on the run, wouldn't getting rid of the phone be the first thing he'd do? He thought so.

Success required a leap of faith.

There was a contingency plan in place, just in case. If at some point — how long, it wasn't clear — Holly didn't bite, Rachel would step in. She'd unblock the suspicious accounts on Instagram and send them each a message. One, if not multiple, of them were likely Holly. Maybe all. Holly could access her Instagram account or accounts from any device, so even if she disposed of her usual phone, that would be a problem solved. If both Plan A and Plan B failed, Mark would create an Instagram account of his own — he wasn't on any social media right now — and reach out to those accounts himself. One of the ideas had to work. They had to.

Mark typed out a succinct but direct text message to the number he had for Holly.

I need to see you. You were right about Rachel.

He showed Rachel. She nodded her approval. This was going to be harder on her than it was on him, but she assured him she could handle it. He felt uncomfortable with it all, but whatever it took — that was his new motto. He hit send. Then they waited.

Twelve minutes later, Mark's phone pinged with a new message. He grabbed it and unlocked the screen as Rachel looked over his shoulder. It was a text.

Where?

The lure had been cast, and the fish had bitten.

Same place as last time?
Fine.
How's 10 a.m.?
What are you doing right now?

Mark turned to looked at Rachel.

"Told you she's obsessed with you," she said. "Are you sure you're up for it?"

"I'll let Tom know."

"And I'll call my mom and ask her to come here while the girls sleep."

Mark nodded, then he typed another message.

Give me an hour.

•   •   •   •   •

An hour wasn't a lot of time, but he couldn't push her off if he wanted her to believe this was genuine. Tom said he'd have men in place. He told Mark not to worry. Mark still worried.

Rachel's mother hurried over, and then Mark and Rachel left together. Rachel sat in the back. When they approached the park, she laid down between the seats, in case Holly was watching.

Between the time and darkness having set in long before, it shouldn't have been a surprise, but Southwestway Park was eerily quiet. Empty. Through the cracked windows, Mark heard a hooting owl overhead and the crunch of gravel underfoot. He pulled into the same parking lot he did last time. Each spot was vacant. Mark trusted that Tom and his team were in place, hiding in the shadows. There was no one else out there to help him if he were to stumble into trouble. If this went poorly, Mark might not ever see Rachel or their girls again. Holly had proven herself to be dangerous.

"You good back there?" Mark asked Rachel without turning. His eyes dashed between the mirrors, hoping to spot Holly before she spotted him. He saw nobody.

"I'm good," Rachel answered. "Are you good?"

"As good as I'll ever be."

"I love you, Mark Starr."

"I love you too, Rachel Starr."

Mark killed the ignition and got out. He left the keys dangling where they were, in case a quick exit was needed. A few streetlights in the parking lot offered him guiding light, enough to find his way toward the familiar post. He leaned against it, like before, with his back to the dark forest. Everything about this left him edgy. Sweat oozed from his pores.

"You came."

Holly's voice made him jump. He waited until she walked out of the shadows and into what light there was before responding. He wouldn't talk to a ghost. "I came."

"Wow, that was fast. I'm flattered. I hope it's not always that quick."

Mark didn't respond.

"So, you've learned the truth about Rachel, have you?" she said.

She was close enough to him where he could reach out and touch her if he wanted to, but far enough away where he couldn't smell her scent. Her green eyes shone, taunting him.

"I think I knew along," he said. "You just brought it to my attention."

"I see."

"Thank you for that. For making me see the real her."

"Which is?"

"Like you said. Selfish. Ungrateful. Unworthy."

Holly smiled. She liked that.

"She's stunning, of course. Which is why I let myself be blinded by who she really is. But now that I know there are two of her, two of you, so to speak, I can get the best of both worlds. The beauty and someone who can truly love me for me, who can appreciate everything I bring to the table. You."

Holly was still. Expressionless. Had Mark pushed it too far? Did he come on too strong?

Then, Holly smiled again. She took a step toward him. "What made you come to your senses?"

He stiffened. "She's crazy. Untrustworthy. Even our girls are scared of her." It was all an act, but even so, saying harsh things about Rachel hurt. He hoped Rachel remembered he didn't mean any of this.

"Smart girls."

"What about you? What about your boys?"

"What about them?"

"Do they appreciate how great their mother is?"

Holly said nothing at first, not for a while. Too long. Eventually, she said, "How do you know about my boys?"

"You told me about them. The first time we met."

"No, I didn't."

"You did. We were standing right here. You told me how great they were." Mark was panicking. He'd overplayed his hand. Holly had caught him in a lie.

"You're lying."

"No, I'm not."

"What are their names?"

"Actually, I don't think you said."

"Liar!"

Uh-oh. Mark was in trouble. He hoped Tom and his men were paying attention. "I'm not lying. I'm not. If you said them, I don't remember. I'm sorry. It was a tense moment."

Holly's face softened. "Maybe you're right. Ryder and Sam. Those are their names."

Phew.

"Where are Ryder and Sam tonight?"

"They're safe. But we're not here to talk about them. Why are we here, Mark? You said you needed to see me."

"I did. I do."

"Why? And why are you asking me about my kids?"

"Holly, I—"

"No. Forget this. I think this was a mistake." Holly turned to leave.

"No, wait! Please."

"Why?"

"Because there's somebody who wants to talk to you."

"Excuse me?"

Mark hollered Rachel's name. His car's back door opened and Rachel crawled out. She walked toward them.

"What's she doing here?" Holly angrily said.

"I'm sorry," Mark said. "But Rachel thinks she can help you."

"Help me? I don't need help."

"You do, Holly," Rachel said with sincerity as she approached. She stood close to Mark. "I don't think you're a bad person, I just think you've been misunderstood. I know about your struggles. When we were younger, your mother called my mother and—"

"She what?"

"Our mothers spoke about you, because they were worried about you. Both of them. We all want to help."

Holly laughed. "Nobody wants to help me. I haven't talked to my mother in over fifteen years."

"I think if you check into a hospital where you can get help, you can find some relief. The doctors at Evansville—"

"Evansville! You must be out of your damn mind. You don't know a damn thing about my life."

"I know you've struggled. I know you act out sometimes, but I know you don't mean it. I know you just want to be loved."

"Is that what you think of me? That I'm some ... out-of-control person? Some fool?"

"Holly, I know—"

"No! No, no, no! You know nothing about my life. You're a spoiled bitch. You have everything. Parents who love you. A husband who worships you. Two beautiful children."

"So do you!"

"No, no I don't. My husband, he's an asshole. He tells me how stupid I am any chance he gets. He criticizes me, picks at my insecurities. He's turned my kids against me."

"Leave him, then. If you're unhappy in your marriage, leave. You can be happy."

Holly laughed again. It was a creepy, emotionless laugh. Callused. "You're so naïve, Rachel. You really are. People like me don't find happiness. That's just not how it works. Maybe in your fairytale of a life, but not mine. We aren't alike."

"We're trying to help you," Rachel said. "Why won't you accept it?"

Something changed in Holly's face. It was as if she'd learned something new, and it was nothing like what she expected. "We?"

"Yes, we. Mark and I."

Fury overtook Holly's face. Her jaw flexed.

"I apologize for bringing you here under false pretenses," Mark said, "but this is your chance to do the right thing."

"You and me, we're family," Rachel said. "I only want the best for you. Please."

"We're not family," Holly said.

The conversation was going just as Mark had expected it would. Rachel would try to convince Holly to do the right thing, knowing she wouldn't, all the while hitting a nerve Holly couldn't resist reacting to.

The best was still yet to come.

Rachel threw up her arms in faux exasperation. "You know what, forget it. If you're too stupid to accept help when help's being offered, then you're on your own."

Holly's upper lip raised in the moonlight's reflection, as if the rage were about to explode out of her.

"This makes perfect sense to me now," Rachel went on, as dramatic as ever, her hands expressive. "I see it all. I can see why your husband looks down on you, Holly. You're infuriating to try to talk to. And your boys? Oh, please. They know an idiot when they see one. That's why they don't respect you. And that's why your husband doesn't love you. And Mark? He'd never love you, even if you were the last person left on Earth."

An angry groan bubbled in Holly's throat. She was close to snapping. One more tiny push would send her over the edge.

"You've heard of mother's intuition, right?" Rachel rhetorically asked Holly. "This is what that means. You're the perfect example of it. This is the reason Mom chose me over you. She knew you'd become … you."

Got her.

Holly screamed, her voice echoing through the park and sending the nocturnal creatures into hiding. "You little bitch!"

The next part was dangerous. Even with Tom and his men—*please, please let them be here!*—nearby, there was no predicting what Holly might do next.

Holly reached behind her back and swung her arm forward. She now held a miniature revolver in her hand.

"Holly, what are you doing?" Rachel said slowly, calmly, the fright in her voice as clear as day. This wasn't a drill.

Holly pointed the revolver at Rachel. "I had the feeling it was going to come to this. You think you can manipulate me? You think you can control me? Think again. I'm not like you, Rachel. I never have been. But I could be."

Holly's face lit up. She looked at Mark now, but kept the revolver on Rachel.

"Do you think your girls would even notice the difference between me and her? You said it yourself: We look the same. There are, essentially, two of us. You, me, the girls, my boys. We could make quite the life for ourselves, don't you think? I can even wear Rachel's clothes to make the girls feel better, if you want. We're close enough to the same size. If I lose five pounds, you'll never even notice the difference. One thing I can guarantee you, Mark, is that no one will ever rock your world the way I can. I'll never say no to you. Never. Anything you want, it's yours. Nothing is off limits. That's a promise."

Jesus. Where the hell was Tom? At what point was enough, enough? He must have had plenty by now.

"Do you want me to kill her so we can be together?" Holly asked. "Just say the word and I'll do it. I won't even hesitate. Trust me."

"Put the gun down and we can talk about this," Mark said.

"No, I'm not going to put the gun down. I want you to answer my question right now."

"I won't answer that."

"Why not, Mark? Don't you love me? That's what you told me last time."

"I thought you were Rachel."

"So, you don't?"

"I don't."

"Well screw this then." Holly turned back to Rachel and gritted her teeth. The revolver shook in her hand. "If I can't have him, no one can. I'm going to put a bullet in your head now. It took me two bullets to kill my husband, but it's only going to take one to kill you. At this range, you'll be lucky if you don't split in two." Holly pulled back the hammer and cocked the revolver. "Nice not knowing you, bitch."

Rachel gasped.

"Wait!" Mark screamed.

The park illuminated. A dozen voices yelled at once and a dozen lights shone in Holly's face. She had no choice but to shield her eyes; she was temporarily blinded. Armed police officers appeared from every angle—from behind trees, in the parking lot, down the jogging path. Amid the chaos, and despite the blinding light, Holly ran toward Rachel, the revolver lowered. Holly wrapped an arm around her neck and stood behind her, using Rachel as a human shield.

"Put your weapon down!" an officer yelled.

Mark didn't know what to do with his body. He was frozen in fear, his feet cemented to the dirt.

"Put your weapon down, now!"

Mark saw the fear in Holly's eyes too. She looked all around her, trapped, her head on a swivel. Rachel screamed.

From behind a couple of officers walked Tom Wilde, a bulky vest covering his front, his hands empty.

"Stop!" Holly shouted at him. "Stop right there!"

Tom complied and showed her his hands, to prove he wasn't armed. As if she'd forget about the twelve other officers surrounding her who were.

"Let Rachel go," Tom said. "You don't want to do this."

"Shut up!" Holly said.

"Come on, Holly," Tom said. "This isn't you."

"You don't even know me!" Tears streamed down Holly's face. Rachel dug her nails into Holly's forearm, desperately trying to free herself, but Holly somehow maintained her grip.

Watching the scene play out in front of him, Mark hadn't felt more helpless in his life.

"Your husband is alive, Mrs. White," Tom said.

"Impossible."

"I spoke with him myself two hours ago. He's going to be fine. That's good news, you know. In the state of Indiana, first-degree murder is life in prison without the possibility of parole. Or capital punishment. Your life would be over either way. Attempted murder, however, and you're looking at twenty to forty years. Twenty with rehabilitation and good behavior. You'll still be young."

Holly seemed to listen, considering. Rachel squirmed more freely now. Holly's grip was loosening.

"Let her go," Tom said.

"I'm not going to prison," Holly said through sloppy tears.

"Someone's going to prison."

Unexpectedly, Holly released her grip on Rachel, who sprinted away and threw herself into Mark's chest. He grabbed her and held her, squeezed her as hard as he could. A police officer ushered them away, behind the barricade of armed men.

"Holly, don't!"

Mark turned around at the sound of Tom's voice, and he saw it. Holly had turned the gun on herself. She held the revolver against her right temple.

"I'm not going to prison!" she said again, this time with more force.

"Put the gun down!" Tom hollered. "Please, put the gun down."

"Tell me I'm not going to prison."

"You know I can't do that. Put the gun down."

The moment was frantic. Mark sensed everyone with a gun tense, their fingers ready to fire in a moment's notice.

"Tell me I'm not going to prison, or I won't tell you where my sons are."

"Don't do this," Tom said.

"Tell me! Tell me I'm not!"

Rachel grabbed onto Mark in a panic. "Those boys! They don't deserve this!"

"Last chance. Tell me!" Holly shouted.

"Holly, don't—"

A gunshot exploded.

Somebody screamed.

Mark told me he loved me. Whether he thought I was Rachel or if he sincerely felt that way about me, it stuck. I can't remember the last time Kevin told me he loved me. Or my boys. Or anybody. Mark was the last one I can remember.

I love you, Mark. I really do. You're everything I've ever wanted …

I love you too …

You do?

Of course.

He said it. As clear as day. He didn't say, "I love you too, Rachel." He said, "I love you too." That meant a lot. I think he meant it and he didn't want to admit it in front of Rachel. Mark Starr is in love with me.

I admit, sometimes my brain latches onto things and can't let them go. This was one of those times. I knew I wanted Mark already. The number of times I've soaked in the bathtub thinking about him. Or the extra-long showers. Or sometimes in the middle of the day, when Kevin and the boys were out of the house. I thought about Mark a lot. I still do.

Mark loving me — being in love, even — was enough to get me to act. I'd had a mini revolver for a while, the one I purchased legally. Don't forget that part of it; it was legal. We've been over this part so many times that I don't feel like doing it again. You know how it goes. If I wanted to be with Mark, Kevin and Rachel needed to be dead. Not divorced. Dead. Only then could me and Mark could start our lives together. I was willing to be the trigger person if my reward was being with Mark Starr. He's worth it to me.

There's not really a clean way to kill your husband. It's all going to go back to the wife. It always does. What's the statistic? When a husband dies, it's almost always the wife, isn't it? Like eight out of ten times. I'm not dumb, despite what Kevin—and my dad—might want to believe. Which left me with two options. First, make it look like an accident. Second, self-defense. The latter is harder to prove, I imagined, but the former was harder to plan. And with Mark's feelings for me out on the table, I felt an urgency to do something sooner rather than later, before Mark changed his mind or Rachel poisoned it further.

Kevin and I were arguing. I don't even remember what about. We argued constantly, so one fight blended into the next. He probably didn't like something I did or didn't do, like usual. I was never good enough for him. I was never good enough for anyone.

"I can't do this with you anymore, Holly," Kevin said to me, his voice shallow. It was dark outside. The boys were asleep upstairs. Kevin and I were in the kitchen.

"Do what?"

"This. Us. It isn't working."

I was shocked. I didn't think Kevin had the balls for that. "Excuse me?"

"I'm not happy. Neither are you. Sometimes you just need to know when to call it quits. I think that time for us is now."

I stood there, frozen, trying to figure out what was happening. How, after all this, was it Kevin who wanted to split?

No way in hell was I going to let that happen. If anyone was going to end our marriage, it was going to be me.

"I spoke to an attorney and she advised me that if we can come to an agreement, we can bypass the courts and a judge will just sign off on it."

"She? What, are you fucking her?"

"Christ, Holly. No. She came as a recommendation from a colleague."

I scoffed. "How long have you been planning this?"

"Planning? I'm not planning anything. I'm trying to do the responsible thing here. I want to come to a financial agreement we're both happy with."

"I don't want your money," I said, which was partially true. I didn't want his money; I wanted all of his money.

"Be realistic. What are you going to do for money? Food and housing and — "

There he went again, talking to me like I was a moron. I was furious. Angry heat radiated off my skin. He'd pushed me as far as he could. I wouldn't stand for it any longer. I rushed out of the kitchen and ran upstairs, ignoring Kevin's irritated pleas for me to talk about this with him, and went into our bedroom. There was a padlocked box underneath our bed. Kevin didn't know it was there, or if he did, he hadn't mentioned it. I grabbed the key from my nightstand and inserted it into the lock. Inside the box was the mini revolver and five bullets, one for each tiny chamber. I grabbed them all and the gun, and I went back downstairs, loading as I descended the stairs. I hid it inside the palm of my hand as I reentered the kitchen.

"Can we do this amicably, please?" Kevin asked me. "I don't want to battle you over this, but I will."

"Shut up, Kevin."

He ignored me. "We can figure out the money, but I'm proposing fifty-fifty with the boys. I know you're more hands on, but they're my kids too. I'm not divorcing them, I'm divorcing you. I'll adjust my work schedule to allow me to pick them up after school a couple days a week. We can work it out."

They're my kids too.

Were they, though?

It was time.

"Look in the mirror sometime," I said. A nasty grin spread across my face.

"What are you talking about?"

"When was the last time you looked at Ryder? He looks nothing like you."

"No, he doesn't. He looks more like you. So what?"

"Maybe there's a reason for that."

"That's a low blow, Holly." He walked toward me, as if he were about to walk out on the conversation—or worse. "If you're going to play games like this, then screw it. You're going to have to scratch and claw for every penny out of me now. That's what you get for being a bitch."

"I already told you, I don't want your money."

"Says the woman who doesn't have any of her own."

"Whose fault is that?"

He shook his head as he walked closer to me.

"His name was Jimmy."

Kevin stopped.

"I used to work with him. Remember that Halloween party years back? The one where you complained about my outfit being too revealing?"

Kevin turned his shoulders and faced me straight-on. I had him.

"You weren't the only one who thought I looked hot that night."

Kevin's face scrunched and turned a fierce red. He balled his fingers into fists.

"Are you going to hit me?" I asked.

He didn't answer.

"Hit me. Do it. See what happens."

Did I want him to hit me? Not particularly. But if he did, that would give me some evidence to show that killing him was indeed self-defense. Maybe this was my chance.

"Jimmy died of a brain tumor three months after he got me pregnant. I never told him. I wish I would have."

Sometimes, even the best laid plans go awry. Kevin didn't hit me. Not even close. He dropped to the kitchen floor and held his head in his hands, trying to process what I just told him. Tears didn't come, but they were about to. He looked pathetic. He eventually looked over at me, spotted the revolver in my hand, and looked up.

"Why do you have that?" he asked. "Do you even know how to use that thing?"

"How hard can it be?"

He sat up. "What are you going to—"

I lifted the revolver and pointed it at him. My hand shook only a little. "Stay where you are."

He stopped squirming and sat back down flat, raising his hands in surrender.

"This is what's going to happen. I'm going to shoot you, then I'm going to claim you left me no choice. Self-defense."

"You have no proof. I've never touched you."

No kidding. It certainly felt that way.

"My word against yours. The woman always gets the benefit of the doubt."

Kevin tried standing up. I didn't give him the chance to. In one swift motion, as if I knew what I was doing, I pulled back on the hammer and pulled the trigger. The revolver's snap gave me whiplash, and I nearly dropped it. My ears rang.

I saw the blood first. It gushed from a gaping hole in his right knee. Maybe it was the shock of it, but Kevin's scream didn't come until a few seconds later.

"You shot me!" He tried standing but screeched in agony, falling onto his back. "You fucking shot me!"

There was a lot of blood in a short time. More than I expected. Since it happened off the cuff, I hadn't prepared with any research ahead of time. I didn't know how long it would take him to bleed out. But considering how much blood there already was, and how fast it was gushing out in clumps, it didn't seem like it'd be long. Just in case, and to help speed up the process, I shot him again. My grip was tighter this time so the recoil didn't surprise me as much. Blood oozed out of his left shoulder.

He screamed again and writhed on the tile.

I knew he was incapable of getting up. With the shot-out knee and now two profusely bleeding bullet wounds, there was nothing he could do. So, I went upstairs, grabbed the boys one by one — Sam first, Ryder second — and carried them downstairs, into the garage, and put them in the backseat of my SUV. Kevin screamed out to me as I did, but his voice was strained; he was getting weak. I figured he'd be dead in minutes.

Remarkably, he wasn't. Somehow, the bastard survived. Apparently, one of the neighbors heard the commotion and called it in. Lucky for him, but it screwed me over. I should have shot him in the head.

So, yeah, that's how it went down.

You know what happened next. Everyone does. Practically every newspaper in the country plastered it on the front page. It was the lead story on all the national news shows for a week. Mark tricked me and set me up. Rachel's still a bitch. A cop shot me in the thigh and dropped me, then the weight of twelve grown men jumped on my back and cuffed me. That about cover it?

I saw the writing on the wall, that it was over, so I gave the cop in charge the hotel room number I was staying in with the boys. They were safe. Obviously. No one thought I'd hurt them, did they? Come on, now. You people don't know me at all.

CHAPTER 43

Three months later. So much had happened, yet so little had happened at the same time — which was just the way Mark liked it. The short-term aftermath of the explosive confrontation with Holly in the park was a lot. Heavy. Mark had trouble sleeping. He knew Rachel did, too. He felt every toss and turn she made during most nights that followed; he felt it because he was awake too, and doing the same.

The girls, thankfully, didn't seem to be bothered. Children were resilient; Mark finally knew what that meant. He and Rachel did a decent job at shielding them from the news and the reporters who'd occasionally show up to the house, so they seemed unaware of what was going on. Mark realized that might not last forever, though. He was prepared to talk about it with them in a way they could understand, if he needed to.

Mark saw a change in them, in the way they interacted with Rachel. It was slow at first. Some days they were timid with her — Maureen, especially — and would prefer Mark if they needed comforting. It hurt Rachel in the worst way. Mark knew that — he could tell — although Rachel didn't talk to him about it. He encouraged the girls to spend time with their mom and to trust her, and eventually they did. He and Rachel sat down with Abagail and Maureen one night and tried to explain the strange happenings lately.

"Mommy has a sister," Mark explained. "An identical twin sister. Do you know what that is?"

Maureen didn't.

"It means they look the same," Abagail said, always the smart one.

"That's right," he said. "Well, Mommy's sister isn't a very nice person. She was trying to trick all of us into thinking she was Mommy. Do you understand?"

Maureen nodded.

"Why?" Abagail asked.

"That's a good question. Unfortunately, I don't have an answer for you. Some people are mean sometimes. This is one of those times."

That seemed to appease Abagail's curious mind, which Mark was thankful for. He didn't want to get into the details with her; she was too young for that. No further questions were asked. Later that night, Maureen asked if Rachel would read her a bedtime story. Rachel emphatically told her she would, tears pooling in her eyes. Everything went back to normal after that night.

The Monday after Holly's confession, attempted murders, and subsequent arrest, Mark went to the office. His entire being wanted to stay home and be with Rachel, but he craved normalcy in his life. His mind needed the distraction and his psyche needed a break. He buried himself in his work during normal business hours. All his clients were happy, Stanley Lyons included, as was the firm. Nobody else threatened to take their money and go elsewhere. Things were looking up.

Maybe it was something he shouldn't have been proud of, but he was: He didn't miss a single day of work in three months following the incident in the park. Usually that would have been nothing, but considering how infrequently he'd been into the office in the days beforehand, it felt like an accomplishment. He even threw Carly a cash bonus and insisted she take a week off, as his way of thanking her for all she'd done for him. Tearfully, she accepted the envelope and the assignment, and she hugged him.

"Thank you, Mark," she said. "You don't know how much this means to me."

He hugged her back. "I think I do."

Mark made it his mission to repay Todd for his continued patience and support, even if his methods were infuriating sometimes. They had lunch at Tony's every Wednesday for a month. Mark tried something different each time, although he was still convinced chalupas, tostadas, and enchiladas were one and the same.

One-upping himself, he let Todd take him out for a beer after work one Thursday night—though Mark paid. It was a dance night for Abagail anyway, so he wasn't missing anything at home. Todd pushed for The Pony, the gentleman's club where Charity worked, but Mark wouldn't go that far. They settled for some bar Mark had already forgotten the name of. He convinced Todd to ask Charity out on a real date sometime, though. Todd was hesitant at first—rather scared, Mark suspected—but he did it. And she said yes. Turned out, Charity was just a stage name— go figure. Her real name was Melissa, and she had two cats, a bachelor's degree in art history, and a pile of student loan debt— hence the evenings at The Pony.

"Do you think she'll like me, man?" Todd asked the day of their scheduled date, a nervous wreck.

"She said yes, didn't she?"

"Yeah, I guess you're right. Hey, do you think she's into trucker hats? Or is that weird?" Todd was still stuck on forty- three of them. He had acquired nothing new since the Vermont maple syrup one.

"I think maybe you should focus the conversation on something else tonight."

"Good thinking, Markster. Appreciate you, dude."

"You too, Todd."

•　　•　　•　　•　　•

Mark and Rachel recommitted to each other. Not just in their marriage, but in their relationship. Every other Friday night was date night. The girls spent those nights at their grandparents' house. Rachel was quick to forgive her parents for their role in what happened. They agreed not to withhold information like that again, and they opened themselves up to answer any additional questions Rachel had. Rachel let them think she learned about Holly from them still; she was forgiving, but she was still out to prove a point. Maybe one day she'd tell them about how she met her sister, or maybe she wouldn't. It was entirely her call. Mark was ready to support her either way.

Tonight was date night.

They went into Indianapolis for a nice dinner. Mark ordered a bottle of the house red. He and Rachel sat next to each other and held hands under the table. He was as happy with her as he'd ever been — and he was confident she felt the same. He saw the sparkle in her eyes when she looked at him. It was like being young again. The spark was back.

"It's been great reconnecting these last few months," he said.

"Yes, I agree. I missed us."

"Me too. I still feel terrible, you know. About everything that happened."

"Don't. There's no need to. We both did things we wish we would have done differently. If I would have told you about Holly from the start, if I would have asked for your help …"

"Like you said, we've both made mistakes."

The waiter came with the bottle. He uncorked it and poured them each a glass, told them their food wouldn't be long. Mark thanked him. The rest of the bottle was put on ice.

"Can we talk about something else?" Rachel asked. She looked tired. Whatever burden she carried about what happened to her at Evansville was still with her. She told Mark very little about it, and he didn't press. When she was ready to talk to him about it, she would.

"Of course. Just one more thing. There's still something I haven't told you."

Rachel leaned away, concern blanketing her face.

"It's nothing like that," Mark said. "Just something that's been eating at me. Indy Guns and Ammo, I went in there."

"Why?"

"I wanted to talk with the owner, to explain what was going on. This was months ago, before I knew about Holly. I offered to pay for the stolen ammunition if he'd promise not to press charges."

Rachel took a sip of wine. She was listening.

"He agreed, but it took a lot more than the cost of the ammo. I wanted to tell you earlier, was going to, but then I saw the green contacts and—"

She held up her free hand to stop him. "No, say no more. I don't care."

"You don't?"

"I really don't. I'm just glad this is all behind us."

Mark sighed with relief. That went better than he could have ever imagined.

"Do I want to know how much? You said it was more than the box of ammo."

"Well—"

"I don't. I just decided. I don't want to know. It's just money. Just promise me something."

"Anything."

"No more secrets. Starting right now."

He grabbed her hand again and held it. "I promise."

"I promise too."

"I'll spend the rest of my life making it up to you, if you'll have me."

"Only if you'll have me."

They smiled at each other.

Their meals came and they ate. Had more wine. Finished the bottle. Mark paid the bill and they left. Outside, a chill was in the air. Rachel tightened her coat and Mark popped his collar. His breath crystallized in front of his face.

"The night's still young. You up for a little walk?" Mark said.

"Sure."

Rachel slipped her fingers in between his as they walked.

"Did I tell you I talked to Tom this week, and he and Helen are definitely coming to Abagail's dance recital next week?"

"Great," Rachel flatly said.

Mark understood her hesitation. She still wasn't sure how to act around Tom, after everything that happened. "It was nothing personal, you know. What happened with Tom."

"I know that."

"If you're uncomfortable with it, I can tell him—"

"No, it's okay. Honest. I have to see him sooner or later."

Mark squeezed her hand. "I almost forgot. You saw the boys today, right? How did it go?"

A few weeks after Holly was arrested, and once her husband Kevin was out of the hospital and back home, Rachel reached out to him. Despite not knowing the boys, they were her nephews—she kept reiterating that to Mark to justify it, and he encouraged her to do what she thought was right. Kevin was receptive but not initially eager. He hadn't known Holly had a sister and had been through quite a lot himself.

Join the club.

Hesitantly, Kevin agreed to meet with Rachel alone first. They met for lunch and they talked, and apparently Kevin bought into the idea that Rachel wasn't anything like her sister. The next time, he brought the boys—Ryder and Sam—and introduced them to their aunt. They were taking things slow. They'd met as a group—Rachel, Kevin, and the boys—a handful of times. Mark hadn't been introduced yet, neither had Abagail or Maureen, and that was fine. All in due time. He was in no rush. This was something Rachel had to deal with on her own, at her own pace, as part of her healing process. He was there to support her in any way he could. The boys had all but lost their mother, so they needed family more than ever right now.

Rachel lit up. "It was amazing. Little Sam is opening up more each time. He was so closed off at first, which I get, but he's coming around. Ryder gave me a hug when I left. He called me Auntie." Rachel smiled. "I just about teared up."

"That's wonderful. I'm so glad it's going well." And he was. Rachel was happy. Happier than he'd seen her in a long time.

On the way back to the car, Mark heard someone call his name from afar. He stopped and turned around, curiously searching for the source.

"Hey, you!" the voice said.

Mark didn't recognize her at first, not until she got closer.

"Mark, right?" she said. She smiled and the cat on her neck stretched. He remembered.

"Sarah, hi. What are you doing here?"

"I just got off my shift at Johnny's. I'm heading to a club to meet some of my girlfriends." She looked at Rachel. "Who's this?"

"This is Rachel. My wife."

Sarah's hand shot out. "Hi, Rachel. Sarah."

Rachel shook it. "You two know each other?"

"I've stopped into Johnny's a time or two," Mark said. "You remember Johnny's? Just a few blocks from the office."

Rachel shrugged.

"Oh, my," Sarah said, gasping. She stepped closer to Rachel. "I hope you don't mind me saying, but you are just stunning. Your eyes, they're beautiful. Has anybody ever told you that before?"

It's all in the eyes.

"I haven't seen anything quite like them," Sarah added. "So blue. It's like they have their own souls with one hell of a story to tell."

Rachel blushed. "Well, thank you."

Mark smiled. Sarah, the future philosopher, didn't know how right she was. An entire story truly could be told just by looking into somebody's eyes.

CHAPTER 44

It's been three months. It feels like three years. There's no way I'm going to make it twenty to forty years in this place. I haven't had a trial yet, so maybe that won't have to happen. My attorney — court-appointed because my cheap soon-to-be ex-husband refuses to pay — says she'll be using battered woman syndrome as her defense strategy. She doesn't sound optimistic, though. Pessimistic, if you ask me. I don't like her.

I'm being held on a quarter-million dollars bail. The judge knew I couldn't afford that, which is why he did it. Dick. I'll be in here until the trial. I'm told that could take one to three years, so there's that. I guess this is my home for a while. Kevin hasn't brought the boys to see me, or accepted my calls, not even once. I highly doubt he will. I sent the boys each a letter last month, but I received nothing back. My guess is, Kevin never even showed them. I'm sure he's putting this all on me, making me out to be the bad guy. He was the one who wanted to get divorced and break up our family, not me. I think he needs to get over what happened. It was a simple domestic dispute. No harm, no foul.

Okay, you got me. Not even I believe that.

I don't know if Kevin believed me when I confessed Ryder wasn't his. I haven't spoken to him since that night in the kitchen, so I don't know what he thinks about it. Maybe he doesn't care. If it were me, I'd want to know. A simple DNA test would tell him. Although honestly, a DNA test isn't required. I know Ryder is Jimmy's. Just look at him. He's Jimmy's twin. Kevin must see it too, that Ryder looks nothing like him.

Well, my leg has healed. Being shot in the thigh hurts like a mother, if you didn't know. The muscle was sore for two solid months after surgery. I just started losing the limp recently. I go to physical therapy upstairs twice a week. Gives me something to do, I guess. The therapist is something nice to look at, so I don't hate it. Between that and coming here, it's like I'm actually busy. Might need a planner to keep it all straight. If only I were that lucky.

"So, Doc, how am I doing?" I ask. "Seeing progress?"

Doctor Vermouth—like the wine—looks at me over the top of his glasses. They just barely rest on his nose, the nose pads so close to his nostrils that he most definitely can smell them. A red thread attaches to each end of the ear pads and wraps around the back of his head. His legs are folded like a lady.

"Progress can be difficult to define," he answers. "Every patient's journey is different."

"How's mine?"

"I think we have a way to go. The journey to full rehabilitation isn't linear. For many, it can be a lifelong journey."

"That good, huh?"

Doctor Vermouth smiles. Apparently, there's a sense of humor behind that stoic, bearded face. Mine's coming back in pieces too, though it's slow.

"How do you feel like you're doing?"

Classic deflection to put it back on me. "Well, I've been honest with you. I think that's a start."

"That's a good observation."

"In that respect, I feel like I've come a long way in a short time. I haven't always been an honest person, you know."

"No?"

"No."

"But you've been honest with me?"

"I have."

Doctor Vermouth maintains eye contact, waiting for me to say something more. But I have nothing more to add.

"Very good," he says. "So, tell me, what's on your mind today, Holly?"

"I've been thinking about my mother a lot lately."

"Have you?"

"I can't imagine doing what she did."

"Which is what?"

"Reaching out to my birth mother to express concerns about me. I've told you that."

"That bothers you?"

"It does. Very much."

"Why?"

"I can't put my finger on it, to tell you the truth. She's supposed to be my mother. Shouldn't she know best? Why reach out to someone who doesn't know me at all?"

Doctor Vermouth keeps looking at me.

"You're not going to give me your opinion, are you?" I ask him.

He offers a whiskery smile. "I'm not. It sounds like something you need to spend more time thinking about."

I hate when he does this. It's like he's trying to teach me a lesson or something.

"How are you sleeping?" he asks.

"About the same. I dreamed about Mark last night."

"Oh?"

"He chose me, of course. In the dream. Just us. No kids. What does that mean?"

"Dreams can represent different emotions. Conscious or subconscious thoughts. Often times, they mean nothing."

"One thing I'll never understand, Doc, is why."

"Why what?"

"Why can't Mark love the both of us? I mean, look at Rachel and look at me. We're identical. We're the same in every way."

"No two people are exactly the same. Not even identical twins."

"So, you're saying she has something I don't?"

"I'm saying you're not the same. There's a difference." The doctor looks down at his watch. He clicks his pen. "I'm afraid that's all the time we have for today, Holly. We'll resume this conversation on Thursday." He grabs his notebook and stands up. "Guard."

An armed guard opens the door and ushers the psychologist away. The same guard comes back for me after. He unhooks me from the table where I sit, my ankles and wrists shackled, and helps me up. His hand remains on my shoulder as I wobble through the security door, down the corridor, and back into my cell.

Inside the cell, I rest my wrists on the cutout in the door and wait for the guard to open it and uncuff me. He does without speaking or looking at me, as if I'm not worthy of his attention. He walks away after, cuffs in hand. I sit down on my bed and think about what Doctor Vermouth said.

He made a valid point, when I read through the lines of what he said. He likes to do that; he likes to make me work for it. Sometimes I don't quite understand. It's like he speaks in metaphors, trying to show me how much smarter he is than me. But today, I get it.

Rachel and I aren't the same. We look the same, but we're different. Mark's in love with the person she is. I could be that person. I could be all that Mark has ever wanted. I already have the looks. A few tweaks to how I carry myself, maybe an attitude adjustment. I can push that stick up my ass a little farther. I can handle that. How hard can it be? And with twenty years behind bars, that gives me plenty of time to fine-tune the new me.

A light bulb goes off in my head.

Now I get it! My dream. Twenty years from now, all four kids will be grown and out of the house. That's why my dream had just me and Mark. Which means …

My dream wasn't a dream at all. It was a premonition.

I'll end up with Mark Starr in the end, just like I always thought I would. I just need to make a few minor changes. The doctor calls it a journey to rehabilitation; I call it something different. An evolution. And that evolution to find the new me, to find the version of me Mark Starr won't help but gush all over, starts now.

I smile at the thought.

Maybe Rachel doesn't quite have everything after all. She's just keeping the seat warm, so to speak, until I'm ready to take a hold of what—of who—I've rightfully deserved all along. One day, Mark Starr will be mine. It's said that all good things are worth waiting for. Luckily for me, I'm a very patient woman.

Dear Reader,

Thank you so much for reading! So, what did you think? If you'd consider sharing a few sentences about your experience with it on Amazon or Goodreads or anywhere you love to talk about books, I'd be grateful. It's a great way to let other readers know if it might be something they'd enjoy as well.

Feel free to reach out to me directly too. I personally respond to all messages.

You can contact me:

@danlawtonauthor on Instagram or X
Facebook at www.facebook.com/danlawtonfiction
via email at info@danlawtonfiction.com.

Also visit my website for updates and to join my mailing list: www.danlawtonfiction.com.

All the best,

Dan Lawton

ABOUT THE AUTHOR

Dan Lawton is an award-winning thriller author from New Hampshire and an active member of the International Thriller Writers (ITW) Organization. He is a somewhat closeted rom-com movie lover and a huge Boston Celtics fan. An antsy person, he's horrible at relaxing, feeling like he should be working on something at all times. Lawton admits to being afraid of snakes, the ocean, and rodents. And if you ever need it, he can talk like Donald Duck.

NOTE FROM DAN LAWTON

Word-of-mouth is crucial for any author to succeed. If you enjoyed *The Both of Us*, please leave a review online — anywhere you are able. Even if it's just a sentence or two. It would make all the difference and would be very much appreciated.

Thanks!
Dan Lawton

We hope you enjoyed reading this title from:

BLACK ROSE
writing™

www.blackrosewriting.com

Subscribe to our mailing list – *The Rosevine* – and receive **FREE** books, daily deals, and stay current with news about upcoming releases and our hottest authors.
Scan the QR code below to sign up.

Already a subscriber? Please accept a sincere thank you for being a fan of Black Rose Writing authors.

View other Black Rose Writing titles at www.blackrosewriting.com/books and use promo code **PRINT** to receive a **20% discount** when purchasing.